A Question of Guilt

Ruth Rowling

Copyright © Ruth E Sundt 2020

This novel is a work of fiction. Names and characters are the product of the author's imagination and any resemblance to actual persons, living or dead, is entirely coincidental.

ISBN: 9798565761122

To all my girlfriends

June 1966
CONVICTION

Kate

Where was Mum? Who was looking after Claire? Bloody Jim again. If I get my hands on him, I thought.

Claire

There was lots of blood. Kate was screaming. Jim smelt bad. Or was that before?

I don't like noise. Kate can be noisy. I switched the radio on. I liked Elvis Presley. I switched the radio on and I sang 'Are you lonesome tonight.' There was more noise and banging. I heard Mrs Hunter's voice. I don't like Mrs Hunter's voice. I turned the radio up and shut the door.

There was lots of noise and banging. And lots of Mrs Hunter. Mrs Hunter lives next door. I began to wonder why Kate hadn't come to see me. She always comes to see me and then she gets noisy and sings all the wrong bits. But Mum came not Kate. She looked at me and went white. Behind the door was lots of noise. Lots of voices that I didn't know. Men's voices. I don't always like men's voices. These men were crowding in the door and I began to get frightened. I turned the radio up even more. Mum was standing in the doorway filling up all the space. Mum said something like my handicapped daughter (that's me) and being frightened. I was frightened. Then Mum said please and lots of other things. The noise and the men went further away. Mum turned back to me. She said my name, Claire, and held my hands. My hands weren't very nice because the blood had gone sticky. The radio was very loud but when Mum turned it off she went more white. There was blood on the switch thing as well.

I think all the men were outside. Mum took me upstairs and started washing the blood off me in the bathroom. She was all panicky. I don't like that. It's not my blood I said, it's Jim's. Mum looked a bit odd. She said my name again then she asked me where Kate was. I think. Or did she ask me if I'd seen Kate. I said that Kate had run away.

When I was fairly clean Mum shut me in my bedroom and told me to stay there. She said it lots of times. That I was to stay there and not to come down and talk to the policemen. I'd never met a policeman before but I'd seen a picture in a book. I always do what Mum says so I stayed in my bedroom and read my book. I had a Bunty Annual and I read the pictures. I read page number three where the first bubble above the girl's head said hello. The next bubble said I'm called Kate. I liked that because I liked reading Kate's name. I liked writing Kate's name as well. But Kate had run away. Then a really sad thing happened inside me and I didn't want to read Kate's name anymore.

Kate

I wasn't used to travelling in a car. It felt squashed and very low down, and frighteningly close to the road in the back of the police car. John Melmerby's father had a car. I'd been in it once when Mr Melmerby had driven past John and me waiting together at a bus stop. He'd stopped and given us both a lift home. Jim didn't have a car.

We were driving up The Old North Road towards the town centre. We hadn't gone back to my house. I started to feel uneasy and remember all the things I was supposed to be trying to do.

'Is someone with Claire?' I asked.

A big policeman screwed himself round to face me from the front passenger seat. He looked blank. I looked at the other policeman in the back seat of the car next to me. He looked blank too. I looked at the driver but he was enjoying himself too much jumping the red light at Clifton Green.

And then I remembered the other big thing I had to do. Or had I already done it? Is that why the police had come?

'Did the ambulance come?'

There was still no response from the policemen.

'I mean did the ambulance come for Jim? Is he…is he…?' The vision of Jim's shoes came back to me and the blood and the mess of scrunched up bone.

'Bloody hell, she's going to be sick again, watch your driving can't you?' said the big policeman.

The panic was rising up in my throat.

'Is Jim going to be alright?' I asked. Well, actually I think I shrieked. 'We have to stop,' I started to shout. 'You don't understand, you have to stop. It's not me who's hurt, it's Jim.' I was banging on the door of the car and trying to open it.

'Bloody hell, we've got a right one here,' the big policeman said screwing round again to face me. 'Shut the hell up missy or else.'

The tone of his voice was like a punch in the face. But the hysteria had taken hold. I continued to bang at the door of the police car. This caused a great deal of panic amongst the policemen such that we all became hysterical.

The policeman next to me was leaning over me and trying to grab one of my arms as I banged ineffectually against the door of the car. The car skidded round a bend and as I lurched into the policeman next to me he clicked a handcuff onto my right arm. It was rough and heavy. I fell back into the seat and started to cry.

'Delusional,' commented the driver knowingly.

'De what?'

'Delusional. Means she's in denial. Thinks she hasn't done it.'

'Hysterical you mean,' said the big policeman sourly.

At least the delusional thought had slowed the driver down.

I looked from one to the other but was too frightened to speak now. I knew what delusional meant and it didn't sound good. And I was deluded, or at least deranged. After all, who wouldn't be? I could only hope that I was completely deluded and that Jim was sitting smirking and smarming, in other words being his usual self, at our kitchen table while Mum made the tea. The thought of Jim smirking and smarming was strangely comforting and I leant back against the cheap plastic of the back seat of the blue and white police car, shut my eyes and cried quietly to myself. Because if he was smirking and smarming in our kitchen there wouldn't be any need for handcuffs, would there, and all this would just be one big mistake.

The siren on top of the police car suddenly started blaring again and we pulled into the police station forecourt with a dramatic sharp turn which flung me against the car door. My right shoulder was nearly wrenched out of its socket as the handcuffed arm pulled in the other direction, because it was attached to the policeman in the back of the car with me.

Other policemen came running out of the police station and one of them pulled the back door open. He looked disappointed when he saw me. I'm not very significant looking. I'm small and mousey and people usually think that Claire is older than me.

'She doesn't look up to much,' he said to the big policeman who had climbed out of the car.

'Come on, out with you,' the big policeman said to me. Then he turned back to the policeman holding the door open. 'Don't you kid yourself, we've had a lot of trouble with this one. Tried to jump out of the car, she did, while we were going full speed an' all.'

I pulled myself out of the car carefully. My shoulder really hurt and the policeman I was handcuffed to had to shuffle out after me. It didn't seem very dignified and he finally gave me a big push so that we both half fell at the feet of the disappointed policeman. I stood up straight and the handcuff fell off. We all looked at it as it swung against the policeman who'd been sitting in the back of the car with me as he also scrambled to his feet. The disappointed policeman rolled his eyes.

'Come on, luvey,' he said.

The big policeman was fussing about the handcuffs and grabbed my arm roughly.

'She's a little devil, a little witch. Get those cuffs back on,' he shouted.

The disappointed policeman touched him lightly on the arm. 'That's enough, Foster, okay.' He turned back to me and indicated that I should go with him and I followed him meekly into the station, looking up at his broad back. I must have been at least two heads shorter than him. He turned round to check that I was still following him when we got inside, then carried on into the depths of the police station with me trailing behind him.

Claire

I didn't want to read Kate's name anymore so I went and stood by the window. I can see the street from my bedroom window. Sometimes I look out of my window to see if Kate or Mum are coming home.

But not anymore.

I looked out of the window and saw an ambulance and two police cars and another car. The men were outside being noisy. Mum was there. I could only see her back. A flat bed thing was put into the ambulance. It had gone quiet and the men had stopped shouting. Mum was all hunched over looking at the ambulance. She wasn't talking to anyone. Mrs Hunter was there. She glanced up at the window and I felt frightened again. I went back to my bed and read my Bunty annual but I didn't want to read Kate's name and the other words were too difficult. I wished Mum would come back into the house and that we could have bacon and eggs for tea.

Kate

The policeman sat behind a desk then turned to face me. He had pulled out some paper or a form from the desk and sat looking at me with pencil poised.

'Name?'

I looked at him blankly.

'Don't play silly buggers. Name.'

I cringed into my dirty school shirt.

'Catherine Howard,' I said. It wasn't a very auspicious name but the policeman seemed as unaware of the implications as my parents had obviously been when they christened me.

'Address?'

'12 Potter's View.'

'That'll be Whitcliff?'

I nodded.

'Yes?' he looked at me sternly.

'Yes,' I said faintly.

'Telephone?'

I shook my head and he looked at me again.

'We don't have one,' I said.

This caused a bit of an impasse; first because he paused to survey me less sympathetically than he had been prepared to do before and secondly because he spent more time writing down something on the form.

'Age?'

'Eighteen.'

'I'll take your word for it,' he said writing it down. 'Okay,' he continued, 'stand up now please, Miss Howard, and come here.'

I hovered close to my chair.

'Here please,' he repeated indicating that I should come and stand by the table. 'Empty your pockets.'

I obediently emptied my skirt pocket – it only had one pocket – onto the table. It contained an old handkerchief, my mother's watch which was too big to go round my wrist but she'd lent it to me for my exam that morning, change from my iced bun and the key to our shed. I stared at the key. What on earth was that doing in my pocket?

'And your shoes, please, up on the desk.'

I undid the laces and took my shoes off. Dried blood made them stick to the floor where I'd been standing. I held them away from me and placed them on the desk carefully, away from the contents of my pocket.

The policeman put my shoes in a plastic bag and the things from my pocket into another plastic bag. He then stood up and went out of the room with the plastic bags, leaving me standing by the desk.

Claire

Has Jim gone? I asked Mum. I asked if we could have bacon and eggs and we did. But Mum didn't answer about Jim so I asked her again. I hoped that Jim had gone because all the blood was horrid. Mum was still white and her eyes were blotchy. I felt another new feeling about Kate and being on my own. I asked Mum if I should go to my bedroom again. I didn't like these new feelings and I didn't like not knowing what to do. But Mum moved her chair next to mine and put her arms around me. I leant into Mum. Her bosoms were warm and soft. I liked being warm and soft with Mum. I liked it that Jim wasn't there. Mum hadn't eaten her tea so I reached over for her plate and ate her food as well. Mum didn't tell me off. She just held on to me.

Kate

When the next man came into the interview room I was sitting on the chair again. He looked at me dispassionately as I drooped on the wooden chair. A policeman in uniform had followed him into the room. The first man was wearing an ordinary suit and carried a buff folder. He was what Mum would have referred to as a plainclothes policeman. He turned to the uniformed man.

'Bring her a glass of water and some tea,' he said, then continuing his perusal of me, he added, 'and put lots of sugar in the tea.'

'Do you want anything, Sir?'

'No. Apart from that bloody duty solicitor. Make sure Cripps is still chasing him up. I don't know why we have to bother with the meddling bastards anyway. They invariably balls it up.'

The uniformed policeman coughed awkwardly.

'Well, what are you waiting for? Get on with it,' the plainclothes policeman bellowed.

He was an ugly man, the plainclothes policeman. He was fat around the tummy, his hair was thin and greying and his moon-shaped face was pasty and oily. He stood at the other side of the desk from me, put the folder down on the desk and took off his jacket and loosened his tie. His blue shirt was stained with sweat under his armpits and the smell of sweat had drifted into the room with him. He was still breathing heavily after his little outburst. But his eyes, although pasty coloured like his face, were intelligent. I returned his gaze with some attempt at confidence. Intelligence was something I thought I could trust.

He sat at the desk and read over the form that the other policeman had filled out. He turned the page over and twisted his awkward body round to reach for a pen out of his jacket pocket from where it hung over the back of his chair. It was quiet for a moment, and then the uniformed policeman who'd been sent to get tea and water came in and put the tea and water on the desk.

'Anything else, Sir?'

'No, just park yourself by the door there and we'll get on shall we?'

He looked threateningly at the uniformed policeman as if he was expected to make some sort of answer or complaint. I looked at

17

him expectantly too in case some new drama would arise, but the uniformed policeman adopted a blank expression. He may have said something soothing and innocuous like, 'Yes, Sir'. The plainclothes policeman smiled a small, cruel smile and said, 'I'm not waiting all night for some half-arsed twit to decide he's got nothing better to do.'

Neither of us made any comment to this statement and the plainclothes policeman rubbed his hands with an air of relish and turned his attention to me.

'Bring your chair closer, Miss Howard. That's right, by the table here. Good. And drink the tea. You'll feel better for it.'

The tea was also pasty coloured and globules of fat floated on the top. I picked up the cup and leant my lips towards it gingerly before giving it an obedient slurp. The sugar was a shock on the tongue, but the man was right, it did make me feel better and I drank it down while he watched me.

'Good. Now, Miss Howard,' he paused and cocked an eye at me. 'Do you mind if I call you Catherine?' By now, in his eyes, I probably looked scarcely adolescent let alone eighteen and old enough to be holding down a job, a husband and even children.

'Everyone calls me Kate,' I said.

'Good. Well then, Kate, Do you know why you've been brought in here? You do know where you are, don't you?'

'I think it's the central police station, isn't it? Down town, just past Woolworths?'

'Yes, well.' Another small smile twisted over his thin lips. 'And do you know why you've been brought here?'

There was a silence. The policeman by the door shuffled his feet and the man turned a warning look towards him.

'I'm not sure,' I ventured at last. There was another short silence. 'But I suppose I was expecting an ambulance so perhaps when you ring for an ambulance a police car comes as well?'

The man opened the buff folder and looked at some papers inside it.

'Who rang for an ambulance?' he asked.

'Well, I did.'

'Really?'

'Well, yes I think so.'

'You think so?'

'Well yes, that's what I had to do. I…I found Jim and…and I had to call for an ambulance because…because that's what you do when someone's…because Jim…' I looked up at him hoping he would help me.

'Because Jim was dead. Is that what you are trying to say?'

'I don't know. I didn't check to see if he was dead. I just ran to get help.'

'I see.'

The man now turned to the other policeman.

'Get Cripps and let's take a statement from her.'

'Sir, I…'

The piggy eyes looked at him menacingly.

'Last time,' the poor policeman tried to splutter.

Piggy Eyes stood up and I wasn't sure who got more scared, me or the other policeman. Anyway he, the other policeman, scuttled out of the room and I drooped back into my chair. The suppressed violence of the big man was making me feel sick again, the fatty tea was hanging like a lump in my stomach and my ears were buzzing. I hoped I wasn't going to faint. The uniformed policeman came back. This time he led a woman into the room and brought another chair with him. The woman was also in uniform. She smiled at me impersonally and sat down at the desk with a pen poised over a note pad. She reminded me of the sewing mistress we'd had in third year. She was thin and neat and middle aged and peered through the sort of tortoiseshell glasses which had gone out of fashion.

The man turned his attention back to me.

'Now, Kate, you are going to make a statement so that we can sort out what happened today.' He looked smugly at the uniformed policeman by the door, then turned back to me. 'Now, just tell me in your own words what you did today, where you went and who you met.'

I nodded, although black dots were now dancing in front of my eyes.

'I got up as usual at seven o'clock because I had an exam this morning. My mother was already up. We just had toast because she was going to the clinic and Jim and Claire were still in bed. Claire was at home today and Jim had to look after her.'

'Alright, alright, steady on. I wonder if you can explain to me who all these people are, Kate?'

'Well my mother's my mother, Claire's my sister and Jim is Jim.'

The piggy eyes hardened.

'Don't get smart with me, Kate,' he said softly.

I looked at him in alarm. I hadn't meant to be clever, it was just the way it came out. I swallowed.

'My mother well my mother's married to Jim and Claire's my sister.'

'So Jim is your stepfather? Is that right?'

I nodded.

'Is that right?'

'Yes.'

'And your mother is usually at home, but today she was going out. You knew she was going out and you knew when she'd get back home this afternoon?'

'Yes, she should have been back by four o'clock.'

'Okay. And you also knew that Jim would be at home all day on his own?'

'Well yes, because someone had to look after Claire as it isn't her day to go to Whitcliff.'

'Claire's your sister?'

'Yes.'

'And how old is she?'

'Sixteen.'

'She's sixteen? Then she doesn't need anyone to look after her, does she?'

'She's handicapped, Sir,' the Sir slipped out.

The man paused at this point while he trawled through the notes in the buff folder. He turned an angry look towards WPC Cripps and the policeman by the door.

'Why doesn't anyone ever get the details right?' he hissed at his silent audience. He turned to WPC Cripps. 'Are you getting any of this down?'

'Yes, Sir.'

He looked sceptical but turned to me again.

'So you got up early this morning and went to school to do an exam knowing that your mother would be out for the day and that

Jim, who is your stepfather, would be at home with your sister.' He sighed heavily. 'So you did your exam and left school at, what? Twelve o'clock? You didn't go to afternoon classes?'

'No, I'm finished at school now. I just did my last exam today.'

'"O' levels?'

'No, 'A' levels.'

He looked at my notes again.

'So, at twelve o'clock you finished your exam and went home?'

'No, Jane had some sandwiches with her and we sat on the bank by the hockey pitch and ate them for lunch.'

'Oh for crying out loud, girl, I'm investigating a murder here not writing a page in the school's year book.'

A murder? Jim had been *murdered*?

Kate

Another man had joined us. He was young and had bad skin. He looked at me nervously and the piggy eyes looked at him disdainfully.

'You should have been here over an hour ago,' the plainclothes policeman said to the young man. He leaned over his desk and glowered. 'But I won't complain about late attendance if you just let me get on with things here.'

The young man made a vague gesture which was taken for acquiescence.

I put my head on my arms on the desk, not really caring any more what they thought. The little black dots were now hopping in front of my eyes and I think I was very hungry – only I couldn't have eaten anything even if I'd been given something. I also smelt. The piggy eyed man smelt. Even WPC Cripps was drooping in her chair. I didn't know what the time was because they'd taken Mum's watch. I daren't ask about Jim but I could hear the man talking and the scratch of WPC Cripps' pencil as she took down the statement.

'Let's take it from Miss Howard leaving school. She arrives home between twelve and two. At home she finds her handicapped sister and her stepfather. Let us say that she hears that her stepfather is in his workshop. She goes to the workshop, hits him over the head with a shovel, switches on the rotary saw on the workbench, pushes him on to it and leaves him.'

If the man was looking at me during this speech I didn't know, as I kept my head in my hands and began to hope that they would all just go away. The young man with the bad skin who was sitting somewhere near me was so quiet I though he must be holding his breath. The scratch of WPC Cripps' pen sounded unnaturally loud. Piggy Eyes continued.

'She goes back to the house and begins to think about what she has done. Maybe she now regrets her actions and returns to the workshop with some idea of trying to save her stepfather. She goes into the workshop a second time. She is overcome with the sight of the dead man, panics and runs away. We have a witness who saw her leaving the crime scene at three thirty and the trail of blood from her shoes alerted the witness to the crime. An ambulance was called for at twenty minutes to four from the victim's own telephone. The witness also alluded to strained relations between the suspect and her stepfather. The suspect was picked up at four thirty where she was found hiding in a telephone box on the Old North Road. The suspect has not denied the charges.'

I sensed that the man now changed position.

'We just need you to sign your name, Kate.' He sounded tired now, not unkind. I raised my head slightly and a sheet of paper was pushed under my arm with a pen. I looked up and around at the other people in the room, my eyes resting on the young man with the bad skin. When I caught his eye he looked alarmed and turned away from me. I looked back at the piggy eyed man and could see the impatience burning under the brief illusion of kindness coupled with his fatigue. I looked unseeingly at the piece of paper under my arm and wrote my name on it. It was snatched up quickly by the plainclothes policeman. I heard the rustling of papers being gathered up and then the scraping of chairs as the young man and WPC Cripps stood up. The man was talking as they stood up. His voice was lowered in a sotto voce whisper.

'We'd better get a medical man in here and check for signs of a struggle or well, you know, anything else.'

Piggy Eyes followed them to the door.

'If you insist,' he said to the young man but his voice had a gloating edge to it. 'You'll not find anything,' he added smugly as I heard them leave the room and then I heard the sound of a key turning in the lock. They'd locked me in. If I hadn't been so exhausted I'd have run after them and hammered on the door. I tried to quell the desire for hysteria and to concentrate my mind on what had just been going on. I'd heard what the man said but I couldn't focus on the words. I stayed leaning with my head on my arms on the desk and hoped that I would fall asleep.

But I didn't fall asleep. I drifted yes, but I was horribly aware of things. Of the room, of the smell of sick, of sweat, of my arms aching and stiff because I wouldn't move, of my feet being cold, of my being cold although it was hot and stuffy in the room. My left side was the worst. I must have bruised it badly when the police car suddenly turned into the police station and my ribs hurt when I took a deep breath. I carefully moved my right hand and felt my left side but it didn't help much and I put my arm back on the table and continued not to sleep. Which was when the door opened again and more people came in. I know there were more people because I could hear at least two different voices.

'Come on, now, wakey-wakey,' one of them said. It was a man's voice. He put a hand on my shoulder. It was a warm hand. I raised my head slowly. 'Miss Howard, Kate is it?'

I nodded. I didn't manage to focus very distinctly on the man. A woman was standing by the door.

'I just need you to stand up for me, Kate,' he continued. 'That's right, good girl.'

He stood in front of me and took my chin in his hand. He turned my head from side to side and examined me carefully.

'Okay. No signs of any bruising on the face. I just need to look at your body, Kate. That's alright with you, isn't it?'

I nodded and a tear was forcing its way through my eyelashes.

He tensed when he found the growing bruise around my ribs and tutted in an interested way.

'Nasty bruise that, Kate,' he said.

He knelt on the floor in front of me and I felt awkward and embarrassed. He raised my skirt and seemed to scrutinise my legs. It wasn't the sort of examination that the school nurse gave us when we had check-ups but something more sinister and intrusive. Nonetheless I had, by this time, concluded that this man was a doctor.

He stood up again and turned to the woman standing in the doorway.

'No bruising on the thighs,' he said. 'I can't think he meant us to make any more detailed an examination, can you?' he addressed the woman.

'No, it hardly seems necessary,' she replied.

And they left, the doctor half turning to me as if embarrassed before he left the room. The door was locked from the outside again and I was now standing in the middle of the room. The warm hand had gone and the tears were coursing down my cheeks. I crumpled onto the floor and curled myself up into a tight ball, tucking my head into my body and my knees up to my chest. It was what I used to do when I was little and Mum was with Claire and no one wanted me.

Kate

I didn't think I'd fallen asleep but I was startled awake by one of the original policemen. Although by now I couldn't remember which of them it was and remembering any kind of sequence of events was getting difficult. He took my left arm rather roughly – the one that hurt – and pulled me out of the interview room. He had a bunch of keys dangling from his belt and started fiddling with them with the hand that wasn't holding me. We went down a long yellow corridor and I tried to wake up and pay some attention to what was going on. There wasn't anything to see, just a locked door made of bars at the end of the corridor we were going down. There wasn't much to hear either. Everything was muffled. There was no noise from the outside world and it was like being in a dream under water. Everything was heavy and slow and there was something suffocating as well as scary about it all.

 The policeman opened the barred gate with one of his keys, pushed me through and locked us in on the other side. The corridor came to an end and eight white doors with hatches in them lined the walls. A drunken old man was singing in one of them and I almost wished that they'd put me in with him so that I wouldn't be on my own. I knew I was going to be put on my own. They were treating me as if I was dangerous. As if they were a bit alarmed, or as though I was alarming rather than just pathetic.

 The cell had a barred window, slime-green walls, a narrow bed with a blanket and a piss-pot. Well, a potty really but a piss-pot sounds more Shakespearean and grandly tragic instead of sordidly banal. The policeman locked me in the cell and I stood looking at the potty for some time. After relieving myself, I lay down on the bed on top of the blanket. I lay on my side and foetus-like I hugged my knees up to my chin and tucked my arms in with my hands under my head. I stared at the slime-green wall and tried to ease the fear from my mind like teasing tangles from hair when it's just been washed. There were gaps in my memory, huge gaps, and they were getting bigger not smaller. I shut my eyes against the aggressive affect of the slime-green wall and tried to think.

Kate

I did my examination. It was the English paper three, the unseen. I'd done the poem. Jane did the prose piece because she said that the poem was too difficult. I'd picked up the half rhyme in the second verse but I'd forgotten to compare it with the half rhyme in the fourth verse. I'd also completely ignored the metaphor about the butterfly. I looked at the green wall. It was unquestionably a horrible green, the kind of green that Jim would have chosen for the bathroom. I teased my way around that particular knot, shut my eyes again and wondered how Jane had got on in her last exam. We'd arranged to meet up outside the theatre café after tea. That is if Mum would let me go out. But that must be long past now. Jane would think that Mum had said I had to stay in. Jane wouldn't know I was here.

Did *anyone* know I was here? Mum might think I'd gone out with Jane without asking and Jim would say that I didn't pull my weight with the family and that I should have stayed at home to look after Claire and not him. He'd missed a day's work and I didn't need an English 'A' Level to get a job or even to go to teacher training college. Jim thinks he knows everything but he knows nothing. Jim wouldn't get me out of here, he'd tell Mum it was my own fault and that it would teach me a lesson to be locked up over night without food. I think I might have shouted this. I was certainly looking at the slime-green wall again.

'I really hate Jim.' I definitely shouted out this time. 'I really hate Jim.' There was something smarmy about him and Mum just didn't see it. Maybe he was clever but because he was clever the rest of us weren't allowed to be. Jim had made me put off my University application and he was going to do it again if I tried to go back to school for a seventh term. He was going to make me get a job, wasn't he?

The lights suddenly all clicked off and the drunken man stopped singing. I couldn't see the green walls anymore but when my eyes adjusted to the dark I could just make out the square of the barred window and a thin edge of light made a rim around the hatch in the door.

I was at the police station and Jim was dead. And if Jim was dead I could apply to University. Unless I had to stay here looking at these slime-green walls forever. Perhaps *I* was dead, perhaps Jim had killed me and sent me to purgatory, or even hell. Jim would have enjoyed that. On the other hand, if Jim was dead maybe I would have to stay at home and help look after Claire. Or get a job and help Mum keep our home going. Perhaps after all it would be better if Jim wasn't dead.

I looked at the faint light behind the barred window, released the grip on my knees just a little and tried to concentrate on the injured, dead or dying Jim. Had I managed to call an ambulance and had that ambulance managed to collect the bleeding remnants of Jim and coax him back to life? And for goodness sake why was that piggy-eyed detective man confusing everything by talking about murder? Who would want to murder Jim?

I called the ambulance, didn't I? I found Jim and I ran off to the phone box by the bus stop and I rang emergency services. Perhaps I got the police instead, then they came and picked me up. They would know where I was because of making the phone call. It was odd though that they didn't find me until so much later and in that horrid phone box on the main road near Potter's Farm. I'm sure I got home at about half past three by which time according to the policeman Jim was already dead. Or dying. Or murdered.

There must have been something I could remember properly. I met John Melmerby at the school bus stop and we travelled home on the bus together. Or was that yesterday? Yes I couldn't have met John on the bus today because he would have been doing another exam this afternoon – like Jane. I do remember I was hungry because Jane had eaten most of the sandwiches and I bought an iced bun on the way to the bus stop. But I don't think I had enough money so perhaps I didn't buy a bun.

I got home and had my usual chat with Claire. She was listening to the radio and we sang a bit of Elvis Presley together. She likes it when I do that but not if I sing too loudly. Claire didn't know where Jim was and I got cross and went to find him in the shed. His 'workshop'. He was making another of his bodged affairs for Mum to admire when she got in from work.

I remembered Jim and the saw and a white bit of bone sticking out from his arm.

Claire

When I woke up Mum said that I was going to Whitcliff. I had to think about this carefully. I asked Mum several times what day it was and every time I asked her she said it was Wednesday which was puzzling because I didn't go to Whitcliff on Wednesdays. If I went to Whitcliff I might get treacle sponge for pudding but if I stayed at home I could listen to Elvis Presley. I asked Mum about the treacle sponge and I didn't like it that she didn't say yes or no. She said maybe or perhaps. I don't like maybe or perhaps. I got dressed anyway but when Mrs Hunter came round and said that she could take Claire to Whitcliff now if she was ready I said I wasn't going to Whitcliff and went into the back room and put the radio on. I turned the radio up so that I couldn't hear them talking but I'd only got through one bit of 'Are you lonesome tonight' when Mum came in with my cardigan. She was wearing her cardigan as well. She said we could get the bus and that if I didn't have treacle sponge she would make me one for tea. I suddenly felt happy and gave Mum a cuddle. It was just Mum and I. It was wonderful. It was so, so, so un-com-pli-ca-ted.

Kate

The Magistrate's Court was packed. We were all waiting in line. Me. The drunken man from the cells the night before. Two youths looking guilty. A man in a suit who kept tugging at his tie nervously. And the young man with acne I recognised from the previous evening. His neck was rubbed raw by his stiff shirt collar. It was hot.

They sent me in first and the young man followed me in to face the magistrate. This was a bit puzzling but no more puzzling than anything else that was happening to me.

The plainclothes policeman (Piggy Eyes) was on one side of the room and I was on the other. The magistrate looked at me distastefully, which as I still smelt wasn't very surprising. Although surely he couldn't smell me from up in his box. They'd lent me some shoes. Big shoes. Mine were evidence they said. I'd eaten a slice of toast with marmalade for breakfast and drunk some more sweet tea. It was becoming a bit of a habit, this sweet tea thing.

The sludgy eyes of the plainclothes policeman avoided mine. He handed some notes to the magistrate and they talked among themselves, and the young man with bad skin joined them. The magistrate kept looking at me, but the policeman didn't. He still had the same jacket on and possibly even the same shirt. There were beads of sweat on his forehead.

'Miss Catherine Howard?' The Magistrate's voice was suddenly loud and unmistakeably directed at me. I looked from him to the policeman.

'Miss Catherine Howard?' the Magistrate repeated crossly.

I looked at him apprehensively.

'You are Miss Catherine Howard?' he asked.

I nodded, then I remembered the policemen getting cross when I didn't answer.

'Yes,' I said, faintly.

'Miss Catherine Howard, you are charged with the murder of James Brown. The crime was committed on 15th June 1966 and a statement is signed by you on the same date giving a plea of guilty. You, the suspect, are to be remanded in custody pending trial. There are no requests for bail.'

This last statement confused me until I realised that he had addressed it to the young man with bad skin and that the policeman answered him in the negative.

And then the Magistrate looked at me again.

'Miss Howard do you have anything to say in your defence?'

My defence. I looked at him blankly. I took a deep breath and ran my mind carefully over his words. Murder? James Brown, well that was Jim. 15th June, that was yesterday. And remanded in custody, well, that meant prison.

'You're putting me in prison,' I said suddenly. My voice sounded loud and a shocked buzzing started hammering in my ears. My legs were shaking and my mouth formed the word why? But no more words came out.

The Magistrate had turned back to the policeman with a knowing look in his lean and aging face. He had grey sideburns. He brought a black mallet thing down on his bench.

'That's all. Next, please,' he shouted.

I was dismissed. Hands clutched at me and led me out of the court. A woman with a different uniform had taken my arm.

'Come on, dearie, let's get you out of here. Jesus wept, what've they been doing with you, you stink worse than a dustbin.'

I turned to look at her. She was about the same age as Mum. Her hair was cut short and it had a big grey streak in the fringe. Her uniform was blue and she wore trousers. She was dangling handcuffs from one hand.

She looked at me disparagingly.

'I don't think we'll be needing these, eh?' she said to me and dropped the handcuffs in her jacket pocket. 'Thank god we won't have to hang around all day waiting for anyone else.'

While she talked she led me away from the court and out through a back entrance where two police vehicles were waiting. One looked like an armoured van. This was the one we headed towards.

'Come on, open up, Bob,' the woman shouted and she banged on the back door of the armoured van.

Bob appeared with a cigarette hanging from his lips.

'That didn't take long,' he said.

'No, well, and this ruddy van is over-kill if you ask me.'

The woman and Bob both turned to look at me. The woman had released her grip on my arm and I just stood waiting, feeling my feet slopping around in the too-big shoes.

'I think you can cancel the armed escort,' the woman said dryly to Bob. 'Eh, murder suspect my arse. How the hell is this scrap meant to have…well bloody hell, it takes all sorts I suppose.' She heaved a big sigh.

Bob removed the cigarette from his mouth and ground it out on the tarmac with his heel. He opened the back of the van with an air of finality and the woman took hold of me again and, pushing me up into the van, climbed up behind me. The van had three rows of seats facing forwards and small windows with bars which offered a limited view out into the world. I sat next to one of these windows and the woman sat next to me.

'Okay, Bob,' she called over her shoulder, 'best get going then, hadn't we.'

Bob banged the grey doors closed and I heard the click of a heavy-duty lock as he pulled the door bolt into place. He walked round to the front of the van and climbed into the driver's seat. The engine started and the dry, insistent smell of cigarette smoke penetrated into the back of the van as he lit another cigarette before starting the engine and driving out of the back entrance of the Magistrate's Court and onto Clifford Street.

I turned to the woman. 'Where are we going?' I asked.

The woman turned to face me. 'Ah ha, it has a voice,' she said. 'What's your name, dearie?'

'Kate.'

'Ah, well, that's a deal less of a mouthful than Miss Catherine Howard. And didn't they tell you where you were going?'

I shook my head.

'Wakefield.'

'Wakefield?' I questioned, bemused.

'Wakefield Prison.'

'Prison? But…'

The woman looked at me less sympathetically.

'Bloody hell, just settle down, dearie, and enjoy the drive. We'll be on the road an hour or so. My name's Dickson, by the way.'

'Oh.'

I turned back to the window. We were already on the edge of town, heading south. It wasn't an area I knew well. We'd once been out this way on the bus to look at some puppies, but Jim had decided that Mum couldn't cope with Claire *and* a puppy, although the puppy was meant to have been mine. I remembered a small terrier with fox-coloured fur. It had kissed me with a black nose and got so excited it had fallen into a wastepaper basket. My cheeks hurt as I remembered the terrier and looked out at green meadows through the barred slits of the prison van.

I turned to look at Dickson instead. Dickson was powerfully built but she had round shoulders and a big soft bosom and would have seemed quite motherly if she hadn't been so physically alert and powerful. Her face was strained and her skin dry and colourless. She probably wasn't as old as she looked. Despite the copy of the *Daily Mirror* on her knee and the swearing, she seemed switched-on and with it. I didn't know if this was a good thing or not. She caught me looking at her and as this elicited an irritated grunt I turned back to the green fields. I hoped I wouldn't cry. I'd decided that Dickson wouldn't be very sympathetic if I did. But I was used to that. I never ever cried if anyone was going to see. At least, I never ever cried in front of Jim.

Claire

I had a family picture at Whitcliff. I drew everyone and then wrote their names. It looked like this.

I was colouring my family picture in. I wrote Mum's name again and my name lots of times. I crossed Jim out very carefully then I crossed out his picture not so carefully. I looked at Kate for a long time and then I put a big red line through her.

We had blancmange for pudding and Lesley let me have a second helping which she wasn't really supposed to do.

Kate

When we got to Wakefield, Dickson took me straight off to the bathrooms with a thin towel and a hard bar of yellow soap. She stayed in there with me – drinking a cup of tea and rustling her copy of the *Daily Mirror* while she glanced at me now and again humphing disconsolately either over the *Daily Mirror* or me.

'Eighteen my foot, you don't look more than twelve and what's more, you look like you haven't had a decent meal in years. Come on, dearie, we haven't got all day.' She sounded cross.

I didn't want the stream of lukewarm water to stop and the soap was so strong that it was starting to drown out the other stale smells which had stuck in my hair and skin. I shook my hair under the water and even applied the soap to that. Jane would have a fit. She was always getting at me to buy proper hair shampoo. She always used Sunsilk shampoo and her hair was thick and glossy. She would shake it out in the sun or under electric lights so that everyone could admire all the chestnut and auburn lights in it. I wondered if mousy hair could be transformed by Sunsilk shampoo.

'Howard, get your arse out of that shower. Madam herself will be in here if we don't look sharp.'

Madam? I wondered, as I was rudely dragged back to the present. I pulled the towel around me and moved over to my sad heap of clothes. Dickson followed my gaze.

'Bloody hell, you haven't got anything else, have you? The family usually turn up with some basics.' She sighed heavily. 'I'll see what we've got in the box.'

The box was a heap of forgotten articles of clothing piled in a dusty corner of the shower-room. It was just like the lost property box we had outside the gym at school. Dickson unearthed a few shapeless garments and produced a pair of jodhpur-style trousers and a blouse printed with pink rosebuds. The blouse was quite small but only had two buttons left. The jodhpurs were enormous. I put them on and Dickson started to laugh.

'Bloody hell,' she said several times and slapped her thigh vigorously. The jodhpurs would have fitted her. 'Well, it'll have to do,' she said when she finally stopped laughing. She wrapped up the remnants of my school uniform, indicated that I would still have to wear the too-large shoes and pushed me towards the door.

'I'll see if we can't get you some food before we throw you to the lions,' she said, suddenly severe again.

Dickson marched me back up a white corridor. Dickson, I noticed, had a big bottom; the kind that wobbles in trousers. She'd have looked better in a skirt. Perhaps prison people didn't wear skirts. We arrived at a small temporary cell. Dickson pointed to a chair inside this cell then went on up the corridor on her own, still carrying my soiled bits of school uniform. She hadn't bothered to lock the cell door. The police cell had been violent with its slime-green walls; this cell was all emptiness. It felt like the sort of place where you could just be forgotten and slowly vanish into white nothingness.

Anyway, I didn't vanish into nothingness because Dickson reappeared in a very short time with a plate of meat pie, carrots and mashed potatoes. I was ravenous. Perhaps it was the effect of being clean or perhaps it was the effect of Dickson. Whatever it was, that meat pie was good. Dickson sat down, watching me again while I ate.

'They wouldn't let me get a cup of tea for you. You'll have to drink that in the canteen. That is if they'll let you in the canteen today. Mind you, I don't think word's got out yet. Bloody hell.'

She took my empty plate and yanked her head towards the door. Although I couldn't make any sense of most of what she said, I was beginning to understand her instructions. I trotted out of the cell and, feeling almost human after the meat pie, I followed her up the long corridor with a little bounce in my step. At least until the shoes fell off, then I had to shuffle again.

We went into an office. I had to sign a slip to say that my school uniform was mine.

'It's not going to be anyone else's now, is it?' Dickson said to the woman. The woman wore a smart blue jacket and skirt, so that answered one of my questions about prison.

'Are you being insolent, Dickson?' the smart woman said.

'No, ma'am,' Dickson said. She'd hardly have said yes, would she?

But the smart woman was more interested in me.

'You may only be on remand now,' she said, 'but it makes no difference with me. Okay?'

I nodded. The 'Okay' was redolent of the aggression the piggy-eyed policeman attached to the same word.

'Prison is prison and the rules are the same for everyone. Understood?' She gave Dickson a hard look. 'We don't have many prisoners on remand in your category so you might have to be on your own at first. But you'll follow regulations like everyone else.'

I nodded. I wanted to ask what my 'category' was but the prim aggression of the woman didn't invite the asking of questions.

'Yes, ma'am,' I said instead, copying Dickson.

'Now take her down to the cells,' she continued to Dickson. 'That small one at the end of 'B' wing will do for now.'

'Very well, ma'am,' Dickson said meekly.

I looked at Dickson sharply. I hadn't expected her to say anything meekly. I was beginning to understand that there was more than met the eye when it came to Dickson – which was an unfortunate analogy given Dickson's size.

The little cell at the end of 'B' wing was yellow. Canary yellow.

'It's meant to be bright, you see, so they don't top themselves,' said Dickson encouragingly.

It had a bunk bed, a potty, which Dickson reassuringly referred to as a 'Pisspot', and a table under the barred window with a chair at either end of it. It wasn't big, but I'm small. I could see the sun shining through the window. I could take the big uncomfortable shoes off. It was quiet. I could sleep. I could…

'Dickson,' I said suddenly as she turned to leave, 'Do you think I could have a couple of buttons?' I indicated the buttonless holes in the blouse, 'and a needle and thread?' and as this request wasn't immediately drowned in derision I added optimistically, 'and a book?'

'Bloody hell,' said Dickson, and she locked me in the little yellow cell.

Claire

On Saturday Mum and I got the bus together. We went into York. It was the first time I'd been into York with Mum on my own. I felt properly grown up like Kate. Kate does everything on her own except when she does things with Jane. I like Jane. Jane came to see us. She talked to Mum and she talked to me. She said something about Kate but Mum didn't say anything about Kate. I told her that Kate had run away and that Jim had gone. I was going to tell her about the blood but Mum suddenly told me that I had to go and find my Bunty Annual. I brought my Bunty Annual downstairs but Jane had gone.

    We went into Browns and Mum bought me a new skirt and a blouse. She said I should have something new because I was going to Whitcliff more days. I didn't like not knowing which days I went to Whitcliff anymore. And Mum didn't talk about things like that. Kate talked about things like that but Kate had run away. I didn't know if I liked Kate anymore.

    Mum bought me a blue skirt and a white blouse with a blue bit on the collar. The shop lady said I looked very pretty. Mum said that I had grown. I liked looking in the mirror in my new clothes. I liked looking at my blond curls and the shop lady smiled at me and Mum put her hand on my head as if she was stroking my hair.

    Mum said lets go to Bettys so we did. I think that Mum was happy too. We both had cheese on toast and Mum ordered a pot of tea for two. Which was odd because I don't like tea. But Mum let me put 3 spoons of sugar in my tea. When the waitress asked us if we wanted anything else I read the words chocolate and cake on the menu card thing and Mum was very pleased. She looked at the waitress and said yes that's what we'll have, chocolate cake for two. Tea for two and chocolate cake for two.

Kate

Someone must have decided that I should speak to my lawyer because someone had told the Governor that I had asked to speak to a lawyer. I decided quite irrationally that that someone must have been Dickson as I couldn't think who else would have done that and Dickson had taken on heroic proportions in my current lost state of being.

The lawyer, Mr Hardcastle, was waiting to interview me in one of the white cells and Dickson's broad back looked distinctly smug as she led me from the canary yellow cell up the long corridors to the interview rooms. Mr Hardcastle. Dickson and I had taken much comfort from the name. I mean, if Charles Dickens called a lawyer Hardcastle, you knew he was going to be tough.

I'd been confined to my cell for a week. Dickson said something about a newspaper and blown-up pictures and nothing better to do than gratify public demand for horror stories. 'As if you could have done any of that,' she had added, shedding more light on her previous hints than I could really bear to think about. Newspaper stories reporting on heinous crimes. The possibility that I had committed a heinous crime was now becoming uncomfortably clear to me. This thought returned unbidden into my head just as we reached the interview room. It was more like a cell. White walls and barred windows. Nothingness.

Dickson and I stopped in the middle of the room and looked at Mr Hardcastle, my lawyer.

'Bloody hell,' said Dickson, under her breath, 'he's still got pimples.'

Mr Hardcastle looked at us nervously. He held out his hand and it was obvious that it was only Dickson's uniform which stopped him from assuming that she was the murderess. He came to his senses just in time and held out his hand to me. Was it possible that he hadn't even recognised me? I recognised him. It was the young man with the bad skin who had followed my charge and remand during the fateful two days of arrest and imprisonment.

'Charles Hardcastle,' he said.

I took his hand.

'Kate Howard,' I replied.

I could feel Dickson bristling with irritation beside me, struggling to contain herself. She took a sharp intake of breath and said, 'I'll be outside if you need me, but as you can see you won't have much trouble with this one. Whatever the papers may say,' she added, flashing Mr Hardcastle a warning look.

'Please.' Mr Hardcastle indicated a chair by the table and walked round to sit on the other side. Bizarrely it seemed like a proper interview. Like an interview for a job or for a place at University. I suddenly wanted to cry. It was so ordinary. This clean-shaven young man with adolescent pimples sitting at a desk with me; we should have been studying T. S. Eliot together, not...I bit my lips. It was becoming a bit of a habit. I wouldn't have noticed, except Dickson had taken to producing Vaseline as well as yellow soap at washing hour.

I sat down and turned my face away from Mr Hardcastle. I couldn't bear to look at his clean (well, spotty actually), ordinary features. He had various papers on the table between us. He cleared his throat again.

'Err, Miss Howard.'

I chewed my lips. He had a nice voice. Posh. Too posh for here. Yes, we should have been reading Eliot together. *A woman drew her long black hair out tight*, was that how it went? *A woman drew? Brushed*?

'I've read through your notes,' the-voice-that-should've-been-reading-Eliot went on. 'But there doesn't seem to be much, well much to go on. I wonder if you couldn't just tell me in your own words what happened on the day your stepfather was killed?'

A tear had forced its way out and was running down my cheek. I shook my head. I tried to look at Mr Hardcastle.

'I didn't do it,' I managed to say. 'I didn't murder Jim.'

Mr Hardcastle looked rather taken aback. He started scrabbling through his notes.

'But, Miss Howard,' he said, 'it's a bit late to say that now. You've already signed a statement saying that you killed your stepfather. We just need to find, er, mitigating circumstances.'

'You can't find mitigating circumstances for something you didn't do.'

He looked at me to see if I knew what I was talking about, to see if I understood what mitigating circumstances meant.

'I mean you can't find mitigating circumstances for something I didn't do,' I explained emphasising the 'I' as if that explained everything. 'And I haven't signed a statement. I haven't signed anything, only for my clothes since I came here.' I was confident Dickson would be proud of me standing up for myself like this.

'This isn't anything to do with your current placement, Miss Howard,' Mr Hardcastle continued. 'It's to do with your arrest and consequent charge of murder, pending trial.'

He continued to shuffle papers and I watched him struggling, trying to decide what to do. He looked up at me again as if summoning courage to continue the conversation. Perhaps people who commit heinous crimes are very scary. Was I very scary? I was more inclined to believe that Mr Hardcastle wasn't very courageous. He resorted to making notes instead. Meanwhile I got distracted and started wondering what *The Waste Land* was actually about. All those images of decay and misfortune and yet one was lulled into thinking it was both beautiful and profound. I stood up and wandered to the window. Mr Hardcastle seemed to jump out of his skin and his pen rolled off the table. I went towards him to pick it up and he hopped up and down, his pimples burning with nervous energy.

'Miss Howard, Miss Howard, please sit down,' his posh voice squeaked. I changed my mind about the reading of Elliot. I didn't think that Mr Hardcastle would be up to it. Mr Hardcastle didn't sit down. He hopped between the desk and the door.

'Er, we're finished in here,' he called out urgently, trying to control the squeak.

Dickson didn't hear him. She was chatting to another prison officer outside.

'Shall I go, then?' I asked.

He moved towards the door, sort of pointing his finger at me like one does with a dog. (They were little Border Terriers, the puppies we went to see. I cut a picture of one out of a magazine and stuck it on my bedroom wall. And, no, Jim didn't like it because the Sellotape made a tear in the wallpaper, but I did it anyway.)

Mr Hardcastle opened the door and leant out looking for Dickson. I leant over the desk and tried to read the papers. 'Seriously delusional. Could be dangerous,' I read. I could hear

Dickson laughing with the other prison officer outside in the corridor and Mr Hardcastle's posh voice trying to attract her attention.

'Hey, you,' he said limply.

I heard Dickson say 'tarar' to the other prison officer and slump up the white corridor.

'You can't have finished already,' she said indignantly when she reached the door.

'Uncooperative,' I read upside down on the desk.

'Er, yes, that's all for now,' Mr Hardcastle said, trying to retrieve his dignity.

'Difficult case,' I read, 'pleads <u>not guilty</u>!' Not guilty had been underlined several times in his nervousness.

Mr Hardcastle was standing over me, holding out his hand. He was brave now that Dickson had followed him into the room.

'That'll be all for now, Miss Howard. We'll be in touch.'

It was like a job interview after all. Don't call us, we'll call you. I stood up and glanced up at Dickson before I drooped again and shuffled out of the white cell in the too-big shoes, the ridiculous jodhpurs and the rosebud blouse.

Kate

I had a visitor. It was a Sunday and Dickson was off duty. Dickson had made it clear that she didn't like being off duty because she was certain I was going to be lynched now I was allowed to join everyone else, (although I don't think Dickson quite understood the exact meaning and hence the implications of being lynched). And despite Dickson's morbid imaginings I didn't have any trouble with anyone. I was easy to ignore and I think that because I looked so unlike the committer of a heinous crime everyone had soon forgotten that I was the perpetrator of one. My fellow prisoners had been outspokenly disappointed. 'That! It couldn't even pinch the baby,' they'd said. Although I'd wished that they could have chosen a less demeaning metaphor to describe my ineptitude.

So they ignored me and I joined the queue of prisoners as we were filtered through into the visiting room. The visiting room consisted of rows of tables and chairs. Prisons didn't seem able to function without tables and chairs – prisoners were always either sitting opposite other prisoners or warders or lawyers and now visitors.

Jane! I saw her before she saw me. I wondered if I was allowed to wave, but luckily she saw me in the next moment and rushed over to sit on her side of the table.

'Katy.'

'Jane.'

Neither of us wanted to cry. I chewed my lips and Jane was suddenly uncharacteristically tongue-tied. The allocated thirty minutes started to tick away on the bland face of the plastic clock on the wall. It was difficult not to sit there and be aware of how different we were; not just present circumstances but how different we'd always been. I was – well, I still am – small, mousey and as insignificant looking as it's possible to be and after lashings of the hard yellow soap my hair was straighter and duller than ever. I had (and still have) no shape, so although Jane wasn't much taller than me she had the neat trim figure that boys seemed to like and lots of hair so that she just always seemed bigger. According to Jane I had nice eyes. They're grey but whenever I looked in the mirror they just looked murky and discontented to me. (Claire has clear blue eyes. She's always had lovely clear blue eyes from when she was a baby. Mine had changed to murky grey but hers had stayed cornflower blue. She was like an advertisement for something healthy.)

Perhaps Jane had been sifting through these differences in her mind too before she suddenly broke the silence. 'My God, what are you wearing?' she exclaimed, her horror at my jodhpurs and rosebud blouse overcoming her awkwardness at the surroundings. Jane was wearing a turquoise summer dress. It had orange and red flowers growing out of the hem and a dark blue braiding around the neck and sleeves. An orange scarf tied back her hair and her flimsy sandals were white.

I grinned and my lips cracked.

'How did you get here?' I asked, thinking that she couldn't have walked all the way from the station or the bus or however you were meant to get to the prison in those shoes.

'Rob just passed his test and Bruce let him borrow his car.'

I looked blank.

'Who's Bruce?'

'Rob's brother.'

'I thought that Rob was just a...' Just a what? A filler-inner until Mr Right came along?

'He'll do for now.'

'Oh.'

'That's so you, Kate. Oh,' she said, mimicking me.

She looked at my clothes again.

'Your Mum hasn't been, has she?'

I shook my head.

'I popped in to see her as soon as I heard.' She glanced at me with an awkward flush. 'And after the newspaper stuff. There were some horrible articles. The Test match was rained off and the papers had nothing better to write about.'

'It rained?' I said, surprised.

Jane looked at me, puzzled for a moment.

'Your Mum's worried about Claire. I'm sure she'd have been to see you otherwise. I mean she,' at this point Jane lowered her voice, 'I'm sure she can't believe that you did it.'

'I didn't.'

Jane looked at me again, but she didn't flush this time and her breathing settled deeper in her chest.

'Of course you didn't do it,' she said, more happily.

A warder patrolled behind my chair. Jane and I exchanged a look. I wondered if we were both thinking about the same thing because I was suddenly taken back to the endless chemistry lessons we had spent eating Poor Bens instead of doing our experiments. The chemistry teacher, a nervous young man not unlike Mr Hardcastle, had walked amongst the large group of adolescent girls trying to be authoritative but really being far too scared of us to either dispense knowledge or command respect. Like the warder patrolling now, he had attempted to give a semblance of control over the myriad of conversations, many likely to be seditious, going on in the room around him. Or in the case of the prison warder, going on around her. I grinned again and Jane pulled a very grown-up white handbag onto her knees and giggled. She opened the bag conspiratorially and pulled a book out of it. At first I looked blankly at the book. I'd expected it to be Poor Bens.

'*Emma*,' she said proudly.

I must have still looked disappointed about the Poor Bens. She pushed the book over to me.

'*Emma*,' she repeated. 'You said you wanted to read it after we'd finished.'

'*Emma*,' I said, suddenly remembering the summer I was going to spend with Jane doing nothing. Lazing in the sun and reading. Reading *Emma*. I was thrilled that Jane had remembered. Tortured, mortified and in despair that she had remembered what we should have been doing. I took the book up to hide the rush of conflicting emotions. I thought that for a moment I was going to shout a string of prison obscenities at Jane. For god's sake, *Emma* was almost an insult. She could have at least thought of something like...well, like what? *One Day in the Life of Ivan Denisovich*? *Escape from Alcatraz* or whatever it was?

The Warder was hovering near us and Jane was looking anxious. Had I said something out loud? I shuffled my feet awkwardly in the too-big shoes, put my head down in shame and confusion and turned over the first pages. *Emma Woodhouse, handsome, clever, and rich, with a comfortable home and happy disposition, seemed to unite some of the best blessings of existence; and had lived nearly twenty-one years in the world with very little to distress or vex her. She was the youngest of the two daughters of a most affectionate, indulgent father, and had...*

'Don't read it now,' hissed Jane.

A bell went. Like a school bell. Jane and I looked at each other.

'Do you think that means time's up?' asked Jane.

I presumed so. I must have looked irritated, angry even. Jane was trying not to cry.

'Look, I'll come again. I'll bring some clothes.' She paused, 'in case your Mum doesn't manage to get here,' she added quietly.

'How is Mum? And Claire?' Things suddenly seemed urgent. Why hadn't I asked Jane these things before?

'Okay. They're okay,' Jane was still whispering. She stood up. Other people had stood up. 'Bye then.'

'And shoes,' I said, 'bring some shoes.'

I stood watching her leaving with the other visitors and then my eyes wandered back down to the opening page of *Emma*.

...and had in consequence of her sister's marriage, been mistress of his house from a very early period. Her mother had died too long ago for her to have more than an indistinct remembrance of her...

'Come on, Howard, we haven't got all day.' The warder hung over me menacingly, suspicious of the book.

Nothing could be more harmless than *Emma*, I thought wryly, and I showed her the title page as if to assert my innocence. For a moment I thought that she was going to snatch it from me but some better part of her, or me, must have prevailed because I turned tail meekly and followed her from the visiting room, still clutching my book.

'We haven't got all day,' I recalled her words dejectedly. I had. I had all day, all week, all month, all year, all decade, all century. When the twenty-first century began I'd be fifty-two. A shrivelled little old woman still reading *Emma*. But wasn't that the life I'd planned for myself anyway? To be a little shrivelled-up old woman living as far away from family as possible, devoting my days to reading *Emma* and her like?

I was marched back into the canary yellow cell. I'd perfected my shuffle into a hup two three shuffle. It was quite effective. The rhythm of the shuffle dazed me into acceptance and compliance once more and my eyes strayed back to *Emma* as I was hustled into my cell.

...caresses, and her place had been supplied by an excellent woman as governess, who had fallen little short of a mother in affection.

I kicked off the too-big shoes and flung myself onto the canary yellow bed. Actually it wasn't canary yellow, it was grey, but it felt like canary yellow, a canary yellow cocoon wrapping me up into the fantasy land of *Emma*. And the sun slanted through the barred window. I looked up quickly to check. Yes, it was sunny, no rain...*Sixteen years had Miss Taylor been in Mr Woodhouse's family...*

Claire

I knitted a whole square bit of knitting. It looked like this.

It was the most knitting I had ever done. Mrs Cartwright and Jane came to see us. Jane was very pleased with my knitting square. She asked me if I could make one for her. I felt very happy about making a square for Jane but I felt unhappy about giving it to her. Mrs Cartwright said that she had lots of old bits of wool and that I could have it all. I like wool. I said thank you and Mum looked pleased.

Kate

I had an appointment with Mr Smith. Mr Brian Smith was my barrister and my trial was due to begin next week sometime. It was about as un-reassuring a name as Mr Hardcastle had sounded reassuring. What would Charles Dickens have called him? Mr Mc? Mr McAdamant. I grinned and my lips cracked. I was following Dickson's broad back up the endless corridor which led from the canary yellow cell. I still thought that Dickson should try wearing skirts, but skirts probably didn't go with Dickson's image. Dickson's image was tough, not motherly. I had a skirt on. Jane had managed to get me some underwear, but that was it. I hadn't really found out why. Anyway, Dickson had cleaned up my school uniform skirt and I still had the rosebud blouse adorned with a full compliment of (un-matching) buttons.

After about five minutes, we turned into the white corridor that led to one of the white interview rooms. I followed Dickson into the interview room and Dickson waved grandly towards one of the chairs, indicating that I should sit down. I stood in the middle of the room and Dickson stood by the door, looking anxiously down the corridor.

'They always keep you waiting these people,' she grumbled. 'They think that no one else has got anything better to do.'

Well, I hadn't, and I wasn't sure that Dickson had either. But I didn't say so.

Dickson kicked the door closed with her foot and sat on one of the chairs.

'Sit,' she said to me. Not unkindly. It was just Dickson's way.

'Shouldn't you lock the door?' I said.

Dickson looked at me scornfully, raised her hand and pointed towards a chair. I sat down. Dickson pulled the *Daily Mirror* out of her regulation jacket pocket and I waited expectantly to see if she would produce a cup of tea as well.

'What are you staring at, Howard?' she questioned belligerently. 'You might be a little freak, but for God's sake try not to show it.'

Dickson seemed to be more nervous than I was. It made me uneasy thinking that Dickson seemed to know something that I didn't. Mind you, Dickson always seemed to know something that I didn't.

Unlike me Dickson was immediately alert to the sound of voices in the corridor. She leapt up heavily, stuffed the newspaper back into her pocket, and reached the unlocked door before the voices did. She peered out into the corridor and made a loud gasping noise of disapproval. I stood up to join her but she merely turned to me crossly and pointed back at the chair. I sat down again. Disapproval and disdain stretched over every fibre of Dickson's broad back. I thought she must burst out of something.

What if she had a heart attack, I thought irrelevantly, that would confuse things.

'Children,' she said loudly, 'no more than children.' She looked back at me. 'No more than children, the lot of them.' She looked at me savagely as if it was my fault. 'Bloody hell.'

Two young men walked past Dickson into the interview room. Mr Hardcastle went and stood by the table and the other man moved past him and sat behind it. They were both carrying large bundles of papers. I looked carefully at the young man now sitting behind the desk. That must be Mr Brian Smith, I thought. I turned my attention back to Mr Hardcastle. He must have had a holiday in the sun as his pimply face was all shiny. Maybe that was why he hadn't been to see me again, because he'd been on holiday and not because he was scared of me and thought that I had committed a savage murder. I resisted the temptation to stare at Mr Hardcastle to see if I could unnerve him. Instead, I turned my attention back to Mr Smith. I was trying hard not to feel disappointed and had hoped that on second viewing Mr Smith would, well, look more impressive, more like a Mr McAdamant. Mr Smith looked all of two years older than Mr Hardcastle and on that reckoning scarcely ten years older than me and given that I struggled to look more than twelve... I sighed sadly. Dickson's opinion continued to be less resigned and less discrete. I knew that she was sucking in her cheeks in disapproval although I didn't look at her. I think she repeated her previous comment.

'Children, look at the three of them, no more than children the lot of them.'

But she can't have, can she? Not out loud in front of them. She would have done in front of me, but not in front of them.

But, oh dear, on first viewing I had to agree with Dickson; the legal team didn't inspire confidence. Mr Hardcastle had a round baby face, although the cherubic effect was spoilt by his spots, and he had long thin legs. Mr Smith had a thin Celtic face and short fat legs. But it didn't look too professional to be peering under the table so I sat upright on my chair, which faced Mr Smith from the opposite side of the desk.

Mr Smith looked at me over his glasses. He wore glasses sometimes, but they must have just been for effect, or to make him look older because he took them off most of the time – especially if he wanted to look at something or read something. Although it was easier to be looked at when he had the glasses on because he had a wall eye and when he didn't look through his glasses it swivelled to the left and then you didn't know which eye to look at. While I was trying not to be disconcerted, he cleared his throat and began the conversation, or perhaps I should call it an interview.

'Catherine Howard,' he said over his glasses. 'Not an auspicious start, is it?' He took the glasses off and I caught his eye, or tried to catch one of his eyes. A glimmer of understanding flickered between me and his good eye and the innuendoes of his remark passed between the two of us in lieu of a smile.

'Um, you indicated to Mr Hardcastle here that you would be pleading not guilty.' His accent was quite strong, West Yorkshire somewhere. Halifax, perhaps. 'Now, Miss Howard, I'd like you to re-consider,' his voice was persuasive and reassuring, but I knew what he was getting at.

'I didn't kill Jim,' I said bluntly.

Mr Hardcastle started to speak, but Mr Smith stopped him before he had said anything comprehensible beyond a grunt that was a prelude to clearing his throat. I wondered if he was still nervous about me. But I needed to concentrate on Mr Smith and not on the rather interesting and distracting possibility that Mr Hardcastle was frightened of me.

'Am I to take it that you intend to plead not guilty, then?'

I nodded. I felt confused about the pleading bit as though one had to ask for permission not to be guilty, but I was sure about the not guilty bit.

'And is there any point in me spending the next half hour in trying to persuade you of the foolishness of this course of action?'

Mr Hardcastle tried to butt in again.

'No,' I said rather loudly. Mr Hardcastle looked disconcerted and seemed to forget what it was he was trying to say.

'Miss Howard, I wonder if you would excuse us while Mr Hardcastle and I step outside for a few minutes to consult.'

I felt confused; wasn't I the one supposed to be being interviewed or consulted? Mr Smith and Mr Hardcastle left the room. Dickson was still standing by the door and she once again kicked it closed with her foot. I noticed that she still didn't lock it. I wondered if she was any less confused than I was.

'Well, what do you think?' she said to me but I knew better than to answer her.

A muffled but rather heated discussion was going on in the corridor. Dickson pulled her newspaper out of her pocket again and we both pretended not to listen. Dickson sat down by the door and I stood up. Dickson made no objection so I drifted over to the window, not wanting to listen anyway. My skirt had shifted round so that it was all skew. Dickson flung the paper down on her chair and joined me by the window. She straightened my shoulders and tidied up my skirt.

Mr Hardcastle opened the door.

'Er all ready again,' he said.

Dickson stayed outside the room this time. I sat down on the chair again. Mr Smith had taken his glasses off.

'Tell me about your family, Miss Howard,' he said, searching my face with his one straight eye. 'Tell me about your sister, or...'

'Claire?'

'...Or your mother, or your stepfather,' Mr Smith finished. 'But, yes, you can tell me about Claire if you like.'

Kate

Claire. Just before Claire was born in 1950, Mum and Dad went to a party. Mum fell over and was rushed to hospital, where Claire was born a week later. With brain damage. I was two at the time so I only know what Mum told me afterwards. But later she dropped lots of hints about Dad and drinking and 'not being able to take any more', so I concluded that perhaps Mum had been drinking too. I don't know how else one would explain it. Mum's guilt, I mean. Jim didn't drink. I think that was the attraction. Well, he must have had something going for him.

I was a terrible baby. At least, that's what Mum told me. I screamed when I was born and I carried on screaming for four months. At four months, I took a liking to mashed carrots and stopped screaming quite so much. I was small and mousey and not very prepossessing. Claire was a beautiful baby. She had blond curls and blue eyes. She drank her milk and slept all day and all night. Mum adored her and would stand over her cot crying and crying because she was so perfect and because Mum had spoilt her. I must remember this because I don't remember anyone telling me.

When I was five, Dad left. 'In the midst of a drunken binge,' said Mum bitterly. In fact what I remember was that Claire had scarlet fever and Mum was terrified she would go deaf 'like Grandma'. Claire had just started to make noises. 'Words,' Mum called them. And she responded when Mum said her name, which I have to admit was rather exciting. Anyway if she got deaf then she would get even more handicapped. So Mum just devoted herself entirely to nursing Claire through the scarlet fever. Dad fed me on spaghetti hoops for a week until he had a blazing row with Mum and left. He never came back. I fed myself on cornflakes and milk (when I managed to open the fridge) for a few more days, until Jane's Mum invited me to stay until Claire got better. 'To give your Mum a rest.'

I stayed with Jane for a week and put on three pounds and grew an inch. Then Jane's Mum took me back home. Claire was sitting up on the living room floor playing with my bricks. Her cheeks were all rosy and her curls neatly brushed. She was wearing a new blue dress with a sailor suit collar. It wasn't one that I'd had. It was new. I think it was the first time I'd seen her sitting up and the first time I'd seen her play with anything. Mum had a dress on too, and lipstick. She had a friend who was staying to tea, she explained to Jane's Mum, and it was so kind of Jane's Mum to look after me and to bring me home etcetera etcetera. The friend came forward eagerly, smiling too much. His warm gaze went straight to Jane as he made to befriend Mum's oldest daughter. Someone pushed me forward and 'the friend's' face fell with disappointment when he understood that I was Claire's older sister and not Jane, who already at five was heaps prettier than me.

By the time I was six, Jim had moved in. I suppose they'd got married because everyone now called Mum Mrs Brown instead of Mrs Howard. Claire took her first step. She was already as tall as me. Jim said that Claire should go to school and Mum and Jim spent the next four years campaigning for Claire to go to 'proper' school. In the end, she started at the special school at Whitcliff the same week that I went to Grammar school. Mum couldn't come to the parents meeting about Grammar school because she and Jim were planning our holiday at the seaside and they had to plan it carefully so that Claire would have everything she needed. I took the 11 plus anyway because Jane did and we did everything together.

I was fifteen when I got my first period and a week later Claire had hers as well. She was round and rosy and her breasts stuck out underneath her blouse. Jane had lent me some sanitary towels so I hadn't had to bother Mum.

Claire was very loving. She would crawl into bed with me and she liked me to cuddle her. She could write her name and work out sums on her fingers. She didn't say much but she could talk – at least, she could say the things she needed to say. When she was sixteen she only went to Whitcliff two days a week. She had grown out of all her clothes and she didn't like me to cuddle her any more. I'd begun to realise that although we'd grown up together I didn't really know her, not like I knew Jane. I felt responsible for her – we all did, at least Mum and I did. Jim thought he was responsible but he really only felt responsible for himself.

I think Claire loved Elvis Presley as much as she loved me.

Kate

'Claire?' I said. 'Claire's my sister. She's younger than me and she's handicapped.'

'And your mother?' Mr Smith continued. He had his glasses on so it was easier to talk to him.

'She works part-time at the clinic but it doesn't always work with Claire's days at Whitcliff. So she's mostly at home looking after Claire.'

'So she's a housewife looking after you all,' clarified Mr Smith.

I looked at him. If that's how he saw it I supposed, but it wasn't accurate. Mum looked after Claire.

'And your stepfather?' Mr Smith was trying to sound casual, but it was difficult to sound casual with a West Yorkshire accent and a rather Dickensian style of address.

'You mean Jim,' I said.

'Yes. How did you get on with your stepfather, Jim, Miss Howard?'

I really hated him. 'Sometimes I really hate that man' I would say to Jane. I chewed my lips.

'I, er, okay I suppose,' I said limply.

'So when the Crown Prosecution produces a neighbour, the neighbour in fact who found the body, and when this neighbour stands in the witness box and tells the court that she frequently heard you and your stepfather 'having words', you are going to be able to tell the court, with conviction, that you got on 'okay' with your stepfather?'

My eyes wandered to a spot about an inch to the left of Mr Smith's head. And if I tell the truth? I wanted to ask him.

'Now, Miss Howard, if there was some part of your stepfather's behaviour that wasn't quite what it should have been. If he showed you attentions that weren't, how shall we put it, appropriate?'

'Jim didn't show me any attention,' I said looking Mr Smith squarely in the eye again.

Mr Smith turned to Mr Hardcastle.

'You're really not helping us much, Miss Howard,' he said.

Soon it would be the trial and all this beastly business would be over. I would get my 'A' Level results and apply to University without Jim's interference. I would be able to explain to the Judge that I hadn't killed Jim. Everyone would realise that there'd been some terrible mistake and I would go home. I could even get a job while I applied to University. I would be able to help Mum now Jim had gone. Maybe Claire could spend another day at Whitcliff and Mum could work an extra day at the clinic. In fact, without Jim to provide for we might even be better off. I hadn't thought about home so much for months. Before, I'd just wanted to get away from it as fast as possible.

'And this case is meant to be cut and dried,' Mr Smith was saying to Mr Hardcastle. He'd taken his glasses back off and his thin Celtic face looked pale and harassed. Perhaps he took the glasses off deliberately to avoid looking people in the eye. He was certainly avoiding looking me in the eye now. He put them back on and looked sternly at Mr Hardcastle. I'm sure he pointed towards the door and said 'Out' very fiercely, indicating that Mr Hardcastle should join him outside again. Although it doesn't seem likely. Perhaps he pointed at Dickson and said 'In' to her. Anyway, whatever really did happen, Mr Smith and Mr Hardcastle went outside and Dickson hovered by the inside of the door. She didn't close it though and when I joined her to listen at the crack she didn't send me back to my chair either.

'I can't believe you allowed the trial to be rushed through,' we heard Mr Smith hiss at Mr Hardcastle.

Mr Hardcastle said nothing and I imagined him looking sheepish.

'I mean, it's clear we should have had a psychiatric report on Miss Howard's mental state,' continued Mr Smith.

I wasn't sure whether this sounded entirely good. Was the plan now to lock me in an asylum instead?

Dickson was whispering crossly. 'Psychiatric report my foot. Sounds more like they should be doing a psychiatric report on everyone else, I should say.'

'Shush,' I whispered to Dickson. She turned her cross look to me but was silent. We leant in towards the door.

'Has anyone stepped forward to speak up for the accused? Who do we have in the way of witnesses as to good character or witnesses as to the facts?' Mr Smith was still doing the talking.

'We've got some excellent reports from her school,' said Mr Hardcastle. The defensive tone he'd adopted helped his voice carry across the corridor and through our partially closed door. He was obviously trying to convince Mr Smith that he had been doing something. 'But it's still the school holidays and Miss Howard is no longer on the school role,' he finished limply.

I didn't think that sounded as encouraging as it should have done. I looked questioningly at Dickson but this time it was her turn to hiss 'Shush'.

'And you've found no witnesses to undermine the Crown's evidence and the police statements?'

Mr Hardcastle said nothing and I imagined him looking sheepish and defensive again.

'If she pleads not guilty,' Mr Smith said dryly, 'we're meant to believe her. You obviously haven't asked her, about potential witnesses or alibis?'

'We talked to her friend, Miss Cartwright,' said Mr Hardcastle.

I looked up eagerly. Miss Cartwright was Jane and Jane could be a witness as I'd been with her after my exam. Dickson gripped my arm urgently and I kept quiet.

'She was very forthcoming,' continued Mr Hardcastle.

'But she parted company with the accused at 12.45. I know, I've read the notes,' said Mr Smith sourly.

I would have felt a lot more optimistic if Mr Smith could have found something to make him sound less fierce. But perhaps he always sounded fierce. Perhaps everyone from Halifax sounded fierce. Dickson and I were not feeling in the least bit comforted by any of this private conversation and I was beginning to wish that I hadn't started to eavesdrop. Mum always said that eavesdroppers never heard anything good about themselves.

'Well, I, er, I hadn't expected her to plead not guilty,' Mr Hardcastle finally said. His voice was hushed and it was difficult for us to hear what he said exactly.

Dickson had clearly heard enough. She made a show of opening the door and stuck her head round it.

'Have you nearly finished?' she asked, 'because it's dinner time and I need to know if I should bring something here for the accused or if she can eat in the canteen with the others.' Dickson managed to purvey a great deal of studied irony into the word 'accused'.

'Christ, you can do what you like with her,' said Mr Smith, sounding ruffled. I peered round the door at my legal team from behind Dickson's bulk. Mr Smith's glasses had gone all askew on his face. 'Yes take her away; we're not getting anywhere. We'll just have to hope that when the trial begins she'll come to her senses. If she has any,' he finished drolly.

Well, I got my lighter tone but I decided that, after all, the fierce words would have been more reassuring. I was getting more and more confused and wished that I hadn't been listening. How, I wondered, could I possibly plead guilty? Although it was apparent even to me that Mr Smith wondered how on earth I could possibly plead not guilty.

Mr Smith came forward to the now officially open door and put out a dry hand for me to shake. Mr Hardcastle didn't. He fiddled with his files instead. I stood with Dickson by the door and tried to read her expression but she wasn't giving anything away.

Dickson and I walked back down the white corridor. The routine was getting familiar and didn't demand anything from me as discouraging as thought. Dinner was shepherd's pie and I put an extra spoon of sugar in my tea because I felt unaccountably hungry and I didn't like the pudding which was sago.

Kate

Dickson and I waited in a small room in the basement of the Crown Court. I wasn't sure whether we were in Leeds or York. I wasn't sure whether York had a Crown Court. I could have asked Dickson but I didn't really want to know. We'd come in a prison van and I hadn't been able to see much out of the window so I couldn't work out where we were going. Everything just looked the same and disconcertingly summery. I'd forgotten it was still sort of summer; late summer, I supposed.

We were early and I think we must have waited thirty minutes before Mr Smith appeared.

'Is the prisoner giving you lots of trouble, then?' Mr Smith asked Dickson as he surveyed her ample proportions compared with my nondescript and diminutive mousiness.

Dickson didn't reckon much to Mr Smith's wit and looked at him disdainfully.

'Hardcastle's got caught in traffic but I think we'll just get on with it anyway?'

I suppose it was a question but neither Dickson nor I answered him.

'Are you coming in with her?' he asked Dickson.

'I thought I would,' Dickson answered carefully.

'I mean, we don't want any trouble in court now do we?'

This elicited more disdain from Dickson. He seemed a lot more chipper than the last time we'd met. I chewed my lip and smiled uncertainly.

'Well, you know the routine,' he continued to Dickson and was interrupted by a knock on the door. Mr Hardcastle came in but someone behind him said, 'The Judge is ready, Mr Smith.'

And Mr Smith and Mr Hardcastle hurried off and Dickson started fussing about my skirt which as usual was hanging all askew. I still only had my school skirt and the rosebud blouse and both felt woefully inadequate for the ordeal before me. Jane had lent me a jacket but it was too big and it was hard not to look pathetic in it. Dickson, however, had decided that just wearing a blouse was too informal for the Crown Court so that the jacket had to do whether it was pathetic or not.

Dickson knocked on the inside of the door where we'd been waiting and someone let us out. It hadn't occurred to me up until then that we'd been locked in. We went up some flights of stairs and then into the court, which was a bit like a theatre. *The quality of mercy is not strained.* I'd seen *The Merchant of Venice* at the Theatre Royal but I'd never studied it so I couldn't remember anything else or even whether I wanted to be like Portia or not. Wasn't she dressed up as a man at this point in the play? But of course she wasn't on trial she was defending Antonio, I thought. I tugged at my skirt and Dickson elbowed me to a bench at the front. The court had gone quiet when we arrived and now people were shuffling and whispering. I think someone tried to take a photograph at the back because I thought I caught sight of a camera and then a bigger shuffle with a court official.

Mr Smith was looking at me over his glasses and Mr Hardcastle was pretending to read some papers. He was red as well as shiny today and his lips looked disconcertingly moist. At least Mr Smith was all dry skin, lips and wit. There were some people in the public gallery but I didn't look in case there was anyone that I knew. I hoped that there wasn't. I wasn't exactly looking my best. A row of people sat behind a bench on the far wall. I glanced behind at Dickson who was still standing as it were on guard behind me. The Jury? My knees went a bit wobbly and Dickson pulled me onto a chair just as someone said, 'All rise,' and we did.

The Judge came in. He was ninety-two and had a hearing aid. I could see it dangling from his left ear. He kept pushing it back in and once he tried to turn it up and it made a loud buzzing noise.

A very sleek young man stood up. He was good looking even to my eyes (I'm very picky). Actually I decided he was tall and handsome with dark hair cut with a thick fringe, but I couldn't possibly have known all that because he was wearing a wig. The Judge was also wearing a wig (which was lopsided) and so was Mr Smith. Mr Smith must have put his wig on between seeing us in the little locked room and arriving in court because I'm sure that he didn't have a wig on when we first saw him. At least I don't think he did, but I was starting to feel confused and hot. I had a quick glance to check that Dickson was still there and that she wasn't wearing a wig. The wigs looked very judgemental. Mr Hardcastle didn't have a wig, but he was judgemental anyway. I leant over to ask Dickson if he wasn't wearing a wig because…but she pinched my arm hard and I shut up.

The handsome young man was telling the court that I'd murdered Jim. Of course, I was going to put him right on that score and then he was going to notice me and I was going to rise to iconic status like Portia. I tried to turn a brave Portia-like stare on the Jury. They were all men apart from one woman who was wearing a bright blue suit, and they were all old.

The handsome young man seemed to have rather a lot to say and Mr Smith just sat there and had nothing to say. The young man was very convincing – if everything had happened as he suggested there was no wonder that Mr Hardcastle was so jumpy around me. Even I was getting jumpy around me by this point. The Judge seemed to decide that he'd heard enough – or perhaps he had not heard anything but had decided it was time he interrupted anyway and he suggested that they got on with the first witness. It was one of the policemen who'd found me in the phone box near Potter's Farm. I was still struggling to concentrate properly until Dickson pinched me again, even harder than last time. I began to listen.

'"There was so much blood," the accused said, "I didn't know what to do," she said,' the policeman was saying.

'And you took this to refer to the body of the accused's murdered stepfather?' the sleek young man said.

Mr Smith leapt up and the Judge waved his arm crossly.

'You assumed that the accused was referring to her stepfather?'

'Yes,' answered the policeman.

'What sort of state was she in?'

'Very confused.'

'Can you elaborate?'

'Well, she went on about there being lots of blood and she was hiding in the telephone box.'

'She was hiding in the telephone box?'

'Yes, that's right, she was huddled on the floor so that we didn't see her at first.'

'At what time was this, PC Foster?'

PC Foster consulted his notebook.

'Half past four,' he said.

'So at half past four you arrested the suspect?'

'That's right,' concluded PC Foster smugly as if it had been a great achievement.

'Did Miss Howard come with you quietly or did she make any more trouble?'

Mr Smith was on his feet.

'Your Honour,' he said to the Judge.

The Judge waved his hand again even more crossly. I think he was struggling to concentrate even more than I was. It is quite hard to concentrate if you can't hear properly and it is even worse if people keep interrupting.

'Was Miss Howard now quiet or did she still seem to be disturbed?' the sleek young man continued unperturbed.

'Well, yes, she seemed to be quiet but then we had a right to-do in the police car.'

PC Foster was not consulting his notebook. The sleek young man looked at him encouragingly.

'Well,' continued PC Foster picking up the encouragement from the young man and warming to his theme, 'she tried to jump out of the car, didn't she? Tried to escape, she did.'

'She tried to escape,' the sleek young man said to the Court. 'And this to you, PC Foster, was indicative of guilt?'

PC Foster looked confused and Mr Smith was reading his notes. I had been expecting him to leap up again to show solidarity with me and to object to the sleek young man. Perhaps his notes were too interesting or perhaps he didn't think that the Judge would let him interrupt anyway.

'That's all I have for PC Foster, Your Honour,' said the sleek young man at which point Mr Smith pulled off his glasses and leapt to his feet.

Ah ha, I thought, he is still concentrating after all.

'PC Foster,' he said, his Halifax accent making at least four diphthongs out of the name. Mr Smith wagged a finger in my direction. 'Are you suggesting that you,' a harsh diphthong which I think Mr Smith emphasised more than usual so that it sounded more like 'yauu' and gave him time to move his pointing finger in PC Foster's direction. PC Foster was big even for a policeman and Mr Smith deliberately arced his arm up so that he had pointed down at me and exaggeratedly up towards PC Foster. 'Are you suggesting that you had problems in arresting Miss Howard?'

Someone sniggered. But the Jury didn't. They were all looking stony-faced at Mr Smith.

'Well,' said PC Foster, glancing at the sleek young man who calmly ignored him.

'PC Foster, did Miss Howard resist arrest in any way?'

'Well, no,' he looked at his notebook. He began to speak but Mr Smith cut in briskly.

'And did Miss Howard at any time attempt to conceal the fact that her stepfather had suffered a serious accident?'

'Well…' he ruffled awkwardly amongst the pages of his notebook.

'And if Miss Howard had in any way been witness to such a serious accident might this not be some justification for her distraught state of mind?'

PC Foster waved his notebook at the court somewhat impotently.

'I have no more questions, Your Honour,' said Mr Smith.

PC Foster looked confused and the Judge thanked him and told him that he could step down now. The Judge had stopped fiddling with his hearing aid which either meant that he had managed to adjust it correctly or that he had switched it off.

'Let's see if we can get another one done before lunch,' the Judge said and the plainclothes policeman with the piggy eyes stepped into the witness box.

Kate

'I wonder, Detective Inspector Slater, if you could piece together the events of 16th June for the benefit of the Court?' the sleek young man asked the plainclothes policeman. 'In your evidence to the court, you will be taking into account the accused's own statement and the evidence you have compiled subsequent to that event.'

The plainclothes policeman, Detective Inspector Slater as I supposed he must be called, gathered his thoughts slowly and deliberately. He had mounted the witness box holding a familiar looking buff folder under his arm. He put the folder down on some sort of shelf in the witness box and calmly surveyed the Courtroom. His gaze passed over me and rested on the Judge and the Jury. I wondered if he managed to make them feel as insignificant as he made me feel. Having ensured the rapt attention of everyone in the Courtroom he began his witness statement. (He'd have made a good teacher. Scary but effective.)

'Shortly after 15.30 on the afternoon of June 16th we received an emergency telephone call from number 12 Potter's View. The call was made by a Mrs Hunter who lives in number 14 Potter's View. Mrs Hunter reported that an accident had occurred at her neighbour's house. Mrs Hunter was very upset as she believed that the accident had criminal implications.'

The sleek young man nodded his encouragement, but Detective Inspector Slater ignored him and carried on.

'We sent a Police car to the address immediately to make sure that nothing was tampered with at the scene of the crime, and myself and Sergeant Davis followed within the half hour. Following directions from the neighbour PC Holder and PC Ramsbottom followed a trail of blood which led to the victim's shed. The victim's shed was locked and a machine was running inside the shed. PC Holder and PC Ramsbottom broke into the shed and found the victim, James Brown either dead or bleeding to death. They radioed a request for an ambulance. An ambulance was already on the way as Mrs Hunter had already had the presence of mind to request one when she made her original 999 telephone call from the victim's house. She had made this call on account of all the blood, you understand.

Sergeant Davis and I reached the scene at 16.15 by which time, acting on the suspicions of Mrs Hunter, another Police car had been sent out to look for the accused. An ambulance arrived at 16.20 and the victim was pronounced dead on arrival at the scene at 16.30. At this stage, death was estimated to have occurred at least an hour before our arrival but no earlier than three hours before this time. Thus death was estimated to have occurred sometime between 13.30 and 15.30. A post-mortem subsequently confirmed this estimation. We took imprints of footmarks made in the victim's blood and as the victim had suffered a heavy blow to the head before falling onto a rotary saw consistent with that which might be inflicted by a shovel we also took possession of a shovel which had been blocking the entrance to the shed where the victim lay.

The victim's wife, Mrs Margaret Brown, arrived home shortly after 16.30 and Mrs Hunter was kind enough to take care of her after we had explained to her what we could of the events which had unfolded. She did not go with her husband in the ambulance. As he had been pronounced dead on the scene there was no point in distressing her further. Official identification of the victim was made later the next day.'

The sleek young man made the most of a pause in the Detective's recital and cut in with a remark to the Judge.

'You will understand that in the circumstances, Your Honour, Mrs Brown has requested not to give evidence at the trial of her daughter, Miss Howard. Mrs Brown herself was working at the York Road Clinic until 16.00 on the afternoon of the crime and caught a bus home with one of her colleagues so there were ample witnesses as to her whereabouts that afternoon and any possible involvement on her part in the crime perpetrated against her husband was ruled out immediately.'

The Jury, as a man, seemed to be nodding sagely and the Judge's hearing aid gave a tentative whistle which the sleek young man took as acquiescence to the assumption of Mum's lack of involvement. Well, as if Mum would have had the presence of mind to kill Jim anyway. I mean, she was besotted with him.

Detective Inspector Slater peered through his piggy sludge green eyes at the Jury before turning his attention back to the sleek young man. Intelligent he might be but I was fast losing faith in intelligence. But perhaps I had misjudged him. Perhaps the initial glint I'd taken for intelligence when I'd first met him had been a glint of power and control. He obviously wanted to have charge of the situation now and he wanted to get on with his story.

'News came through to us that the suspect had been apprehended at some distance from the crime. Sergeant Davis secured the evidence of the shovel and the shoe print and I interviewed Mrs Hunter after she had settled Mrs Brown with a cup of tea. Mrs Hunter confirmed that she had seen the suspect running from the scene in a state of agitation at the same time as the paper boy had delivered the paper. In fact, the suspect had run into the paper boy without seeming to even notice. Mrs Hunter believed the suspect to be a "rather hysterical young woman who frequently caused a good deal of stress and unhappiness in what was otherwise a lovely home." Mr and Mrs Brown were a "devoted couple" and had tried their best with Mrs Brown's daughter. But Catherine, or Kate as the family call her, constantly caused trouble with Jim and Mrs Hunter had heard her make "violent threats" to her stepfather on more than one occasion.'

Detective Inspector Slater paused again.

Violent threats? Well, I had told him to go and jump not so very long before (it could even have been that very morning) but that was because I couldn't find my bus pass and I had to get to an exam and he wouldn't give me my bus fare. Mrs Hunter had always been a nosey old cow. And what did she know about Jim and about our family? She didn't have to live with him.

Dickson was pinching me so I had no option other than to stop mentally re-running my favourite threats to Jim and listen to D.I. Slater. I suppose it was a good story, if that was all it was. I think I sighed audibly because Dickson pinched me again.

Piggy Eyes carried on.

'In addition to this witness, Sergeant Davis confirmed that the wound on the victim's head was consistent with both the shape of the shovel and with evidence of blood and hair found on the shovel. Finger print evidence later confirmed that the suspect had indeed been the last person to hold the shovel. The suspect's shoe was also an exact copy of the print found in the victim's blood both inside and outside the shed where the victim was found. And the key to the shed was found in the suspect's pocket. This evidence, together with the suspect's statement accepting responsibility for the crime, was presented at the Magistrate's Court and the suspect was charged and remanded in custody until this date. There were no appeals for bail.'

Accepting responsibility for the crime? What was that supposed to mean? Feeling responsible was not the same as being guilty. I looked over towards Mr Smith. He didn't see me looking at him but he was writing notes. And had I made a statement that first night at the police station? I mean everyone said that I had so perhaps I did.

It was Mr Smith's turn now.

I tried to go through the Detective's evidence and what he said had happened. I could take his word for what had happened after I ran off to call an ambulance, although I didn't believe that Mrs Hunter would have had the wit to call both the police and an ambulance. And anyway the shed was locked – or so they claimed – so how could she have known what had happened to Jim? How could she have known to call an ambulance? No, I called the ambulance. After all, that's why I was in the phone box. What time had I got home? About three thirty? So that was after Jim was supposed to have died, wasn't it?

But I was missing Mr Smith's cross examination of Piggy Eyes and a change in the tone of Detective Inspector Slater's voice brought my attention back to him. He was less suave – if such a man can ever be said to be suave – although not ruffled, just more sort of indignant.

'I assure you that there were no lapses in police procedure on the night of Miss Howard's arrest,' D.I. Slater was saying to Mr Smith. 'There was an element of confusion in Miss Howard's demeanour, but she was calm and well able to answer questions. She was of course provided with appropriate nutrition and support. The duty solicitor, Mr Hardcastle, was called in and there was at all times a WPC present.'

I looked up puzzled from my tight little nook by Dickson. Was there? I mean, had there been? A WPC and Mr Hardcastle? Had they always been present, as D.I. Slater put it, during my police interview? I tried hard to remember.

'A doctor made a full examination and assessment and Miss Howard was calm and willing to sign a statement which gave a full account of her movements leading up to the death of her stepfather on the same night as the arrest was made.'

The piggy eyes gleamed with intelligence (or control), if eyes that look like stagnant water can gleam. He was sweating inside his jacket, at least I imagined that he was sweating inside his jacket because there were beads of sweat on his forehead, but he still seemed completely unflustered. Mr Smith consulted his notes and nothing was said for a while. The Judge fiddled with his hearing aid in case he had missed something. But there was only silence until someone at the back coughed and the Judge was reassured that his hearing aid was working.

'Is that all, Mr Smith?' he said.

Mr Smith turned back to Detective Inspector Slater. This time he kept his glasses on, which meant that he could look him straight in the eye.

'So you are confident that Miss Howard, a girl of just eighteen who has just in some way been witness to a terrible crime,' he corrected himself quickly, 'or accident, was in a fit state to sign a statement on the same evening?'

'Yes,' came the cold reply.

'And she was fully aware of what she was doing? Of what was going on?'

'Miss Howard, as you must know Mr Smith, is one of the top students at the girls' grammar school, of course she knew what was going on,' continued the cold responses.

Mr Smith turned to the Judge.

'Yes, that's all, Your Honour,' he said.

The Judge did some scrabbling about and stood up. A young man in a black robe sitting at the front of the Court near the Judge suddenly stood up too and shouted out hurriedly, 'All rise,' which meant that everyone else stood up and that Dickson hauled me up by Jane's jacket sleeve.

'Session closed,' said the Judge. 'We'll reconvene at two on the dot,' he finished, looking at Mr Smith.

He left the Court and the rest of us followed. Well, the rest of us went out. I didn't follow because Dickson took me out via a different door and led me back down to a cell in the basement of the County Court.

Kate

It was my turn now. It was only the second day of my trial and the whole thing could soon be over. Just like that. Two days.

I was put in the witness box, or was it the dock because I was the person on trial? (Dickson put me right on this point afterwards. Apparently, I was sent from the dock to the witness box and I was in the dock because I had committed a crime but as I hadn't actually committed a crime I obviously preferred to forget that I was sitting in the dock at all and how could the Jury be expected to abide by the maxim that a prisoner was innocent until proven guilty if the prisoner started by sitting in the dock?)

Dickson followed me and I turned to tell her that it was my turn in the witness box not hers but she looked at me fiercely and I understood that mine was *not to reason why,* mine was *but to do or die*. What an unhappy quotation or knowing me an unhappy miss-quotation. I climbed into the witness box and Dickson followed and sat discreetly behind me. At least, she attempted to sit discreetly behind me. Dickson never did anything discreet in her life. I wondered if this was so that she could carry on pinching me at critical moments, although surely such a thing couldn't have happened, could it? It would be perverting the course of justice or some such thing.

I was my own chief witness so Mr Smith began, not the sleek young man. I did the swearing in (taking the oath I suppose I should say – everyone knows the stuff: *I firmly believe,* or is that the beginning of the Creed? I've never really been to church and Creed or oath it all seemed more than a bit insincere to me just now and it certainly hadn't in any way curbed D.I. Slater's elaborations of events).

I'm sure that at this point Dickson did pinch me and I looked up attentively and handed the Bible back to the young man in the black robe. The Judge's hearing aid whistled a bit as he tried to adjust it. The Jury, still acting en masse as it were, all looked up at me intently. Mr Smith stood up, took his glasses off and looked at me reassuringly, which was a bad start because I didn't know which eye was being reassuring. However, there's nothing better than a Halifax accent when it is being reassuring, I tried to convince myself optimistically. I chewed my lips. It didn't seem appropriate to smile any more. I suppose there might have been more formalities but anyway Mr Smith turned to me with his kind voice.

'Miss Howard, I wonder if you would be so kind as to take the Court through the events of 15th June in your own words. Take us through the day as you remember it.'

'Er, from the beginning?'

'Yes, that would be fine,' the gentle voice continued.

'Like breakfast and stuff?'

'Yes, breakfast and stuff is fine,' he smiled putting his glasses back on. I liked the glimmer of intelligence in his thin face when he smiled and now he had his glasses back on it was easier to look him in the eye. I chewed my lips.

'We're waiting, Miss Howard,' butted in the Judge with an accompanying whistle.

My voice cracked a bit so I had to um and er and clear my throat.

'Mum and I were up early because it was her day at the clinic and I had my last exam. Which meant that Jim had to look after Claire. Mum and I ate cornflakes...' Well, actually I couldn't remember whether we ate cornflakes or not.

'Did Jim often look after Claire?' asked Mr Smith.

'No, Jim wasn't capable of...'

'Just answer the question please Miss Howard.'

'No, usually Mum or I look after Claire and Mum tries to get her days at the clinic to coincide with Claire's days at Whitcliff.'

This time the sleek young man butted in.

'Is this really necessary?' he asked.

'But that day Jim was looking after Claire?' questioned Mr Smith.

'Yes.'

'So you went to school and sat your exam?'

'Yes, it was English paper three. There was a difficult metaphor about a butterfly.'

The sleek young man twisted in his chair in an irritated way. Mr Smith broke in quickly. 'And you finished at twelve o'clock?'

'Yes, we finished at twelve. Jane was waiting for me. She had another exam that afternoon and we'd arranged to meet during lunchtime. Jane had some sandwiches and we sat on the edge of the hockey pitch.' But we hadn't had that much time. Perhaps we didn't go all the way to the hockey pitch. Perhaps we just sat on the bank above the car park? I looked at Mr Smith, but he wouldn't know, would he? 'Jane had an exam at one o'clock so she went back to school.'

'So you left Jane at 12.45?'

'Yes, I suppose so.'

'And then what did you do?'

'I don't know. I'm not sure.'

Mr Smith looked less calm and reassuring now. He didn't come up with any helpful questions.

'I er, I think I thought I'd wait until Jane had finished and then I decided I would go home.'

'And what time did you get home?'

'At three thirty.'

'And what did you do when you got home?'

'I went in to see Claire. I remembered that Mum wasn't home and that Jim was looking after Claire. I couldn't find Jim anywhere and then I did find him. He was working in his workshop instead of looking after Claire. That made me angry because...' Mr Smith was looking at me with an appeal in his eyes. I haltered, confused suddenly, then floundered on. 'And then I found him all bleeding and hunched over the saw bench. I was worried about Claire but I ran off to phone an ambulance. The policemen found me in the phone box after I'd called the ambulance.'

'Was Jim dead when you found him, Catherine?'

'Yes. No. I'm not sure. Yes, he must have been,' I looked at Mr Smith helplessly.

'Did you kill Jim, or in any way do anything that might have caused him to die or get hurt?'

'No, I didn't kill Jim,' I said confidently.

The Judge looked at Mr Smith.

'Is that all?' he asked.

Mr Smith nodded. He smiled at me and I shrank back against the witness box, trying to derive some comfort from the bulky presence of Dickson still discreetly sitting behind me.

'We'll rise now then and reconvene at one thirty, precisely,' said the Judge to Mr Smith.

The black robed young man leapt to his feet.

'All rise,' he shouted, to be sure that the Judge had heard him.

Kate

'So at, let us say one o'clock, having just left your friend Jane Cartwright, you go home.'
'But I didn't go home.'
The sleek young man ignored me.
'And you arrived home at about two o'clock? Would that be about right?'
'Well yes, no, I didn't get home until about three o'clock, I mean half past three.'
'You are not sure? You could have got home at three or half past, or half past two, or two o'clock? You are not sure, so you say.' Mr Smith shuffled in his seat but the sleek young man ignored him. 'You are not sure, or you can't remember?'
I didn't say anything and neither did anyone else.
'I'm sure I didn't get home until three thirty,' I said.
'But you left your friend at 12.45?'
'Yes.'
'And your friend had an exam?'
'Yes, it was…'
'Just answer the question please, Miss Howard. And you are asking the Court to believe that you just sat around doing nothing for an hour, even two hours and then just went home?'
'Well, yes.'
Lots of people stirred and the Judge turned his hearing aid down. Or perhaps he turned it up in the hope that we were now getting to the interesting bit.
'Let me put it to you, Miss Howard.'
I noticed Mr Smith sit up on the edge of his seat.
'That when you left your friend at 12.45 you went straight home. You knew that Jim and Claire were at home on their own. You knew that Claire would be easy to distract or keep out of the way. You had had enough of your stepfather and you wanted him out of the way.' There were lots of distractions at this point but the sleek young man carried on speaking above the noise. 'You came home and took the first opportunity you had which was to trap your stepfather in the shed, hit him over the head with a shovel and as he hit the rotary blade you set it running and then left him to bleed to death.' We were all listening again, as if spellbound by the sleek

young man's story. 'You went back in the house and then became worried, perhaps even full of remorse for this terrible crime and then you did, as you say, go back to the shed and find your stepfather dead or dying. But you did not, as you claim, ring for an ambulance, you panicked and ran away, leaving your disabled sister alone and leaving your stepfather to die.'

Mr Smith finally led the rising noise and managed to get the Judge to stop the sleek young man. Everyone went silent after that. They all seemed to be looking at me.

The Judge turned to me and said, 'Have you anything to say, Miss Howard?'

'Er,' to what exactly? 'I wouldn't have gone home if I'd known that Jim and Claire were home alone,' I said.

The sleek young man almost shouted in his glee.

'So you didn't know that they were at home on their own? But just this morning you explained how that morning you and your mother had got up early and left Jim and your sister alone because it was your mother's day to work at the clinic. Is that right?'

'Yes.'

'And now you claim that you didn't know that they were home alone?'

'Yes.' I drooped guiltily.

'Right, now let's go back to you finding Jim, as you claim, at three thirty. You go into the shed and find your stepfather dead or seriously injured, you don't know which?'

'No.'

'You find a seriously injured man who as far as you know could be dying and not already dead?'

'Yes.'

'And what do you do?'

'I er I was worried about Claire. I didn't know what to do. I decided that I should call an ambulance in case he was still alive.'

'But that's not what you did, was it?'

I looked at him puzzled.

'There were lots of things that you didn't do weren't there, Miss Howard? The first thing that you might have done is to switch off the rotary saw? But you didn't. The second thing you might have done was to make sure that rescue services could access the shed as quickly as possible. But you didn't, did you? In fact, on the contrary, you locked the shed and put the key in your pocket. And then you say you were worried about your sister, so one might have expected you to go straight to a neighbour and get help so that someone could call an ambulance and someone could look after Claire. But you didn't do this, did you? You didn't even go straight to the telephone in your own home and call an ambulance. In fact, what you did was run away with the key to the shed in your pocket – leaving your stepfather for all you knew dying and your sister on her own with him.'

I'm sure that the woman juror with the bright blue suit gasped. It was a terrible description of events. And it was confusing. I was starting to forget what had happened. I remembered that Claire had been listening to Elvis Presley on the radio. Or had I made that up too? Had I caused Jim to die? I looked at the sleek young man and felt really frightened for the first time.

'But Jim was already dead, wasn't he?' I asked in a small voice. I don't think anyone was listening.

'You weren't very fond of your stepfather, were you, Miss Howard?' the sleek young man said quietly.

I twisted my mouth. This wasn't the time to go into that.

'In fact you didn't like him, did you? You had often told your friends that you hated him, hadn't you.'

I nodded my head. It was all too horribly true. I had hated Jim, but…but I wasn't going to be allowed any buts, was I?

'I wonder what it was that made you hate him so much? So much that you decided to use this one opportunity when he was alone in your home to kill him?'

A horrible silence had descended on the Court. Why did I hate Jim? I looked up, angry, tearful, desperate. Did I speak or did I just stare into that terrible silence? Jim had never liked me. He had always preferred Claire. And he never let me do anything with Mum. I never went out with her, shopping or anything like Jane did with her mum. He was sort of cocky and clever and wildly incompetent. And he would say snidey things to put you down and appear to be all loving when other people were there. And he gave me the creeps. And what made it worse was that everyone else seemed to like him. I mean just for one take Mrs Hunter. And Mum just doted on him. It didn't seem natural. She didn't dote on me.

Kate

Dickson didn't say much on the way back to Wakefield. She rustled a copy of *The Press* loudly and I looked listlessly at the grey walls of the prison van. I had been so sure that these trips to the Crown Court were going to have been the beginning of the end. I didn't even strain my neck to look out through the barred window. It was just fields and things and summer somewhere out there. We were due back at the Court again in the morning for the verdict.

'England are 150 for 2,' said Dickson.

Did that mean it was a Thursday then? I thought.

'I suppose this'll be my last night in the remand cell?' I said, more for something to say than anything else.

Dickson looked at me, then turned her attention back to *The Press*.

I'd grown almost fond of my canary yellow cell. I'd read *Emma* and *Daniel Deronda* and tried to write a few sonnets. It was more cheery than my room at home. Jim had insisted on putting up wallpaper, because it protected the plastering better than just having paint. Of course, he did it himself. The pattern had horizontal lines which were meant to cross over each sheet but the lines never quite met so every time I looked at it I was reminded of Jim and another of his botched jobs.

I'd been planning this last night of confinement ever since I'd arrived. I was going to pack my things together this evening so that I would be ready to go free straight away after the judgement in the morning. I hadn't seen Mum since we ate cornflakes together on the morning of the day that Jim died. Or was killed. Or was murdered. Or had a horrible accident. No one had mentioned the possibility of an accident. I wondered why. I looked at Dickson, but she was ignoring me so I knew that this was not the time to ask her. I would have to work it out for myself. I looked at Dickson's *Press* and at her broad back spilling over the seat in the back of the prison van. It must be because of the blow to Jim's head made by the shovel. I thought about the shovel. I mean, I had picked the shovel up, hadn't I. But Jim was already dead when I forced my way into the shed, wasn't he?

'Nothing in tonight,' said Dickson. 'They're probably waiting to do a full page spread tomorrow.'

I looked at her, but she was still ignoring me.

'Dickson, what have I done?' I asked her. What a question! What I meant of course was what had I done to upset her, as she didn't seem to be speaking to me. But philosophically speaking the question started to grow in my mind with huge ramifications until Dickson brought me back to the present with signs that she was about to communicate something to me.

She rustled *The Press* and peered round at me.

'Don't be daft,' she said.

What was that supposed to mean? I wondered.

'You and those two daft apeths representing you. My god, you couldn't organise a piss-up in a brewery between the lot of you. What do they teach you in school these days? Poetry?' she scoffed. *The Press* rustled. 'Bloody hell,' she said and folded *The Press* up in a big mess.

'Can I have a look?' I asked.

She handed the evening paper over silently.

I read it randomly and abstractedly. Someone had complained because of the mess from the ducks in the Museum Gardens. And a duck had menaced some small child. Some strange weed only found in Sparta had been identified in a pond in a local village. I looked again, that can't have been right. Sparta? I must have made that up. *The Press* was so boring you had to make up bits here and there. Jane and I used to do that in English. We'd had to write an article for *The Press*. We'd sat in Jane's bedroom and gone through the stories in *The Press* one evening making them more and more outrageous. Then we wrote our own. The teacher made us do it again but we sent our original story to *The Press* and it was published. Luckily, our teacher didn't see it, or if she did she didn't say anything. To cap it all Jim had gone round to all his friends (well, all one of them) telling them about this really strange story in *The Press*. I couldn't remember what it was about though. How odd. It had been so funny at the time, like the most important thing in our lives and I couldn't remember what it was we had made up.

I looked at Dickson's broad back still ignoring me and went back to *The Press*. There had been an organ recital at the Minster. And they were doing *The Importance of Being Earnest* at the theatre. I'd like to have seen that. Perhaps tomorrow. Perhaps tomorrow

Jane and I could get cheap tickets and go and see *The Importance of Being Earnest*.

I looked at Dickson's broad silent back and frowned. It wasn't like Dickson. Usually she talked too much. I didn't understand most of what she said, but I liked the way she said things. I liked the way her voice got all indignant. And I liked the way she swore. No one swore at home and I'd liked to have been able to swear like Dickson. I'd like to have sworn at Jim. I chewed my lips because I didn't want to smile at Dickson when she seemed to be so disapproving. And she obviously wasn't going to tell me what I'd done. You couldn't ask Dickson the same question twice.

When we arrived at the prison Dickson deposited me with the warder on duty and went off home. Still without a word. I sat in my canary yellow cell for the last time and re-read the end of *Emma*.

...having once owned that she had been presumptuous and silly, and self-deceived, before, her pain and confusion seemed to die away with the words, and leave her without a care for the past, and with the fullest exultation in the present and future...

Now I had to look forward to my future. Tomorrow everything would be put right. Dickson could sulk, but after tomorrow I wouldn't see any more of Dickson anyway.

Claire

I asked Mum if Kate had gone too, like Jim. Mum said yes. I went to my bedroom and read Kate's name in my Bunty Annual. Mum made treacle sponge for tea.

Kate

We'd spent a lot of time in the grey prison van, Dickson and I. More time than in the Court. More time than in the canary yellow cell. Dickson still wasn't saying much. We were sitting together at the front in the back of the prison van because another prisoner was being moved to York. Or was going to the Court as well. It was York. I knew it was York now because of *The Press*.

The van pulled up in the usual place at the back of the Court and Dickson led me to our room in the basement of the Court building. Mr Smith was already there.

'Is she prepared for this,' he said to Dickson.

'No,' said Dickson.

Mr Smith looked at Dickson, as if waiting for more.

'I thought you might have, you know, discussed things with her.'

'No,' said Dickson.

'I thought…'

'Never mind what you thought. I haven't and that's that. It would be like discussing thieving with a three year old. Anyway, I'm not meant to talk to the prisoner,' she said primly. 'That's your job,' she added maliciously.

It was the judgement today. I knew that. They didn't give me credit for much. Mr Hardcastle joined us. Mr Smith turned to him.

'She's got no idea,' he said, his Halifax accent drawing out the 'no' so that it sounded like naaw and made the 'idea' sound awkward. As if people with Halifax accents didn't like ideas.

Dickson was now ignoring all of us and, hearing someone approaching down the steps outside our room she took me off to the Court before the usher called us. Mr Smith and Mr Hardcastle followed disconsolately. It was the same routine; Dickson and I huddled in my corner and Mr Smith sat on a bench with Mr Hardcastle, and the sleek young man had taken up his position opposite Mr Smith. The Judge came in with his whistling hearing aid and we all stood up. I had to go and stand in the witness box or dock or whatever it was. And then sometime later Dickson led me out and Mr Smith and Mr Hardcastle gathered in my room underneath the Courtroom. At least I presume that Dickson led me

81

out and I presume that we went into the Court because for a moment I got rather confused because there we all were again. Mr Smith and Mr Hardcastle looking downbeat and Dickson not talking to anyone. I tried to summon some words along the lines of 'What has happened?' or 'Is that it now?' but I don't know if I actually said anything. Mr Smith, however, did speak.

'Are you alright?' he asked.

I nodded. I looked from him to Mr Hardcastle to Dickson and back again to Mr Smith. I'd been found guilty hadn't I? I'd been convicted for murder. For murdering Jim. But everything had gone blank and that was the second time, the first time being when I found myself in the phone box by Potters Farm. If that was the second time. Perhaps there'd been other times. Perhaps this going blank was becoming a habit. It was rather convenient if you didn't want to remember something and rather inconvenient if you were trying to explain your actions to the police or a Judge or a court or whatever. So if I'd started having these blackouts perhaps after all, perhaps I did…this was not a thought I wanted to finish. I looked at Dickson and forced myself. Perhaps I had killed Jim. Everyone else thought I had, didn't they.

I looked at Dickson meekly, and as no one said anything else she got up and I followed her up the stairs and into the prison van. So this wasn't the end, was it? This was the beginning.

Claire

One day when we walked back to get the bus home from York I stopped to watch the man shouting Press, Press except it didn't sound like Press it sounded like uhhr uhhr but I knew it meant Press because I asked Mum what he was shouting. There was a picture on the board thing by the man and I tugged and tugged at Mum because I thought it was a picture of Kate but Mum was pulling me the other way. I told Mum about it being Kate but Mum seemed cross. When we sat on the bus I thought about it again. I asked Mum if she didn't like Kate. Mum looked a bit odd. Mrs Hunter from next door got on the bus too. She was very excited about something and Mum got quite cross with her and pointed at me. I'm sure that she told Mrs Hunter to shut up. I sometimes say shut up when I'm listening to Elvis Presley and Kate sings the wrong bits and then Mum says that it isn't polite to say shut up. I would never ever ever say shut up to Mrs Hunter.

DOING TIME

Claire

A big van thing came to get me to take me to Whitcliff. Mum called it a bus. It was yellow and it said **WHITCLIFF SCHOOL BUS** on it in big black writing. It came on Mondays and Tuesdays and Thursdays and Fridays. I wore my new skirt and my new blouse. I got cross with Mum because she made me cover it all up with my cardigan because she said it was getting cold. I wouldn't go on the van bus thing but the man driving the van bus thing was very kind. He said I could sit next to him at the front. So I did. He is called Mike. Mike called the van thing a bus so I did too. Mike told me that it was his job to drive the school bus and to look after it. I thought that he must be very clever to drive a bus. Even Kate couldn't drive a bus.

Kate

I'd got used to toilet cleaning duty. In fact, I rather liked it. When you got used to the strong woman smell which especially pervaded the toilets it wasn't so bad at all. In fact it was almost comforting because that was what Claire smelt of; woman. Toilet duty was always foisted on the smallest or most vulnerable prisoner. That is to say it was done by the prisoner who couldn't or wouldn't object. So no prizes for wondering why I got lumbered with it. I had big rubber gloves and industrial bleach. The bleach oozed down the toilet bowl and all the horrors were washed away, sometimes with a bit of encouragement but always in the end washed away.

To start with Big Bertha had followed me into the toilet section of the bathrooms. Ostensibly Big Bertha was meant to clean the sinks. Big Bertha was affectionately (or discriminatingly) known as Big Bertha because she was huge and fat. Her arms tapered from enormous shoulders down to normal sized wrists and her thighs tapered down to normal sized ankles and her prison smock stretched tight over her huge bosom. Big Bertha was impressive and I thought at first that perhaps she was in charge and that she was there to oversee my work. But then when someone else new arrived in the prison Big Bertha shadowed her instead of me. It was because she wanted to suss out the new arrival. Was this newcomer a rival for her position as Big Bertha? Because in a way I suppose Big Bertha was in charge. She was the boss. Everyone did what Big Bertha said and everyone was much more frightened of Big Bertha than of the prison warders. Even the prison warders were frightened of Big Bertha.

I don't know why. She never did anyone any harm. She sort of watched over us and maintained her rule with an easy hardness. Big Bertha had killed her husband, without apology and evidently with a great deal of satisfaction, because he had persecuted her for twenty years. Bertha slept in the bottom bunk in my cell and I slept in the bunk above her. A woman called Margaret slept on the top bunk opposite me but I can't remember if there was anyone in the bunk beneath her at this stage.

Big Bertha had a sister who came to visit her once a month and a daughter who sent her letters and sweets. She loved toffees. Big Bertha's world was very female. Well, you couldn't really blame men for giving her a wide berth now, could you? Especially if they were the persecuting kind and in Big Bertha's world all men were the persecuting kind. I wondered if she'd killed other men. Her father perhaps? I don't think she had any sons which was just as well and I never heard of any brothers. But her father was dead which was suspicious enough. I mean, someone only had to die and you could be put in prison for murdering them.

The idea of false accusations and the general man hating hadn't made me think any better about Jim. And I was convinced in my more rebellious moments that it was probably more his fault that he'd died than mine and here was I in prison because of Jim. It was typical of Jim to get someone else and especially me into trouble. It was a sort of low down snidey Jim type of thing, getting people falsely accused of wrongdoing. After all, he'd falsely accused me of wrongdoing just about every day of my life and now just about every day of his death.

A few weeks after I arrived in C block I got a letter that Mum had sent on from school. It was dated a month earlier and it contained my 'A' Level results. I'd got three As.

I stood reading this letter for some time, wondering if there was any gratification in these three As. There was no note from Mum. In fact, I still hadn't heard anything from her at all. But I was soon distracted from thinking about Mum because Big Bertha was standing over me in a very threatening way. My getting a letter must have inspired her, because she was asking me to read some letters from her daughter. She had fifteen letters and apparently she hadn't been able to read any of them. You'd think that her daughter would have known that she couldn't read them, I thought indignantly. Anyway, I read the letters. Big Bertha had a grandson (whoops, not good news) and a grand daughter (better) and a son-in-law who wisely had chosen to move away from Leeds and lived in Liverpool with his family. Hopefully, when she was released Big Bertha would go back to Leeds and not move to Liverpool. Big Bertha's sister lived in Leeds and she visited Big Bertha regularly. I saw her often as Jane came to see me a lot and sometimes Big Bertha and I would stand together waiting to see our visitors.

Big Bertha had been the bleacher in a laundrette. If one can be a bleacher. Maybe that was why she hung around the toilets. Maybe the smell reminded her of happier times. Although if you'd had to kill your husband perhaps it hadn't been happier times. So we had bleach in common. And a legitimate hatred of men called Jim. Big Bertha's husband had been called Jim, I think. She called him a bag of shit and other worse things so I called him Jim in my head although I'm not sure Big Bertha ever called him anything beyond the many expletives at her command. When Big Bertha talked about her husband it was best to go and clean the toilets. No one ever stopped me cleaning the toilets. Even the warders didn't stop me cleaning the toilets although this activity sometimes had to take place after midnight because Big Bertha had woken up and remembered all about her husband and lots of warders had to rush to the scene and hold her down. Luckily, the daughter never mentioned her dead father so reading her letters to Big Bertha was almost a pleasant experience.

'Dear Mum, We finished early at the canteen today and I got time to go to the shop before Trudy came home from school. Malcolm got a pay rise last week so I got the extra big toffee selection from Woolworths for you. Adam lost two teeth last week. (Well, with all those toffees … but I didn't say this out loud to Big Bertha.) Trudy has been learning how to knit. I'm hoping she'll take after you and be a good knitter. (This gave rise to two thoughts, both of which I deemed it best not to pass on to Big Bertha: Bertha knitted!! And her daughter 'hoped' that Trudy would take after her grandmother?) Auntie Beryl is coming over at the weekend and she has promised to bring us some of your old patterns.

Love from Deidre.'

Claire knitted. At least I presumed she still knitted. I wondered if she still just knitted or if she'd progressed to knitting something. A scarf perhaps, or a tea cosy. We'd all knitted tea cosies in our last year at primary school. Jim had used my tea cosy on the teapot in his shed. Apparently it was too scruffy to have in the kitchen and it had tea stains all down one side because Mum's old teapot which Jim used in the shed leaked around the spout.

Big Bertha sat chewing on her toffees and I suppose she listened to Deidre's letter. When I'd finished she took it and looked at the writing almost fondly, then she folded it up and stashed it away with all the others. One day Deidre sent some photos of them all. Big Bertha spent ages looking at the photos. She didn't listen to her letter but she did show me the photos. Trudy was wearing a short orange frock with red and brown squirls on it. Adam had a green knitted jumper on (presumably not knitted by Trudy, but perhaps by Auntie Beryl). Malcolm had short, fair hair and was wearing a cheap suit and Deidre had a sort of Buffon hair-do and looked very fashionable.

I didn't have any photos of Mum or Claire. Jane brought me one that her mother had taken of us both when we were fourteen. We were all dressed up ready to go out to the theatre. We'd been allowed to go to the Saturday matinee on our own. It was the first time we'd gone into York on our own on the bus. Jane's mother had given her half-a-crown and we bought a ginger beer each in the interval. It was *Romeo and Juliet.* Jane fell in love with Romeo for a week afterwards and I learnt Juliet's speeches and wondered what would have happened if she'd fallen in love with Mercutio instead. I kept the photo safely hidden in *Emma*. I'd read *Emma* fifteen times at this point.

I suppose Big Bertha was my friend. At least, you could trust her and it was easy to tell when she was going to think about her husband and then you could just sneak off out of the way. Big Bertha was a lifer. It must have been quite a killing, the killing of her 'Jim'. I wondered if everyone else thought that my killing of Jim had been 'quite a killing' and if I was a lifer.

Of course, this was the sort of thing that I was meant to know. This sort of proper information as Dickson would have called it that had nothing to do with poetry or Jane Austen. But as I'd blanked out when my verdict was given I really didn't have a clue about what had happened. Dickson had said nothing. She'd just taken me back to the prison, found the smallest regulation prison dress she could lay her hands on, sort of poured me into it, then sent me on my way, as it were, up the prison ladder to proper full residence status. Said bright blue prison dress which drooped down over my shoulders, hung well below my knees with a saggy waist band that awkwardly encircled my hips, was the regulation dress worn by all prisoners. Dickson had said nothing. It still hurt. I'd thought that Dickson and I were friends. I hadn't seen Dickson since the day of the verdict, but then Dickson didn't work in 'C' block.

Claire

I am writing a diary at Whitcliff. Today I wrote

> I went Bettye. I had Chocolate Cake. KAte cant drive Bue.

Lesley helped me.

Kate

Jane leant over the table conspiratorially. Big Bertha was sitting at the next table. She was eating toffees and her sister, Beryl, was knitting.

'Now, what worries me is, assuming that you didn't kill Jim, who did? Because whoever did do it is still at large.'

Jane was wearing a long woollen cardigan with large orange buttons. The cardigan was also orange and had a twisted pattern running down the front. I glanced across at Beryl's knitting. It was green, like a school uniform colour.

'Kate, are you listening to me,' hissed Jane frustrated.

I dragged my eyes away from Beryl's knitting.

'What if I did do it?' I said.

'Don't be daft,' said Jane.

'Yes, but what if...'

'There's no way you could have killed Jim,' professed Jane stoutly.

I looked at her uncertainly. Everyone else thought I'd killed Jim, and maybe I had. All it needed was for me to have had another blackout. I didn't like to contemplate my blackouts. There was the one in the telephone box and the minor one when I wasn't sure whether I was just saying stuff in my head or shouting it out at the court. There was the one surrounding the sentencing. All the things I should have known about lifers and sentencing; all the things that Dickson wouldn't talk about. There seemed to be a pattern of getting hysterical and blacking out so if I blacked out in the Court then the chances were that I was also hysterical. Which meant carrying on. Like I did with Jim, shouting and stuff. So I could have had one of these hysterical outbursts in the Court, something like shouting that it was all Jim's fault, that he'd done it on purpose sort of thing. This was the kind of thing that I should know. Dickson should have told me. Bloody Dickson. I don't think Jane was there for the sentencing. I think she'd started working by then. I hoped she hadn't been. Could I have asked her what happened? I wasn't sure. Although Jane would have understood. Perhaps. But better not to have put that understanding to the test. I had to believe that Jane understood even though I knew that she couldn't possibly understand. It was just the same kind of understanding that she applied to being loyal about hating Jim even though she couldn't really see why anyone should hate him. Jane was incredibly loyal. Because I could have had a blackout, got all hysterical and well, done Jim in. I shook myself and tried to follow Jane's line of enquiry.

'But who else could have done it?'

Jane thought she'd got my interest at last. She leant over the table again and took a deep breath.

'You know your mother just got a big insurance pay out. Apparently Jim had a life insurance policy.'

Jane knew all about insurance these days. The job she'd got was with Yorkshire Life and she worked in Piccadilly. I thought she was mad not to go to University. She'd got good 'A' Level results too. But Jane had never intended to go to University. She'd talked about it because I'd talked about it but she'd never intended to go. She'd even got a place at Nottingham to study psychology. I smiled at the thought of Jane studying psychology.

'Kate, it's not funny,' said Jane sharply.

I shook myself.

'Mum couldn't have killed Jim. She had an alibi.'

'She might have paid them off, or made it up.'

'She'd never have killed Jim anyway.'

'If you'd been married to Jim you'd have killed him, especially for £10,000.'

'£10,000? Wow. That must be the only sensible thing Jim ever did.'

'Maybe it was a scam,' continued Jane.

I looked bewildered.

'You know, your mum and Jim meant to stage Jim's death and then run off with the money together.'

'You can't stage a death with a circular saw,' I said dourly. 'And anyway they couldn't have run off anywhere. What about Claire?'

Jane looked scuppered for a moment and then the bell went. I stood up immediately to be ready to follow Big Bertha out. It was a tricky moment, leaving the visiting room. People tended to get emotional and then they would start looking for someone to pick on. But no one picked on anyone within the vicinity of Big Bertha and

Big Bertha herself was going to be happy as the large bag of toffees would be accompanying her to the cell.

'I'll see you,' said Jane, suddenly desperate at having to see me in my ill-fitting prison uniform going back into the prison.

I tried to smile, but Big Bertha rose to her feet and I said goodbye hastily to Jane and hurried after Big Bertha so that I was able to attach myself to her as she walked out of the room chewing her toffees. She noticed me as we went out into the corridor. She smiled complacently and looked down at me.

'Want a toffee?' she said.

My jaw dropped about a foot. Big Bertha never shared her toffees. I dug my hand into the bag and pulled out a large toffee éclair.

'Thanks, Bertha,' I said and we both sauntered down the corridor sucking noisily on toffee éclairs.

Kate

Not long after this, Eileen was put into our cell. There might have been someone before Eileen but I can't remember anything about her so perhaps there wasn't anyone else ever. Just big Bertha, Margaret, Eileen and me. But I do know that Eileen arrived just before Christmas. I'd got Jane to get me a bag of Thornton's special toffee to give to Big Bertha and Eileen didn't like this.

Eileen was small and round and homely. She had short dark brown hair which had originally been permed.

'You and I can be friends,' she said when she arrived. She leant towards me and said in a stage whisper. 'Well, Bertha's not up to much is she?' Eileen tapped her head to indicate that Big Bertha was stupid. I was glad that Bertha was well out of earshot of Eileen's stage whisper. 'Not much conversation to be had from Bertha now is there,' continued Eileen, laughing a light tinkling laugh.

I smiled uncertainly.

'Now, I heard on the grapevine,' began Eileen, 'that Bertha killed her husband accidentally. Can you believe it? She didn't know her own strength and strangled him in flagrante,' she added for effect.

I was pretty sure that Eileen didn't know what 'in flagrante' meant.

'And Margaret obviously didn't kill her mother. Poor Margaret. I mean someone posh like Margaret shouldn't be in here. Although for my own sake I must say I was rather relieved to see that I was going to have some decent company, if you know what I mean. Especially when the first person one sees is Bertha. I mean, look at the size of her. She has hips like an elephant,' Eileen tinkled.

I wondered whether I was 'decent' company.

'Oh yes, you and I are going to be such friends. You know, I have 'O' Levels in Needlework and Religious Education. And I'm going to make sure that you attend the Adult Learning Centre. It's no good sitting in here and not getting ahead. One day you'll be out of here and you'll have me to thank for that. Now, after Christmas I'm going to enrol you for the Domestic Science class. I'll come along too and help you so you needn't be afraid. And I'll work next to you so I can do your practicals for you to make sure you get a good pass. Things like that count you know. When you go before a Parole Board, they'll look favourably on an 'O' Level in Domestic Science. It means you can do useful work so they'll let you out.'

I liked the idea of being let out.

'We'll get Margaret to join our club. Her needlework will be excellent you know,' continued the tinkling. 'People of her class still learn these things.'

Because of this as it were fresh view of Margaret I was beginning to think that perhaps I'd misjudged her. (Although at this point I'm not sure that I'd done any judging of Margaret. Margaret didn't say much and neither did I so there hadn't really been much to go on.) However, if I was to be influenced by Eileen on the subject of Margaret, perhaps I was to believe that she was a kind of modern-day Jane Austen heroine. Poor by circumstance and wrongly accused, with a faithful lover waiting who would greet her at the prison gate on the day of her release and at last lead her up the aisle so that they could spend a long and happy old age together.

'And we must sit with Margaret at lunchtime so that you can learn proper table manners from Margaret and myself.'

Margaret and me I corrected silently.

'Although really this prison food will be the death of me one of these days. Constitutions like Margaret's and mine can't manage all these suet puddings. And the gristle in the stew, did you ever see anything like it?'

Quite frankly no. Mum was a reasonable cook as long as she stuck to basics.

Eileen's quick glance suddenly caught sight of Bertha lumbering over in our direction. Eileen jumped up and started pulling at me.

'Come on, quick, look as though we have to go somewhere in a hurry,' she said as she dragged me past Big Bertha.

'Sorry, Bertha, got to rush. Catherine and I have so much to do,' tinkled Eileen as she rushed us past Big Bertha and on in the vague direction of the library.

The library would have been quite a soothing destination.

'Oh Lord,' exclaimed Eileen crossly. 'I can't be doing with all these books. It's so morbid. Come on we'll go somewhere else.'

I was starting to miss Big Bertha's quiet company. Eileen propelled us into another part of the open recreational area and barged our way into the group led by Amy Smith who were in for petty crimes like theft and prostitution.

This tinkling went on until Christmas unless I managed to team up with Big Bertha before Eileen got her claws into me. But Eileen still hadn't given up all hope of us being best friends as I was perhaps marginally more communicative than Margaret.

Christmas slipped into the calendar of our daily routine. Jane had wrapped the Thornton's toffees in a big pink bag with ribbons and a gift tag which said 'To Bertha from Kate' on it. I presented it to Big Bertha when we'd all been filed back to our cells after the Christmas church service and prior to our Christmas lunch. In the excitement of the pink wrapping and Bertha's quiet delight I forgot about Eileen and when we were called to lunch I happily went to the canteen with Big Bertha. Eileen was sitting on her own on the edge of Amy Smith's group. I was feeling suddenly magnanimous – after all it was Christmas – and I tried to call her over to sit with Bertha and me, but she didn't seem to notice.

Later she was waiting for me in the toilet.

'Don't you ever, ever do that again.' She pushed her fingers up my nose and kneed me in the stomach. 'You little turncoat, toadying to Bertha. You know what they say about Bertha don't you? Well, don't you, you little bitch?' She spat at me. I was pinned against the wall. She suddenly thrust her hand inside my pants and I sicked up the whole of my Christmas lunch all over her.

After that I had to be careful of Eileen, as well as following the intuition which made me be careful of Margaret, despite her promotion to Jane Austen heroine. It could make simple things like a trip to the bathroom rather complicated, and the more interesting hidden parts of the library were now completely out of bounds for me. If nothing else I was going to be able to write Mills and Boon romances if they ever let me out of here. Because they were popular they were kept under the strict eye of the librarian, thus the Mills and Boon section of the library was the only safe place to be, especially if one had not managed to latch onto Big Bertha. I wondered if writing Mills and Boon romances would be considered a 'useful occupation' by the Parole Board.

Kate

'But if your mum didn't do it, then who did?' Jane was still like the proverbial dog with a bone when it came to Jim's murder. I mean, did it really matter any more? Although I suppose if I hadn't killed Jim then there was a circular saw murder maniac on the loose somewhere in York and it was all very well for me not to care tucked away safely in prison; safe at least from that particular mad man – or woman.

Big Bertha didn't have a visitor today and to be quite honest I was more worried about how I was going to get from the visiting room to our cell in one piece. At least two other people had carefully noted the absence of Big Bertha.

'Can we talk about something else for a change?' I said to Jane.

Jane was wearing a lime green skirt with a matching short coat and plastic shoes. I didn't like the plastic shoes but Jane insisted that although she agreed that in themselves they were rather ugly, they went with the rest of her outfit so well. Her cream top had short sleeves and a roll neck. In fact Jane was looking pretty good despite the shoes.

'Did Mark bring you again today?'

'Alan.'

Wasn't Alan Big Bertha's son-in-law? No, that was Malcolm, I think. Or Adam? Was that her grandson? I must pay more attention when I read the letters from Bertha's daughter to her.

'Really Kate, do you ever listen to anything I say?'

Every word. Like manna from heaven. I smiled apologetically.

'It's just that I'm not sure about the name Alan,' I said.

I'd decided that people called Alan were at risk from Big Bertha despite my confusion over the names. Although perhaps a man by any name was at risk from Big Bertha. That is if anyone was at risk from Big Bertha. Personally, I was beginning to wonder if we hadn't all underestimated Big Bertha, or overestimated her when it came to her killing capacity. She wouldn't let us kill spiders. But spiders are the ultimate female predator aren't they? So it could just be that she looked after her own kind. Was that why she looked after me?

'Alan's already got promotion,' continued Jane somewhat randomly I thought.

'Er, what does Alan do?'

'Katy! Honestly. He works in the sales department at Rowntrees.'

Well that couldn't take much cop could it – persuading people to buy chocolate. Okay I admit it; I was a bit jealous of Alan, or Mark or whatever his name was. I know he drove Jane over to see me but she used to come at least every three weeks when it was Rob who drove her and now it was well over a month since her last visit.

Time didn't just go round and round, it went on and on. Only I was a time warp. Jane was 19 pushing 20 and I was still only 18 because the button had jammed on my time machine.

'I was wondering if I should try reading Trollope. You know, all the *Barchester Chronicles* and the *Pallisers* series. They could keep me going for several months if I'm lucky,' I said.

Jane looked pleased.

'Brilliant. I'll try and find some shall I? And bring them in next time?'

'You might be able to get them second hand,' I said, suddenly anxious. I couldn't expect Jane to buy twelve books for me; it would cost her a fortune.

'Oh, don't worry about that,' said Jane, 'I'll get them for your birthday or take them out from the library.'

The library sounded a dodgy idea.

'I don't need them all at once,' I said.

'Then I'll just get you one for your birthday,'

'And in the right order,' I said.

'In the right order.'

'You know what the right order is?'

'Kate, just leave it to me, I got three 'A' Levels as well you know.'

'Sshh,' I said in sudden panic.

'Sshh what?' said Jane, at least lowering her voice.

'No one knows.'

'No one knows what?'

'About the 'A' Levels.'

Jane looked puzzled.

'Does it matter?'

'Yes it does matter.'

'But?' Jane looked at me carefully, suddenly remembering that prison wasn't a weekend at Butlins. 'I'm sorry, Kate,' she said. And we both knew that she wasn't sorry about the 'A' Levels – she was sorry for me, for this whole horrid mess. 'I do know it must be awful, it's just…'

If I started blubbering I was going to be massacred big time on the way back to the cell.

'How are Mum and Claire?' I asked, an unwanted indifferent tone hardening my heart.

'Oh, okay I think. I haven't seen them for a while but my mum bumped into your mum last week and they were doing fine. Your mum's got her days at the clinic shifted to the same days that Claire spends at Whitcliff.'

'She's still working, then?'

'Yes. Mum says that the money won't go that far if it's all they've got and that your mum is very sensible to keep her job on. And if anything happened to her it would be something to help Claire, you know.'

I didn't know. But then I don't think Jane did either, she was just repeating what her mother had said. The bell went to warn that visiting was over and I was out of the visiting room and down the corridor to our cell before Jane had managed to check her make-up, speak or wave goodbye.

Claire

Mrs Cartwright came to see us. She brought me some wool. I put my new skirt on and Mrs Cartwright said I looked very pretty. Mum made tea. I didn't have any tea but I did have 3 biscuits. I chose a big ball of blue wool and then I got my knitting needles out and Mum cast on 20 stitches for me. Mrs Cartwright said lots of things and she had 1 biscuit. She said that Jane had a very nice boyfriend. She said that Jane's boyfriend took Jane to see Kate. Mum didn't say anything. I said that I had a very nice boyfriend too and Mrs Cartwright and Mum laughed.

When Mrs Cartwright had gone I asked Mum if Jane went to see Jim too. Mum looked at me in an odd way and didn't say anything for a long time and then she said my name, Claire, and then she said you mustn't ever talk about Jim. And I said not ever ever. And Mum said not ever ever. Then I asked if I could talk about Kate but Mum didn't say anything. She tidied the tea things away and I ate another biscuit.

Kate

I didn't see Jane on my birthday but I did get a present. *The Warden*. Everyone, led by Eileen, thought that it was called 'The Warder' and Eileen began a rumour that I was plotting something. It also elicited the most attention that Margaret had ever paid me. She picked the book up carefully, turned it over and read the back cover. Big Bertha picked it up and threatened to destroy it in conjunction with Eileen's head, announcing in a loud authoritative voice that it was called *The Warden*, you daft cow, not 'The Warder'. I looked at Big Bertha in disbelief. No, one mustn't overestimate – or was it underestimate – Big Bertha.

Kate

I didn't clean the toilets any more. Jeanette, my psychologist, said I had to be given a job which helped me socialise more. Reading Big Bertha's letters didn't count as socialising, besides which Bertha didn't have sessions with Jeanette. But Eileen did and Eileen made it clear to everyone and anyone who listened or not, that I was a vicious anti-social being with warped predilections hidden beneath my quiet exterior. Although I'm not sure that even Eileen's posh voice managed to put it quite like that.

Basically, Eileen hadn't spoken to me for over a year now. And Eileen not speaking to one was noticed. Now if it had been Margaret... The fact that Margaret didn't speak to a soul apart from asking politely for someone to pass the salt or the water or whatever small item she might need at the table – yes, Margaret did have perfect table manners – didn't seem to cause anyone any concern. Although sitting at the table with Margaret was the only place that it was possible to feel comfortable with her. But that was just me. Everyone else accepted Margaret's gentility as being a safeguard against all ills or ill-intentions. When Margaret wasn't eating she was embroidering and someone who embroidered had to be sane, civilised and good. Both inmates and warders alike were, despite themselves, impressed with good breeding (as Eileen would have put it).

Jeanette, of course, knew about my 'A' Levels so she recommended me for library duty. I was made junior librarian under the command of the librarian. The complexities of this promotion cannot be exaggerated. Eileen was furious. She was still dishwashing and scrubbing kitchen tables and she soon pointed out to everyone that I had been given a favour and a promotion which wasn't right. No one had ever wanted to be junior librarian before but now it was deemed to be the most wanted job in the prison. At least for a day or two. When it came to applying for turns to do the job in a rota no one put their names down. Not even Eileen.

Library duty was easier to expedite than cleaning the toilets had become and I had frequently been in trouble for being lax in my duties as I could only clean the toilets when I was sure that Eileen and one or two others were safely engrossed in some other activity. This meant that the toilets were only ever really clean on Monday and Wednesday evenings when *Coronation Street* was on. Although I had noticed for some time that Big Bertha had taken to spending rather a lot of time in the toilets, as it were on guard against evil intent.

Library duty was easier in that it was harder to intimidate someone in the library as it was part of the other communal working and living spaces but on the other hand I was given a timetable of days and hours when I had to work. I had to be there and everyone else knew when I would be there – alone. However, at about the same time as I was made junior librarian Big Bertha took a liking for Mills and Boon and when I turned up for duty her large bulk would also take up position by the door, in full sight of all comers to the library and she sat there for hours, days and months reading Mills and Boon. If I achieved nothing else, I indirectly helped Bertha up quite a few rungs of the literacy ladder. I still had to read her letters though.

Jeanette was about ten years older than me. She had neat dark hair and wore trouser suits. It was hard to concentrate during my sessions with her as I kept thinking that this was what Jane could have been doing and then I would hypothesise to myself the kind of questions that Jane would have asked, what I would have answered and how she would have reacted to my answers – on the assumption that I hadn't known her before, of course.

'I see your friend's been to see you again,' Jeanette began. (You have a very loyal friend who comes to see you a lot don't you, that must be nice, I imagined the psychologist Jane saying.)

'Yes.' (Yes, it is. It reminds me that it is possible to be normal, to live a normal life, I imagined replying to the psychologist Jane.)

'Has she always been your friend,' Jeanette continued. (Have you known each other for a long time? asked the friendly sympathetic Jane of my imagination.)

'Yes.' (We met on our first day at primary school. Jane sat next to me although she knew two other girls and I didn't know anyone.)

'Do you have any other friends, Kate?' asked Jeanette. (And did you make lots of other friends once you had started school?)

No comment. (Yes, but we were never as close to anyone else as we were to each other.)

'Why do you think that is, Kate,' continued Jeanette assuming my silence to mean no. (Why was that? continued the imaginary Jane soothingly.)

Still no comment. (Because we understood one another, because Jane understood things without me having to tell her all the time and she didn't ask questions. It's not nice being constantly asked by other five year olds, where's your daddy? And then by six year olds, is that your new daddy, then? Oh, how I could have poured my heart out to this perfect Jane psychologist.)

'You're not making this easy for me are you, Kate?' At which point Jeanette decided to change tack. 'Do you know why your mother hasn't been to see you?' (I see from your records that you haven't had much contact with your family. Would you like me to find out how they are for you? said the imaginary Jane, making even this most hurtful of wounds something one could talk about.)

It was hard to pretend indifference and make any kind of reply to Jeanette. (Yes, I'd like to know how Claire is. I think that my mother thinks that I killed Jim, I could have said to the imaginary Jane.)

'Do you think that's because of what you did?' (I'm sure that it's been very hard for her losing her husband and she is probably worried about Claire.)

'I didn't do anything.' (Yes, she is probably worried about Claire.)

At this point Jeanette was just Jeanette again and the hypothetical Jane faded from the picture. It needed all my concentration to deal with Jeanette's pained look. The look that meant that if I could just admit to everything then everything would be alright. I would be the most popular girl at school, the most popular prisoner in the whole of Wakefield, be welcomed into the bosom of my family again...

'I think you should start doing needlework with Margaret, that is, when you are not on library duty. I think Margaret needs a friend too and she would be a good influence on you. I understand that it might be difficult to always get along with Eileen but you can't have any difficulties with Margaret. I've noticed that you often sit near her at meal times and I think that is most commendable. Well, Kate, that's it for today. I'll see you next week and I'll be keeping a look out to see how you are getting on with Margaret.'

Claire

I learnt another song. We all learnt it at Whitcliff. I listened to it on the radio instead of Elvis Presley. It is called The Beatles. I sang we all live in a yellow margarine and Mum talked to Mrs Hunter in the kitchen.

Claire

It was a Thursday and Lesley wasn't at Whitcliff. It was a man. He said that Lesley was poorly. He had a black beard and a big loud voice. He stood at the front of the room and talked a lot. I didn't like his talking so I put my hands over my ears. He kept smiling at us and his mouth was horrid and red and wet. His voice got louder so I started to sing we all live in a yellow margarine. I blocked my ears and put my head on the table and sang. But someone got hold of my arm. I could smell him. I didn't like it so I pulled my arm away from him as hard as I could and I hit at him with my other arm. My chair fell over and the man fell over. I hurt my knee. I made a big noise like crying and I ran away. I ran away like Kate. I ran down the road where the yellow bus drove but I got a big pain in my chest bit and I had to stop. I sat down in the road and wished that Kate was there. Then I wished that Mum was there and then another man came and stood over me. He didn't say anything and after a bit I looked up at him. It was Mike. He had a big bucket of soapy water with a sponge sticking up on the top. Why have you got a big bucket I asked him. He said that he cleaned his bus on Thursdays. I asked him if I could help him and he said that I could watch. I followed him to his bus. He rubbed the sponge all over the bus and I sploshed the sponge about in the water and gave it to him. A woman came down the road. She saw me and came rushing over. Claire, Claire she said what are you doing here. I'm cleaning Mike's bus I said. Mike gave me the sponge and I sploshed it about in the bucket and when I gave it back to Mike the soapy water sploshed all over the woman's stockings. Claire, Claire she said again we have to talk about what just happened. Her voice went nasty. I put my hands over my ears and watched Mike. She said something else, she said lots of things then she looked cross and went away again. Who is that person I asked Mike. Mike knows everything. Oh that's Sally Mike said. Sally's alright said Mike. I looked at where Sally was walking away from us and I wasn't sure that Sally was nice but I looked back at Mike again and decided that Sally was alright. After a bit Sally came back. She had my coat. I smiled at her and said thank you. She looked a bit odd then she smiled back. She patted me on the arm and said there there then you're a good girl Claire. Yes Mike was right Sally was alright. Sally said that I could stay with Mike until it was time to go home. I sat on the bus and Mike showed me all the bits on the bus. I liked the horn best and he let me toot it 3 times.

The next day I drew a picture of Mike.

Kate

The next day I took my well-worn copy of *The Warden* and sat next to Margaret in the day room. Margaret had taken an interest in *The Warden* and I could sit next to her and read it with at least some pretence of solidarity. At least with enough pretence to show Jeanette that I was making an effort. Eileen did not like this new development. She plonked herself down on the other side of Margaret.

'Oh, you are skilled aren't you, Margaret,' she started babbling. It was one of her posh voice days today. Her Margaret voice. 'My Aunt used to do fine embroidery work too. The Rev. Arthur Plumber much admired her work once at a church fête, you know.'

I wondered if there really had been a Rev. Arthur Plumber or for that matter if there had been an aunt. Margaret had grown up in a vicarage and the reference to the Rev. Arthur Plumber was as much in deference to Margaret's background as to the truth.

Margaret said something polite about the finer points of embroidery and how difficult it was to get the best quality thread these days. Would that be referring to these days in general or these days in prison? Her long thin body hunched over her embroidery, perhaps to protect it from Eileen's effusions.

'Oh I couldn't agree more,' continued Eileen. 'Only just the other day I was desperate for some embroidery thread, but it wasn't to be had, neither for love nor money.' She leant in close to Margaret and indulged in her favourite stage whisper. 'I think someone is taking it,' she said dramatically.

Margaret was sharp on the inference and on cue she turned to me. Her pale eyes looked towards me without really registering interest or colour. Did she turn to me to acknowledge blame or to refute Eileen's possible hint that I was the embroidery thief?

'That's not my favourite Trollope,' she said. 'I prefer *Rachel Ray* and the *Palliser* novels. One can have too much of The Church. But I remember my father enjoyed it. He always recommended it to his curates.'

Whoa. I hoped that Jeanette was watching this. I didn't know that Margaret could spin so many words together at once. She had been brought up in a nursery where little girls were to be seen and not heard. At least that's how I imagined that she'd been brought up; the reality had probably been something closer to poverty and repression. But if she carried on chatting like this I'd be earning my first ever brownie point from Jeanette. This was not going to make things any easier with Eileen but I couldn't please everyone and I'd got more adept at dealing with Eileen than I had at dealing with Jeanette.

'I haven't read *Rachel Ray*,' I said.

'Then I can recommend it for you,' said Margaret with a polite smile. Her lifeless eyes travelled discreetly down my throat, taking in my exposed Adams apple (do women have Adam's apples? My Eve's apple? Anyway, my neck and throat) and the thinness of my neck and consequent narrowness of all air passages. 'It is a breath of fresh air,' she said dreamily.

It was a long time since I'd had to suppress the desire to chew my lips. I swallowed, then regretted it. I felt the bulge of the involuntary swallow as it forced its way down my throat, fixating the pale eyes.

'Thank you, Margaret,' I said politely, 'I'll ask my friend to get a copy of it for me.'

'I'd lend you mine but all my books went when my mother and I had to move out of the rectory.'

I didn't want to hear about Margaret's mother. Margaret was 'in' for smothering her mother with a feather pillow and there was much debate about the likelihood of her ever actually having done this. She had however been convicted of murder, hadn't she? But then, so had I.

'Do you like Jane Austen?' I asked.

'Well, I don't know do I, I never met her,' Margaret smiled again. 'But I did much enjoy her works, yes.'

Oh, please be watching all this, Jeanette. I wasn't sure that I could go through all this again another day.

'I think my favourite's *Emma*,' I said.

'Oh, really?' said Margaret. 'I've always preferred *Persuasion* myself, once one has got over being in love with Mr Darcy, of course.'

'Does one ever get over being in love with Mr Darcy?' I said lightly.

Margaret looked suddenly interested and looked at me properly for the first time, and I noticed that her eyes were a light pale blue colour.

'No,' she said, 'one doesn't. Not even a Captain Wentworth could compensate for a Mr Darcy.'

Just as the conversation was actually becoming interesting, by which I mean almost personal if drooling over Jane Austen heroes can count as being personal, Eileen started muttering and fussing. She was leaning over Margaret's sewing to try to get her attention.

'And such lovely colours,' she said.

Margaret's eyes went blank again and she turned away from me and fixed her attention on Eileen's throat and I went back to *The Warden*.

Well done, Kate, you just managed a prolonged conversation with the most taciturn prisoner in the whole of 'C' block in full view of everyone, I thought, and deeming that I had done my social stint for the day I slowly edged away from them both until I was well out of hearing of Eileen's incessant chatter.

Claire

The next day was Saturday. I bought a big sponge with some money that Mum gave me. I bought it all on my own while Mum watched. We had Welsh rare-bit and tea and chocolate cake at Bettys.

But then Mum came to Whitcliff one day and Sally said that I couldn't go on Mike's bus anymore. Mum got cross and said why not and Sally said that I was 20 now and that it was a school bus which took the children to the school and Mum said that it took people to the day centre as well and Sally said that it only took children until they were 20 and that after that it was not allowed. Mum said that it was ri-di-cu-lous. Mum then said something crossly about Mike and Sally said that it was nothing to do with Mike but yes that was another issue and that did she realise how pretty Claire was and Mum gave me a hug. Mum then said in a nasty voice could Claire still go to school oh sorry I mean the day centre just like before and Sally said of course. Mum said but but then she didn't say anything else. She sighed. I put my head on her bosoms and she carried on hugging me. Then Mum said so Claire can still go to the day centre 4 days a week and do all the things she does now and Sally said yes of course again until she's 24. And Mum asked what happened when she's 24 and this time Sally sighed and said then she'll probably only be able to come 2 days a week. Mum said that it was ri-di-cu-lous again and Sally said I know but that she didn't make the rules. Mum said and Claire's coming on so well these days and Sally said yes she's doing very well and did Mum want to look at her diary and that she's drawn a lovely picture of Mike and written Mike's bus without any help from anyone. And then Mum said how on earth am I going to get her here though and Sally said couldn't she walk. Mum shook her head. And she can't get the bus on her own can she Mum sort of asked Sally and Sally said de-fin-ite-ly not Mike was quite harmless but what if she chatted someone else up and Mum got cross again and said she didn't chat anyone up and Sally said but you can see that she's very and a word I didn't understand.

On Thursday I didn't go on Mike's bus. Mum and I got the bus that went to York but we both got off at Whitcliff and Mum walked up the road with me. I had my new sponge with me. It was in a big bag. Mum asked me if I knew the way and if I could get off the bus on my own and walk up the road to the day centre and I said yes of course I could. That afternoon I said I didn't want to write my diary I wanted to be outside. So I went outside with my sponge and helped Mike clean his bus. Mike was very pleased with my sponge and he let me clean the back bit of the bus all by myself.

Claire

Mrs Cartwright came to see us. She said that Jane was getting married to Alan and that Jane would be coming to see us herself to give us an invitation to the wedding. Mum looked very pleased and said that that would be very nice and that Jane had always been a good girl and that she deserved to be happy. Mrs Cartwright gave me some more blue wool and Mum made 20 stiches for me. Mrs Cartwright told me I could do purl as well. I had to knit and then I had to do it all sort of backwards. Mrs Cartwright and Mum got very happy and laughed and said I was very clever. Mrs Cartwright asked me what I was going to make and I said I was going to make a scarf for Mike. And I did. I cut out a picture in a magazine and made it look as much like this as I could.

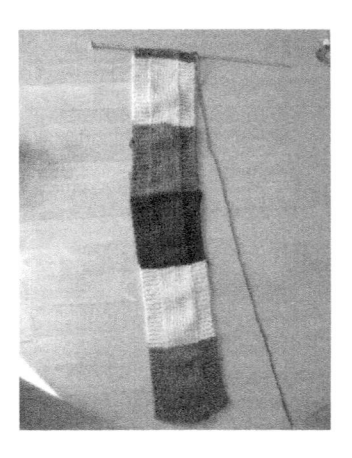

Claire

Jane came to Brown's with us. She was very happy. It made me feel happy. She said that we had to get Claire a new dress. I tried on 2 dresses. The first one was a blue dress but Jane said I had to try on a yellow dress. I stopped being happy and said I didn't want to put the yellow dress on. Jane talked some more and I put my hands over my ears. Then Jane said you don't have to try the yellow dress on if you don't want to but it would look very pretty on me and was perfect for a summer wedding. I took my hands away from my ears and Jane said I should think of something really nice that was yellow. I thought of Mike's bus. I put the yellow dress on. Mum and Jane said it looked very pretty. I looked in the mirror and thought that I looked pretty but I said I wanted the blue dress.

Kate

'I'm not sure that *Emma* is my favourite Jane Austen novel anymore,' I said to Jane. It was a bright June day. Jane was wearing white trousers which hugged her bottom, flat pumps and a sleeveless white top covered in spots which were all sorts of sizes and colours. She had a long chunky cardigan flung over her arm which was bright turquoise and a matching handbag. She was also bursting with news. Although she hadn't actually told me anything yet, I could just tell.

'Maybe it's because I've read it so much since being in here. Maybe I should give it to you to take away from me for a year or so then when you give it back to me again I'll enjoy it more than ever.'

Jane wasn't listening. I smiled across at Big Bertha. She and her sister Beryl were both knitting. Bertha was allowed to knit now. Beryl was knitting the usual uniform green jumper and Bertha was knitting a bright orange cardigan. I knew because I'd helped her to ball up the wool. And anyway, she took it everywhere with her.

'You got engaged, didn't you?'

Jane jumped guiltily.

'To Mark,' I continued.

'Al...' Jane started to say, and then she caught my expression and started to laugh with relief. 'I wanted to wait. Until you could, well you know, be bridesmaid, but...'

'It's okay,' I said, and meant it.

'We got engaged on my birthday.'

'Are you sure, Jane, I mean you're still a bit young aren't you?' I couldn't help thinking about all those dreams we'd had, all those things we'd been going to do before. Before what? Before marriage or prison?

'I'm twenty two, you know,' she said, almost indignantly. Other people must have made the same comment.

Twenty two? Then I must be twenty two too. I was a couple of months older than Jane.

'I've never met him, have I?'

Jane shook her head.

'I could bring him in to meet you. I mean Alan said that he would like to. If you...'

I looked at her. I wasn't sure.

'Have I changed?' I said.

'I don't know,' said Jane. 'Sometimes, but sometimes you're just as you were.'

'Yes, that's how I feel too. You should have done psychology after all,' I said suddenly, remembering all those sessions I'd had with Jane/Jeanette.

'I'll still come and visit.'

But not as often. I couldn't expect Jane's life to stop because mine had.

'I'd like to meet Alan,' I said.

Although I'd have to speak quietly or call him Mark the whole time if Bertha had a visit from Beryl at the same time. I'd told Bertha that Jane's boyfriend was called Mark. Just to be on the safe side, having got myself all strung up about the name Alan. I decided not to explain this to Jane.

'Would you really?' she said.

'Yes.'

The bell went. Jane's eyes were shining. I was glad I'd been brave. She leant over the table and kissed me on the cheek. She had clean hair and clean skin. Big Bertha was gathering up her knitting so I had to be quick.

'Give my love to Mark,' I said jauntily, feeling suddenly filled with my old self.

Jane checked her make-up and we kept waving as she followed the other visitors to the exit door and I stuck close to Bertha. The euphoria was short lived and my old self slipped away as I tagged on to Big Bertha. Or did it? What was my old self? Someone who ruthlessly murdered people? Someone who was so incompetent they didn't manage to murder someone without getting caught for it? Someone who, even worse, didn't murder anyone but who got put away for it anyway? Or the bolshie teenager who picked fights with parents all the time. If Jim counted as a parent. Or sulked. Was that old self so very different from the present self? That sulked. That didn't manage to get anything right, make friends, understand the other prisoners. Listen to them. I just read books and remained hidden. Was that what I'd been like before?

Claire

Mum and I got the bus to the big building that Mum called a Church to go to Jane's wedding. Mum had told me lots and lots about the wedding. She said that there would be lots and lots of people at the wedding and that it might be noisy. Sally said there would be lots of people and that there would be lots of noise. She showed me lots of pictures in a book. She said that the person in the white dress was the bride. She showed me pictures of lots of people looking at the bride. I asked if a wedding was a nice thing. Sally said that it was a very nice thing but she looked as though it wasn't. Mike said he'd been to a wedding and that it was very nice. Mike smiled when he said this. He said he drank orangeade and ate ice cream and two pieces of cake. I told Mike that I liked weddings too.

    Mum held my hand when we went into the church. We sat down on a long wooden chair. There were lots of people sitting down as well. Everyone was whispering and looking round. Mrs Cartwright saw us and waved at us. Mrs Cartwright was sitting right at the front. Lots more people came then there was a big music noise and everyone stood up and looked around. I looked around and saw Jane. She was walking towards us with her father. She had on a white dress and was smiling. I remembered that she must be the bride in the white dress. I was going to tell Mum this but Mum was crying. There isn't a bridesmaid Mum said. Someone turned round and looked at Mum crossly and Mum got a handkerchief out of her bag and blew her nose. She had to try and do it quietly because the big music noise had stopped and a man at the front who was looking at us began to speak. He was wearing white too. Is he the bride as well I asked Mum but the person in front of us said shush again and Mum squeezed my hand so I didn't ask any more questions.

    When we cleaned Mike's bus on Thursday I told Mike that I drank lemonade and ate 6 strawberries and something called lemon me-ringue pie. There was a nasty cake but Mum made a chocolate cake when we got home and put butter cream icing in the middle and on the top and then she put lots of Smarties on it.

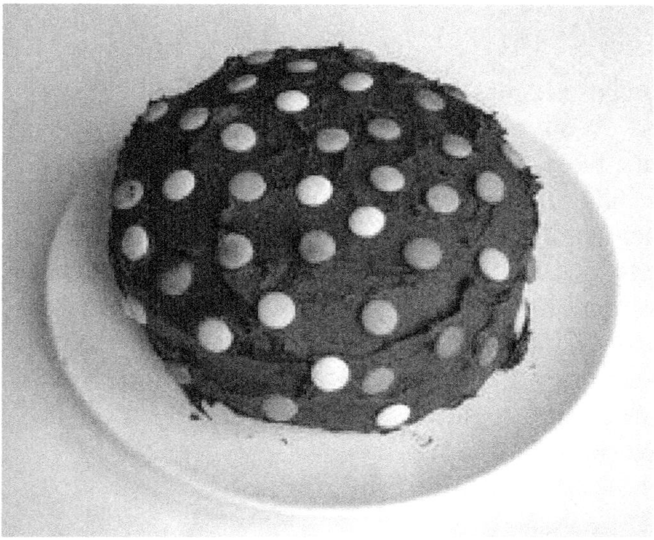

Kate

Jane's wedding album caused quite a stir. Eileen spoke to me for the first time in ten years. Well, not actually ten years. Three years, four years, something like that. There was an uncomfortable moment when Big Bertha noticed from the comments that went with some of the photos that Mark was actually called Alan. But Bertha wasn't too phased by such a detail. Bertha's world had never been perfect. Margaret showed a polite interest until she got near enough to note that Jane's wedding dress hung several inches above the knee and that the intimacy obvious between Jane and her new husband wasn't one that had been wont to glow in the eyes of newly weds in the safe Jane Austen world of Margaret's past.

'That's a pretty girl,' said Eileen as I turned over the next page.

I stared dumbly at a picture of Mum and Claire as all sorts of emotions knocked me about in the chest. Jane hadn't told me that Mum and Claire had been invited to the wedding. It probably hadn't seemed a big deal to her, just a natural part of the invitation list.

'Who is it?' continued Eileen with her new-found ability to speak to me.

'A cousin of Jane's,' I said quickly, still staring at the page.

Eileen had lost interest and she turned over the next page for me and provided a running commentary for the rest of the album.

Claire had continue to blossom. She still had her blond curls and it took an expert eye to classify her as disabled. She was full grown and had what Jane Austen would have called a full figure and was what Richardson might have described as buxom. Meaning sexy. She was still hunched in the shoulders but no one cared about that any more. The neat twin sets which had hung over into the sixties with girls in slim trousers and straight backs had been replaced with blouses and skirts which stretched around full hips and rounded shoulders to accommodate more comfortable breast sizes. Even Jane had 'blossomed' into these new fashions and a fuller figure.

Mum looked older. She looked old-fashioned but she also looked old. Tired.

There was no place for me. Not even any room for Jim. Mum and Claire fitted together; the blooming girl and the devoted mother deep in their own little world. Safe. No Jim and no me. It almost looked like a plot. But who had written the play and who had decided to edit my part – and Jim's for that matter - out of it?

When Eileen had finished with the album, I climbed up to my bed and went through the photos carefully, searching all the faces for clues to confirm my own existence. Jane of course was as familiar as ever and I'd met Alan a few times now. He was nice. They were nice people. Jane's mother looked just the same and that caused me some pleasure. But of course it was only a picture and she wasn't looking at me in it but at a stranger holding a camera. Jane's father I didn't know so well. There was a lovely photo of him and Jane arriving at the church. Jane was leaning on his arm and he looked every inch the proud father. Jane didn't have a bridesmaid. So there was the shadow that was me. Spot the missing figure in the picture and you'd got me. But Jane's cousin (her real cousin, not her pretend Claire cousin) had had to sign the register in lieu of me and subsequently sit at the front of the church and walk down the aisle with the best man, be in lots of the photos and sit at the high table at the reception.

It was obviously a posh do. Jane was an only daughter and she hadn't done anything expensive like go to University so her parents were obviously longing to splash out on her. And in theory this would be their last chance. The church was our local church – or would have been if we'd gone to church, but I didn't recognise the hotel where the reception was. Most of the pictures were taken in what must have been the hotel's garden so apart from a few sights of the church nothing else was, or felt familiar.

I should have been able to recognise some of the people. There were three of Jane's grandparents. Jane's father's father must have died and I supposed I must have known but I couldn't remember. People were slowly disappearing from my world. Jane's cousin I knew, and I recognised a couple of friends from school. And who was that? A neighbour of Jane's perhaps? The rest I supposed were friends from work, Alan's family and friends. New friends that Jane and Alan had made. There were even children born since I'd been in prison.

I shut the album slowly. It was like seeing the consequence of one's own death. Everyone in the end carried on. The slight shadow that was me as Jane walked down the aisle with only her father for support was almost forgotten. Live bodies had expanded and filled in the space left by the dead. Like Claire had expanded and filled Mum's world. I couldn't help but wonder how much room I'd taken even when I was in the land of the living. I mean I'd shouted and created a fuss and made myself be seen when I'd wanted to, but the small space that had actually been occupied by me had been easy enough to fill.

I slipped off my bed (I still slept in the bunk above Big Bertha as Big Bertha said that the others woke her up, but really it was because Eileen and Margaret felt it was beneath them to associate so intimately with Bertha, so Eileen and Margaret shared the other bunk with Margaret on top as she'd been there longest) and walked sadly down the steely prison corridor.

I had to open the library at two o'clock and for once I didn't care who followed me into its dimly lit spaces. I didn't care what became of me. I had thought of time as standing still but the harsh reality was that time didn't stand still it just went on and on. Time out in the 'real' world and time in here. It went on. I was a sad woman sitting in a library that nobody cared about in an institution designed to lock people away. Forever. Down that linear time line. So time hadn't stood still waiting to welcome me back into its everyday folds, it had gone on without me and forgotten me. There was no longer a place for me 'out there'.

Claire

It was my 21st Birthday. Mum said it was a very special day. She said we could have a party and that she would make a Smartie cake. I asked if we could have lemonade and Mum laughed and said yes we could have lemonade. She said we would have ham sandwiches and crisps. I like crisps. They are a very special treat. Mum said that Mrs Cartwright and Jane would come and I said is a party when lots of people come like when it is a Birthday at Whitcliff and Mum looked pleased and said yes it is just like that. Then Mum said Mrs Hunter could come and I said I didn't want to have a party and went to listen to The Beatles on the radio.

Seven people came to my party and then Mum and I came to my party so that was nine altogether Mum said. Mr and Mrs Cartwright came and Jane and Alan and Mike and Sally and Mrs Hunter. Mum said I had to be nice to everyone and that I had to be nice to Mrs Hunter. Mrs hunter gave me a big bottle of bubble bath called badedas. Mr and Mrs Cartwright gave me a string thing with a blue heart on it. Mum called it a neck-lace and said it was very pretty and very kind of them. Jane and Alan gave me a blue dress with lots of little white flowers on it. Sally gave me a book about knitting and Mike gave me a new sponge. Mum had to clear a big space on the table so that Mike's sponge could be in the middle.

Mum made 24 ham sandwiches and 12 buns. Mike and I ate 4 sandwiches and 2 buns and then everyone sang Happy Birthday to Claire, Happy Birthday to Claire, Happy Birthday to Claire, Happy Birthday to Claire and we ate the Smartie cake.

When everyone had gone I counted up all my presents and said that there was one missing because there wasn't one from Mum. Mum smiled in a very pleased way and said that that was because there wasn't one from Mum yet but tomorrow a very big special present was coming.

It was called a tel-e-vi-sion.

Kate

That night. I remember it as being that night although it was probably sometime later because Margaret's Parole Board was nearly a year after Jane's wedding but because of the time warps I constantly got caught up in I associated that night with Jane's wedding, or with her wedding album which for me was the same thing.

Margaret had seemed to be more normal during the months before her Parole Board but that night I woke up from a gothic nightmare straight from *Jane Eyre* and felt a cold breath on my face. I know a breath should have been warm, but it wasn't, it was cold. I decided not to open my eyes and look and waited for whatever it was to pass. Which it did. The next morning when I joined Margaret in the day room – the habit of joining Margaret most days and sitting next to her with whatever book I was currently reading had stuck – I thought something was different about her. Margaret wasn't the sort of woman you could scrutinise so I had to make discreet sideways glances. Could she have had her hair done without us noticing? Or changed her glasses? (She had to wear glasses now to do her embroidery and when she wore them her pale eyes were magnified behind the lenses.) No, she looked just the same. But she didn't say anything. Normally she would have passed some polite comment on my choice of literature.

Any chance of identifying this curious change that wasn't a change was thwarted by the arrival of Eileen, who invariably joined our quiet corner if there was nothing else going on. Since she had been allowed to knit again Bertha had established her own group of knitting friends. I joined them occasionally but I didn't have any knitting and that upset the others as they thought it gave me too much time to pass comment and criticise what they were doing.

'Such a nice time of the year,' began Eileen. 'I love it when the first snowdrops begin to emerge and daffodils pop up all over.'

She was obviously in her tinkly mood. I did wonder where Eileen got some of her ideas from, her conversation could be so middle class. I mean, how did she know that that's how people like Margaret talked? Eileen grew up in a slum in Bradford. No snowdrops and no daffodils and an abusive father. But perhaps he'd been schizophrenic too. I wasn't supposed to know about the schizophrenia but she'd been carefully given a pill every morning after a new inmate had suffered the same induction into lonely toilet visits that I'd suffered from at Eileen's hands. Although that poor girl had not managed to be sick all over Eileen. I'd avoided hearing about what had happened, although the gory details had circulated for a month. But it had perhaps encouraged Bertha's protective instincts towards the weak and feeble (i.e. me) and increased Eileen's sessions with Jeanette.

Jeanette, in an attempt to awaken my sympathies for my fellow men (or in our case our fellow women, men being less involved in our world than in a nunnery) had instructed me to be more understanding towards Eileen because. Because... and here my noncommittal silence had led to more revelatory comments about Eileen than really was ethically correct. My sympathies had not been aroused but my interest had and I took a keen interest in Eileen popping her pill every morning. If the pill wasn't popped one knew to keep well clear of Eileen for the day. And it did happen. New Warders, change of duty rota, human error. One pill amongst so many to be remembered day in and day out for year upon year was in the manner of these things bound to be forgotten occasionally.

Anyway, Eileen had had her pill this morning and perhaps a bit extra as she was particularly chatty and waxed lyrical in Margaret's ear for, oh, at least two hours.

'Oh don't you just love it when the spring flowers come into bloom. I so love the spring. The days get longer and one just longs to get out into the garden.' (Into the garden? Whenever had Eileen had a garden to get out into? Or as the pill slowly deprived her of her own warped-though-it-was-character, did she in desperation have to take on someone else's? And was she now unwittingly taking on Margaret's character and thus saying the sort of things that Margaret might have said in another, happier, life?)

'And the birds singing. Don't you just love to hear the birds singing? Did you ever see such a lovely morning... ?'

Of course poor Margaret had seen such mornings, many of them all her life until fate had killed off her father and left her alone with a sickly mother. On top of which she suddenly had no home as the vicarage had to be given up with the death of her father and she and her mother were moved to functional but otherwise inadequate church housing and were in receipt of a functional but otherwise inadequate pension. These details I accrued or invented as we sat together pretending to communicate. (One does of course have to assume that nothing worse than fate did kill off her father but Margaret had had much less incentive to kill her father than I had had to kill Jim and I still tried very hard against all the odds to believe that I hadn't killed Jim. *Ergo*.)

But I needn't have worried about Margaret's sensibilities because I now realised what it was that had changed about Margaret. She wasn't looking at us anymore and I doubt if she was listening to us either. She was looking at our throats, calculating air channels and showing a concentrated interest in the human breathing apparatus, fascinating as it was. Like she used to do. What had led to this reversion? The impending Parole Board? And I thought of the cold breath on my face just the previous night. I was going to have to watch Margaret again. Margaret and Eileen's pill. I looked longingly over towards Big Bertha's knitting circle and wondered if, after all, I shouldn't ask Jane to buy me some knitting things.

Kate

'Margaret went before her Parole Board yesterday,' I said to Jane.

Jane was wearing red bell bottom trousers which were a bit too tight. She had a white loose cheesecloth top with wide sleeves and things that dangled. And long white boots. Her hair was a mass of tight permed curls. Alan hadn't come today. He was mowing the lawn of their new semi in Acomb. But it didn't matter because Jane had learned to drive as soon as they came back from their honeymoon. (They'd spent their honeymoon in another posh hotel in the Lake District but these days they'd graduated from posh hotels in England and they spent two week's holiday in Spain every summer. They flew there and changed their new English pounds and pence into Spanish pesetas. If Margaret did pass her Parole Board, how was she going to calculate all this new pounds and pence business?)

Margaret's Parole Board.

'Oh,' said Jane. 'Isn't Margaret one of the women who share your cell?' And then suddenly she looked more interested. 'Do they happen often these Parole Boards?'

'No.'

'Oh, so it doesn't necessarily mean that you might have one soon?'

'No.'

Pause.

'I'm a lifer.'

Perhaps there was much more doubt over Margaret's killing of her mother (or to be more specific, smothering of her mother) than over my killing of Jim. (I admit I didn't really understand the implications or the workings of a Parole Board.) Or perhaps a Parole Board recommendation was easier in Margaret's case because unlike my case where Jim's rather bloody demise had been all over the newspapers, Margaret's quiet smothering of her mother had hardly been noticed. In fact, come to think of it, how *had* it been noticed? Did some vigilant doctor notice suspicious bruising on the face of an old woman who was dying anyway? Or did Margaret go strange, as per now. Or perhaps Margaret confessed, overcome by guilt, before the fascination set in. The fascination of realising that she herself possessed a God-given power over life and death. (Indeed I hadn't, as I say, understood the implications of a Parole Board.)

Jane looked at me disconsolately. As the hypothetical mad man (or woman) with a penchant for circular saw massacre had not struck again, Jane's case to free me and re-open the investigation into who really did kill Jim had petered into nothing. And if she'd really believed it was Mum, she wouldn't have invited her to her wedding. Would she?

'What does it mean,' Jane asked, 'being a lifer?' She'd obviously decided not to follow up the idea of a Parole Board, but then Jane probably knew even less about Parole Boards than I did.

'I'm not sure.' It was my turn to be disconsolate now. 'I think it just means a very long time.'

Was Jane thinking of me at this point or of the 'very long time' she would have to spend driving to Wakefield?

'I found an easy knitting pattern,' she said suddenly, brightening up. 'I asked Alan's mum – she has a whole workbox full of patterns – and she gave me this.'

I took the pattern from Jane while she busied in another bag fishing out wool and knitting needles. I hoped she'd cleared the business of the needles with the visit warder. The pattern was for a jumper. It looked a bit like the kind of school jumper that Beryl always seemed to be knitting. However, the needles were enormous and the wool was a chunky twist of blues and greens and a brave flash of orange. I was almost encouraged; could my passport into Bertha's knitting circle also turn into a new interest for me and the beginnings of a glittering career in knitting?

'I brought some toffees too,' said Jane

I was impressed. Toffees would be a secondary useful intro into the knitting circle. Sometimes there were heart-warming flashes of Jane's old self. The old self that had responded to me rather than the modern sensible self that had settled down with Alan and made her predictability seem boring as well as reassuring. Although who was I to talk of being boring? And what would my life now be like without Jane? She was my only link with anything. And what did she get out of her long drives to Wakefield? Well, yes, driving practice, but what else? She didn't need a good conscience so it must just have been for me. It was hard to entirely lose one's faith in humanity when someone like Jane just did a nice decent thing once in a while for someone else without any other motivation or reward.

'I thought I should start reading something else,' I said.

'Oh,' said Jane.

'You know, history or something.'

She brightened up again.

'Oh, I'll find something shall I? What do you think you'd like to read?'

'I don't know. Anything.'

This was not the sort of thing that daunted Jane. She loved projects and the vaguer the better (something had to have drawn her to me in the first place).

'Oh, I was promoted last month,' she said after a pause while the idea of history hummed between us.

'Oh.' Promotion was too far removed from my world.

'I think Alan's quite keen to start a family, but he'll have to wait a bit longer now,' said Jane with a glint in her eye.

My god, babies. I hadn't thought of that, stupid as I was. After all, marriage usually led to babies.

'Your mother will make a great grandmother,' I said to hide my shock.

'I know,' said Jane still being coy, 'but she'll have to wait as well.'

How old was Jane now, 24? 25? And here was I, still 18. The bell went. Jane bundled the rest of the knitting stuff over the table and we parted with the friendly hug which had become our way of preserving the friendship against all the odds and avoiding the embarrassing goodbyes and futile waves across the tables and chairs of the visiting room.

'I'll bring some history books next time I come then,' said Jane.

I watched her go. There was no rush, no need to hurry any more. Eileen had had her pill that morning and I'd realised that Margaret's wasn't a waking threat. And all the other inmates were so used to me by now that they hardly noticed my existence; fresher newer prey had long since come their way.

Kate

Catherine Howard. Jane had found me a biography and a copy of the play. She'd even been to see it at The Theatre Royal so that she could tell me all about it. The country was wild about the Tudors at the moment as Keith Michell had breathed new life into Henry VIII. Although the more I came to understand about Henry VIII, the less new life breathed into him the better. What a tyrant and a monster he was. Apparently he was so fat and bloated when he died that his body not only smelt to high heaven but there was so much foul gas inside him that his body exploded before they'd managed to wrap him up in a coffin and bury him. And poor Catherine Howard was expected to have physical relations with this man. She was under orders to be sufficiently intimate with him to produce an heir. Whoever dreamt up that little scheme should have been locked up.

And there's Catherine herself, was she really a raving, sexy beauty? This isn't exactly what her portraits convey. Unless fashions have changed. She looks more like her cousin Anne. Hurt, betrayed and trapped. Personally I think that if Anne Boleyn was passionate about anything at all it was about Protestantism. But that's another story. And who has told the stories about these women? Men, politicians and kings. Even Queen Elizabeth the First didn't go into raptures about her mother whom after all she wouldn't have known or remembered. But back to the portraits of Catherine Howard. There is the sketch by Hans Holbein (the younger) of Catherine which does look more convincingly like a young woman and less like the queen she was turned into in the other portraits thought to be of her.

So I'm supposed to believe that Catherine Howard was a young girl stupid enough to sleep around before getting married and then, after marriage to a king notorious for his brutality, tyranny and wife swapping, she is stupid enough to carry on sleeping around. That she found Henry himself repulsive is not hard to believe and I think that at least in that I am at one with my namesake. And in having had my life turned upside down at eighteen. There she is bumbling along, expecting like any other girl of eighteen to flirt a bit, learn a bit and get married to some tall dark handsome man. Perhaps even, like Jane, believing herself to be in love with one or two of them before an Alan comes along. But a fifty-year-old king, overweight, ulcerous and with numerous associated health problems is not what one expects. Already twice widowed and aged thirty two it is perhaps possible to contemplate such a spouse (Catherine Parr) but not at eighteen. One should more think of locking him up than her.

I'd always been happy in the belief that I had nothing in common with my namesake – other than feeling embarrassed with the connection to someone so stupid and ignorant; the ultimate dumb blond. And what I read only seemed to reinforce that view. But the evidence didn't quite make sense. I mean, there are all these testimonies as to her pre-contract and sexual relations before her marriage and then various theories as to her infidelity afterwards, and the assumption is that all these accusations are true despite her own denial of all of them. That is what is surprising; she denies all of them. (And by the way, Parliament had to change the law so that they could behead her, which sounds again more like the act of a brutal tyrant than an act necessary to national security. I wonder if and when that law was repealed?)

All of which began to make me think. Everyone assumed that I had killed Jim. I mean, even I wondered – I excluded Jane from this 'everyone' but Jane wasn't going to get to talk to Judge and Jury was she and nor was she going to run any Parole Boards. I wondered if poor Catherine had had a friend who didn't denounce her? There are no records of anything like that of course. Any counter evidence would have been thoroughly suppressed and destroyed. Although there probably wasn't any. After all, Jane didn't constitute evidence did she? However loyal and passionate she might have been in my defence, it wasn't evidence to prove my guilt or innocence. There was nothing that could be written down. It was all just based on a look, a hug or a squeeze of the hand. There was no evidence to be passed down through the vagaries of history.

So despite the fact that both Catherine and I claimed innocence, our claims were totally brushed aside by the law. If I had 'killed' Jim a year earlier I too could have been hung on the basis of other people's evidence. Such thoughts were not conducive to peace of mind, but they did make a re-reading of Catherine Howard a much more interesting occupation than I had expected.

Catherine denied all the claims made against her, even though for example, accepting her pre-contract to Francis Dereham would theoretically have led to the annulment of her marriage to King Henry and a happy retirement into obscurity with her first 'husband'. Her only incentive to deny pre-contract was because there wasn't one. It seems odd at this point of sentencing to death not to have stretched the truth a little, but when one is there being judged by all sorts of people one thinks differently. It matters more what you believe and the only thing you have left is your belief in yourself. I was meant to plead manslaughter or provocation or something – I was never quite sure what or which – but I couldn't do that to myself – I couldn't admit to a crime that as far as I was aware I hadn't committed. That is in the end all one has and that belief in oneself seems to mean more at the time than life or death. Not that suddenly seeing the block or the rope wouldn't tempt one into a momentary relapse from such heights. But if Catherine didn't do anything wrong then she was a girl of much greater integrity and courage than history has ever given her credit for.

The result of moral courage, however (if I can claim such heights for myself and my namesake) is one version or another of non-existence. One can pretend that there is something glamorous about death (although personally I just think that it is terrifying) but one can't pretend that there is anything glamorous about prison. Actually, that's not quite true. People do pretend that there is something glamorous about prison (Little Dorrit's father – sorry, can't remember his name). Anyway, there isn't.

Mmmm. I was a little bit worried that dwelling on Margaret's obsession with breathing passages was also making me a little bit obsessed with death. Or was I just questioning the meaning of life. Or did I just have too much time to think without any proper guidance? It is very difficult to think on one's own. One has no clue as to the truth of any of one's thoughts. Knitting was better; when it went wrong I could not only ask advice but I could un-pick it and start again. If I ever got out of here someone was going to have to give my thoughts a lot of un-picking.

Claire

A Horrid thing happened. It was Thursday so Mike and I were going to clean Mike's bus. I was very happy because I had another new sponge. But Mike wouldn't let me clean his bus. He said that girlfriends didn't clean buses they did other things. He held my hand which was quite nice and I thought I could lean into his bosoms like with Mum but then he started touching all sorts of other bits of me and I said I didn't like those bits being touched and he said it was what girlfriends did. But I knew I didn't like this kind of touching so I said no. Mike held on to me and I shouted no, no, no. Then I hit Mike so he fell against his bus but there wasn't any blood. I ran back to the Centre and got my bag. I bumped into a chair and hurt my leg. I cried a lot and went to the proper bus stop on the road and hoped that Mum would come.

    Mum did come but before she got off the bus to come and collect me I got on the bus and sat down at the front. Mum looked at me with a worried face and asked me if I was alright. I said no, Mike was horrid. I said I didn't like Mike any more and Mum said poor Claire, never mind, lets go home and make tea. Mum and I held hands and I liked that.

    Mum didn't eat her part of the tea. She said she felt a bit poorly and could we go to bed early. I said we could go to bed after Top of the Pops and Mum said okay. The next morning Mum said she was poorly again and I said I was poorly. Mum said we could stay at home and I said yes I liked being poorly and staying at home. Mum said she would ring up Sally on the telephone and I said on Jim's telephone then I felt anxious because I wasn't supposed to talk about Jim but Mum just said yes she would telephone Sally on Jim's telephone. I said should I go to bed if I was poorly but Mum said no I didn't have to if I didn't want to I could look at pictures in my magazines but that she would go back to bed because she felt very tired. I sat on my own and I didn't like feeling sad about Mike so I got out all my Birthday presents and looked at them then I looked through my magazines and found pictures which were nearly like my presents I got when I had my big birthday party a very very very long time ago.

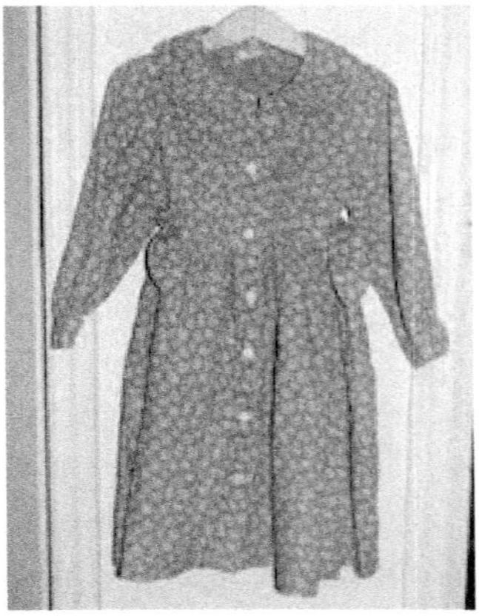

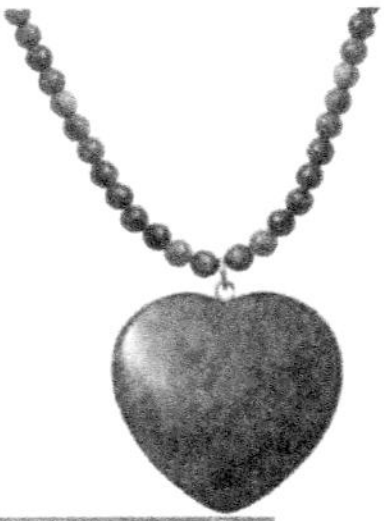

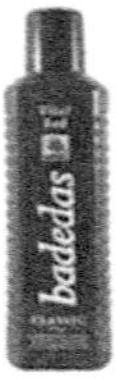
badedas

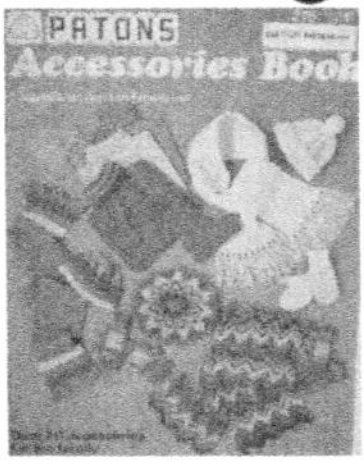
PATONS
Accessories Book

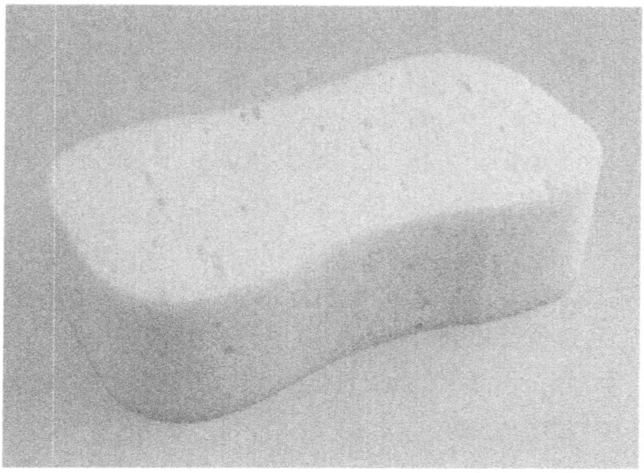

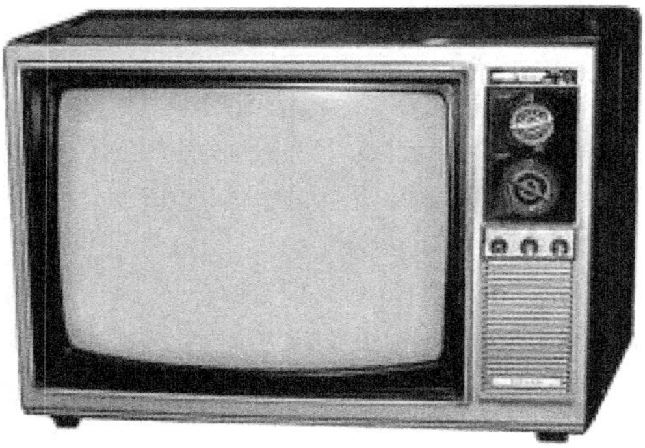

Kate

It was Margaret's last night, forever, in prison. Imagine having to spend it with Big Bertha, Eileen and me. Eileen had been quiet all day and I hadn't actually seen her take her pill that morning. I'd stuck to Big Bertha and knitted my jumper and I'd carefully managed not to see much of Margaret either. So I didn't know whether her impending release had affected her or not. Although it was always difficult to tell if Margaret was affected or not by anything. Was she excited about being released, or not? She was supposed to have a job in an old people's home. I hoped that that was only a rumour. Just because that was all she could do didn't mean that it was the best thing for her to do. In fact, the last place in the world I'd have committed Margaret to was an old people's home. But I think a suitable job was a strong recommendation to the Parole Board. I wonder who found such a job for Margaret. Jeanette? But I don't think that Margaret had sessions with Jeanette. Margaret wasn't 'ill', and there was 'doubt' over Margaret's killing of her mother. Doubt meant that no one really believed it (apart from a Judge and Jury…) I mean no one here really believed that Margaret was guilty – unlike the rest of us, who were all guilty. I suppose Dickson would have explained it all.

    I'd seen Dickson once a year or so ago in as much as a year or so ago had any meaning to me. She was showing some bigwigs round. Well, they were female bigwigs who talked like Eileen did when she tried to talk to Margaret. They wore hats and proper shoes and jackets that were tailored to fit rather than the clothes that we wore which were tailored not to fit. They liked the library. At least, they liked the library because I looked small and unthreatening. They liked it less when Big Bertha appeared to read Mills and Boon armed with knitting needles. I think Dickson might have said something to me, but I was distracted by the bigwigs and the knitting needles.

    Dickson would have explained to me about Margaret and Parole Boards in her own inimitable way. She would have said something comforting like you can't really have read all those books and be such a moron and then she would have explained that Parole Board hearings were about recognising guilt and not being a danger to society. The logic of which would mean that I was a danger to society and Margaret was not. Working in an old people's home where there were lots of sick and defenceless old women. Was I just being moronic or had everyone else missed the plot? Dickson wouldn't have missed it. Whatever else I'd lost, I hadn't lost my faith in Dickson even though she had lost her faith in me. Dickson would have understood about Margaret, I think. Anyway what did it matter, Margaret was off and that was that.

And my original thought? Did she want to leave? Was stupid really. Anyway, whatever she thought, she had quietly packed her few things into a neat holdall. I wondered where that had appeared from. Had someone bought it or had it been kept in the prison for safekeeping? I wasn't sure how long Margaret had been in here for. All I knew was that she'd been in prison longer than me (so far).

Apart from being worried about the old people and hoping that that was just a rumour, I felt rather happy about Margaret's release. In fact, everyone usually felt happy when someone was released. Yes, there was jealousy but mostly there was happiness because it meant it was possible. But that's not why I felt happy about Margaret's release. I felt relieved. And fell soundly asleep as soon as the warders switched the lights off. Which is why the cold breath that re-awakened the *Jane Eyre* type nightmare was as shocking as it was frightening. Was this a repeat of a nightmare or was I awake? I determined not to open my eyes as I didn't want to see what it was that was breathing on me, if there was anything breathing on me. I tried to pretend to myself and the thing that I was asleep. Or perhaps I was asleep so that when Eileen started screaming I either woke up or admitted I was awake in time to see the shadow that can only have been Margaret calmly ascending into her bunk above the screaming Eileen.

Bertha sat up with a start and banged her head.

'Shut up you daft cow,' Bertha shouted.

'I don't think she had her pill this morning,' I said, staying safely on my top bunk. I don't know if Big Bertha heard me or not and I don't know if Big Bertha understood the significance of the pill but she got up anyway and started calling for help by our cell door.

Eileen was screaming murder. Literally. Murder. They're trying to kill me. In as much as she was screaming anything coherent.

Margaret sat up in her bunk calmly. Had she been up at all? Had there been a shadow that was Margaret or had I just imagined it? Dreamt it?

A warder followed by two more came at last. Having successfully enlisted help, Big Bertha retreated back to her bed. They didn't know what to do with Eileen who was into third degree hysteria by this point. I think one of them slapped her in the face – which, although it sounded rather brutal, did stop the hysteria.

'Someone tried to kill me,' said the recovered Eileen. But she was close to the edge. I'd seen her like that too often before. She'd definitely had no pill the previous morning.

She started to look wildly about. She couldn't see Margaret as she was above her so her wild gaze rested on Big Bertha first. But one didn't accuse Big Bertha of anything however unhinged one was becoming. Then she inevitably got to me. Her finger pointed and shook in my direction.

'She did it. She tried to kill me. She's always had it in for me. Right from the first. She's a sneaky dirty cow. She just wants one thing. She hides in the bathroom and gets young girls and does dirty things to them, she…' and so the tirade went on.

The warders looked from Eileen to me and the balance was in Eileen's favour. They wanted to shut her up and I was an easy scapegoat. Despair rushed up in a huge engulfing wave. Not again. Not again. I couldn't bear it. I could feel panic, hysteria and breathlessness begin to overtake me. I don't think I actually did or said anything because into the mounting mists of my blackout I heard Big Bertha say.

'She didn't do anything.'

I pulled myself together and watched the others all turn to Big Bertha.

'If anyone did anything then it wasn't Kate.'

At that moment I think I loved Big Bertha.

One of the warder's took control of the situation at last.

'How do you know?' she said crossly.

'Because I sleep as lightly as a mouse and if Kate so much as blinks an eyelid then I wake up,' said Big Bertha fiercely. 'And I didn't wake up until she,' and here she pointed at Eileen disdainfully, 'started screaming.'

The lead warder looked uncertain. A few eyes turned in Margaret's direction but Margaret looked far too refined to have done anything so unladylike as to have caused all this stir and hysteria. The warder looked back at me and still looked crossly at Big Bertha. Big Bertha filled the pause with perfect timing.

'She,' Big Bertha said jerking her head in Eileen's direction, 'she didn't have her pill yesterday morning.' And this was a definite accusation of mishandling and incompetence levelled at the warders en masse. And yet further confirmation, as if I needed it, that Big Bertha was all knowing and all seeing despite appearances.

This explanation took root quickly especially as Eileen looked distinctly mad by this time. The warders conferred hurriedly among themselves and one of them went off to find a nurse or doctor or some sort of medical orderly. Eileen was shouting obscenities and the two remaining warders had to concentrate their energies on holding her down. Big Bertha got up calmly off her bed and sat on Eileen's feet. This didn't help Eileen's madness but it did help them restrain her.

The warders talked about the usual upset and jealousies when someone was being released until the dispatched warder came back with someone else and the four of them, with Bertha still sitting on Eileen's feet, forced a pill or two down Eileen's throat and after five more minutes Eileen suddenly went woozy and fell asleep. She fell asleep for 28 hours. (Perhaps they over-did the pills a bit and perhaps Eileen *had* had her pill the previous morning...) Anyway, she missed Margaret's quiet departure, and Big Bertha and I spent a rather subdued day together. And it wasn't because we were tired. We were worried. Margaret really had got a job in an old people's home. And a live-in one at that.

Claire

The next day I didn't want to be poorly any more. I went into Mum's bedroom and said could we go to Bettys. Mum didn't say anything then she said of course we could go to Bettys and she got out of bed. We held hands again on the bus and Mum squeezed my hand and said I was a good girl and what would she do without me. I had Welsh rarebit and chocolate cake and tea at Bettys but Mum just had a cup of tea.

Kate

Bertha and I were now fast friends. We knitted and shared toffees. I gave her my greeny blue orange creation and she gave me some purple wool and a pattern for a long cardigan. This was way beyond my expertise but well within Bertha's. On special occasions Jane brought us Thornton's special toffee and Beryl bought Bertha chocolate éclairs, milk chocolate éclairs.   Eileen was sucking out the personality of another poor victim but Eileen herself was rather 'poor' these days as she now had a pill in the evening as well. Which perhaps wasn't fair because if I had been awake, i.e. not dreaming when the cold breath hovered above me then someone had perhaps also breathed a death wish over Eileen. Unless Margaret's inspiration had been less esoteric and more, how should one put it, more physical in its intention. But enough of Margaret. Margaret was not my problem. Margaret was somewhere safely many, many miles away from me.

My study of history (largely through biography as Jane thought that the covers on history books looked too dull) had now got to James II. We skipped Cromwell for the same reason. And who wants to read about Cromwell anyway, especially from within a prison? From where I was coming from, freedom and licentiousness were much more appealing than a fundamentalist puritanical state. So there were none of Malvolio's sentiments for Bertha and me – we didn't think that because we were virtuous there should be no more cakes and ale (for all those people who were not in prison. No indeed, let them frolic while they may).

And just as my opinion of Catherine Howard had become rather turned about upon itself so did my view of the Jacobites. One had so wished to romanticise about the Jacobites and we had all learnt such rousing Jacobite songs from our radio-led music lessons in primary school. Bonny Prince Charlie and Speed Bonny Boat and My Highland Laddy (but was that a pro-Jacobite song or not? I always got confused with the bit about King George upon the Throne. And Jane used to get cross with me and said that of course it was and made me sing the questions while she sang the answers back which meant that she never had to give me a reason for it being pro-Jacobite other than that she liked singing it in a sentimental way.)

So with all this prejudice in his favour, King James had to be pretty awful to lose my respect. There he was messing around with French princesses and Catholicism and having more children when he already had two perfectly serviceable daughters who were sure to make better queens than the spoilt darling that his little James must have been. So there's King James messing things up so much that even I could believe that Cromwell hadn't been so bad after all. And to top it all, he goes stirring up the Irish by getting all the Irish Catholics to pop over to England to fight for his cause. And being game for a good fight the Irish Catholics did pop over and everyone wonders why there is an 'Irish Problem'. Even I know about the Irish problem. Anyway, not surprisingly the Irish are too disorganised to help very much and the English end up being more biased against them than ever. William of Orange becomes our big hero and some kind of Satanist in Irish Catholic folklore.

James III as never was, is effete and inadequate to the nth degree and Bonny Prince Charlie just an opportunist who out-ran his luck. Imagine being doomed forever to the appellation of Bonny. He didn't look very bonny in the pictures in Jane's history books, just rather small and insignificant. And apparently he was anyway an alcoholic who died, not romantically young but when he was sixty-eight, no doubt as a result of alcohol poisoning.

Alcohol abuse was not a happy thought for me. I looked at Bertha stolidly knitting away and wondered what abuse had led her to kill her husband. Her violent outbursts were a thing of the past, which presumably meant that whatever frustrations had caused them were also a thing of the past. I wondered if my father had died of alcohol poisoning. If indeed he had died at all. Dying in my imagination and vanishing from my world was not the same as dying, I don't think, although being forced to leave a world as we know it sounds a lot like dying to me. He had of course been a drunkard. Which probably meant that if not dead he had been on his way to an early grave. And was that to be the first and last time I ever thought about my father?

Uncomfortably and inevitably such thoughts led me on to thinking about Claire and Mum. Which was very painful although Jeanette still hadn't understood this. And once I had dragged Jeanette into my mental state or lack of mental state it was high time to get back to knitting.

I'd managed to untwist rather than twist the ropy pattern thing that was meant to run up the front of my cardigan. I leant toward Bertha. Bertha sighed happily and tutted in a motherly sort of way.

'You do two over and two under and only twist once, see?' she said demonstrating on her own knitting.

'Okay,' I said, now worrying about the fact that there were two lots of stitches to take out – my mistake and Bertha's demonstration. I hated taking stitches out although you'd think I'd have become immune to it by now. The knitting seemed so vulnerable once it was off the needles and once you went too far with the unravelling it could go on forever. Bertha took the knitting from me after she'd unravelled her own and calmly put mine to rights.

It was time to open the library. Bertha stayed knitting as even she had had enough of Mills and Boon. I had a rummage in the murky depths which was still something of a novelty and I was ever in the hopes of finding something readable. I found some Wordsworth poems and sat down to read them for two hours while no one else came near the place.

Sometimes I fell into a trap of believing that I was happy.

Kate

Jane was wearing a smock and a coloured hair band. She looked remarkably well.

'You're pregnant,' I said not able to hide the shock in my voice.

'Yep,' said Jane happily patting her tummy.

'You said you were going to wait,' I said glumly.

'We have waited, silly,' she said

How old was Jane now? Twenty six may be? Was it possible?

'Does Alan mind?'

'Of course he doesn't mind.'

Silly question.

'You're not going to have too many are you?' I was reading a rather romanticised tale about Queen Victoria and Prince Albert.

'Kate, you are funny sometimes.'

'I don't mean to be,' I managed to say rather than just think. I spent so much time just thinking that sometimes I didn't know the difference between thinking and talking and Jane's visits were so precious that I put a lot of effort into talking and thinking at the same time.

'Well, aren't you going to ask how I am, and when the baby's due and what we're going to call it?'

'You can't plan what to call it when you don't know what it will be.'

'We have lists of boys' names and girls' names so you can think of some for us.'

'You don't drink, do you Jane?' I said suddenly.

Jane looked shocked and surprised.

'But if you have too many different names you won't be able to choose one,' I said quickly to cover up my question. 'You couldn't even decide what ice cream to have when you were younger,' I continued, trying to be jolly and not think about babies and alcohol.

Jane forgot her shock and laughed.

'I wasn't that bad,' she said happily.

She was fishing in her bag and then produced some wool. Pink wool.

'I thought you might like to knit something for the baby,' she said.

Pink?

'How do you know it's a girl?' I said suspiciously.

'We don't.'

'Well?'

'Well what? Don't tell me you're that prejudiced Kate,' she said censoriously. 'Boys are meant to wear pink, to bring out their feminine side.'

Well, I knew what Bertha would say to that. I would have to tell Bertha it was going to be a girl. Which Bertha would swallow, but only because it came from me. Eileen wouldn't. Eileen had been hovering around our knitting group lately as her new friend had finally wrestled her personality back from Eileen and to be on the safe side dumped Eileen at the same time. As a consequence, Eileen had been hanging round the toilets until she had temporarily been given an extra pill at lunchtime as well as at breakfast and dinnertime.

'But couldn't it have been blue to bring out the girl's more masculine side.'

'Trust you to be difficult,' said Jane smiling.

'I think blue's a nicer colour than pink, that's all.'

'Really, Kate, sometimes you are the limit. Give it back to me and I'll get you some blue wool.'

'No, it's okay,' I answered a little desperately. 'Get me some blue as well and if I manage to knit this I can knit a blue one too.'

Then we'd all be happy. Especially Bertha. Bertha and possibly even Eileen would accept the explanation of knitting two cardigans for the baby – a pink one and a blue one just in case. We all tended to approve of schemes which wasted time, or took up time as we liked to think of it in our more positive moods. (If indeed that was how Eileen saw it but what with Eileen's fragile mental state and her pills Eileen's opinion really counted for very little.)

'Claire's knitting something for the baby,' said Jane suddenly.

A little spasm twisted in my cheek.

'Claire's knitting something, I mean not just knitting,' I managed to say.

'Yes, isn't that good!'

I wondered what colour Claire had chosen for the baby or what colour Jane had chosen for Claire. And did Claire chose things like colours now as well as knit?

'It is good,' I said slowly, trying not to feel desolate with loneliness and the feeling of being so forgotten, so left behind. It was good that Claire was getting more and more of a life; after all it wasn't at the expense of mine, was it?

Jane looked at me carefully.

'Your Mum was a bit poorly last month,' she said noncommittally.

I answered in the same vein.

'Oh? Is she okay now?'

'Yes, I think so. She hasn't mentioned it any more to my Mum anyway, at least as far as I know.'

She was still looking at me carefully.

'I'm sure that my Mum would say if there was anything, if there was anything to worry about,' she said.

As if I cared.

Claire

Lots of things happened. I had a Birthday and Jane came to see us. She said she was having a baby. Mum looked very pleased and I said was she getting a baby and she said yes and I said where are you getting a baby from and Jane giggled and Mum said from the hospital and I said oh did babies come from the hospital and Jane giggled again and Mum said yes very firmly. I asked Jane how many babies she was getting from the hospital and Jane laughed properly and said just the one thank you would be enough to be getting on with and I asked if it was funny getting a baby because I sort of didn't like Jane laughing and Jane stopped laughing and said no it wasn't funny but that it was a very nice thing and because it was such a nice thing she was very happy. Then she said she wanted me to do something very special for the baby and I said what and she said she wanted me to knit the baby a cardigan. I felt pleased and I said that I would like to knit a blue cardigan and Jane said I thought that perhaps you would like to knit a blue cardigan so look I've brought you some wool isn't it nice and I said yes it was very nice because it was and Mum said Jane was very kind but we could have bought the wool ourselves and Jane said that she liked buying the wool and Mum said she would help me and then she said when was the baby due which sounded odd because that's what people say about buses.

Kate

'I'm going,' announced Big Bertha.

I assumed that she meant she was going to the toilet, not that she usually told me if and when she was going anywhere. Not that there was anywhere to go. I was concentrating on casting off on the shoulder and knitting on the neck line with the insipid pink wool I felt obliged to battle on with. It better had be a girl after all this. On the other hand it probably wouldn't matter as I'd never get the wretched thing finished in time anyway. Jane was four months due when she told me, and that was in February, or was it March and now...

'I'm going,' repeated Bertha a little crossly.

I looked up at her.

'Leaving. Leaving here,' she continued aggressively.

I dropped a stitch I wasn't meant to drop.

'You haven't had a Parole Board,' I said, almost accusingly.

'No, the likes of me don't get Parole Boards.'

'Then how can you be leaving?' I mean she couldn't just walk out like that, without a boo to a goose as it were, now could she?

Bertha calmly turned her knitting around and continued with a purl row. Sometimes I still marvelled at how calm, almost majestic, Bertha could be these days. When you remember what she could be like, when just a passing thought could turn her into a homicidal maniac cracking her large knuckled fingers into action.

Bertha looked at me severely. I wasn't concentrating. When she'd got my attention back again she continued carefully, so that I would understand.

'I've done my time,' she said.

'You mean?'

'Yes.'

(This was about the longest conversation Bertha and I had ever had.)

I was devastated. Bertha picked up my knitting and sorted it out for me.

'How long?' I said crossing a boundary into the past which one never crossed.

'Fifteen years,' said Bertha without rancour.

'Fifteen years?' Was that what I was down for? I couldn't remember. I might be down for longer.

'I thought you were a lifer,' I said.

Bertha looked at me.

'Don't you think that fifteen years is enough?'

'Well yes, I don't know. What did you do?' It slipped out.

'Don't you know? Most people know everything about everyone in here.'

'Yes, no, sort of. It never mattered.'

'And it does now?'

I was silent.

'Do you think I'll do it again, like Margaret?'

Now here were several things that required thought and commentary. It was the first time we'd mentioned Margaret since Eileen's hysterical night and Margaret's departure. It was a bit uncomfortable when Bertha put it like that, suggesting that we both knew that Margaret wasn't safe. That Margaret was, well to put it bluntly, was a murderer. Anyway, Margaret wasn't the point just now.

'I only had one husband anyway,' continued Bertha in the gap left by my thoughts. 'Although if I still had him, or another like him I'd do my time again and willingly.'

'No, of course you won't do it again,' I finally managed to say. 'When are you going to be released?' I asked.

'Tomorrow.'

'Tomorrow?'

So that was that, no more Bertha. Bertha was well overdue for release, I had to think positively. Bertha had a family. Bertha would be fine. Bertha might even enjoy the rest of her life knitting jumpers and following her grandchildren as they grew up. Even enjoying great-grandchildren in time, who wouldn't know about or judge anything from Bertha's past. I stood up quietly and went to the library. There was a set of miscellaneous pamphlets and booklets that I had long wanted to go through and sort out. Once I was safely hidden in the murkiest depths of the library I sat down amongst the dust and cried for two hours.

Kate

'I don't think that Bertha was a very good influence,' said Jeanette.

Shouldn't Jeanette have left as well by now, been promoted or moved on somewhere else? I couldn't believe she was that devoted to us prisoners.

'I didn't like to say anything at the time,' she continued. Jeanette had graduated from trouser suits to big earrings (which I thought rather dangerous given the unsocial tendencies of her patients), a grey streak in her hair and pale cheesecloth blouses.

Well, one wouldn't have said anything against Big Bertha 'at the time', would one? No one had ever said anything against Bertha. Bertha had commanded respect. Or fear. Unless it came down to the same thing in the end.

'But now you will have an opportunity to find some new friend and do something more useful with your time.'

Was the waste of time Bertha or knitting?

'We are beginning a pilot scheme to train prisoners so that they will be better prepared for life outside when they have done their time here.'

I wondered if Jeanette was trying to be diplomatic; 'done their time' like any other public duty.

'But I haven't done my time, have I?' I asked despite my usual vow of silence when dealing with Jeanette.

'No, but it is still a good idea to be prepared.'

For what? Be prepared for what? They weren't going to let me out were they? Not only had Jim's murder been particularly horrific but I hadn't admitted it and was therefore both deluded as to my own actions and unremorseful about what I had done. (Mind you, Bertha had also been unremorseful and they'd let her out, hadn't they. Perhaps her murder had been less brutal.)

'We need people to be on a trial scheme so that we can develop a proper programme of education and rehabilitation for prisoners.'

I looked at Jeanette sharply. So that was it. They needed me because I was one of the few prisoners who could read, let alone understand anything about what it was like to be educated. If I could remember. The reading bit was okay, but it was a long time since

I'd adhered to any of the rules of being educated, having just let my own thoughts dominate and run riot in my head, not needing to take any heed of scholarship, reason or evidence.

'Okay,' I said. 'What are we going to do?'

'We already have literacy and numeracy courses but of course they haven't been relevant for you.' Jeanette obviously wanted me to co-operate, badly, as she was being unusually nice, even patient with me.

I waited.

'We'd like to have a trial programme teaching prisoners basic office skills like typing and computer skills.'

Computer skills? What on earth was that? I wasn't going to gratify Jeanette by asking her.

'Okay,' I repeated.

'It may mean that you can't run the library,' Jeanette said cautiously.

'No one uses the library anyway,' I said.

Jeanette looked relieved. She obviously thought that I was dependent on the library. She hadn't quite realised that the problem had been that I'd been too dependent on Big Bertha, not the library. I almost felt interested in this typing course thing. But I wasn't going to let Jeanette see that.

'We are going to start with just six of you next week. It will be all morning from Mondays to Fridays.' She was looking at me anxiously.

I shrugged. I was hardly doing anything else, was I? And Jane never visited me in the week anyway, so as far as I was concerned we could have worked all afternoon as well.

'Will there be homework?' I asked.

Jeanette looked a bit startled.

'I mean, will we be able to practice things like the typing at other times of the day?'

'Well, Kate, that's a good question, we hadn't really thought about that possibility. But I'll certainly look into it.'

Jeanette looked pleased. Very pleased. She obviously felt that at last she had got through to me and had found something to interest me and 'bring me out of myself' as she no doubt would have put it. Still, it wouldn't do any harm to have something positive on my record sheet for a change. Hanging round with Big Bertha and her cronies obviously hadn't done me any favours with the authorities, even if it had raised my kudos with the other in-mates.

Claire

Mum came to Whitcliff and we both sat in a special room and talked to Sally. Sally said I couldn't come to Whitcliff any more and Mum got cross and Sally said it wasn't that I couldn't come to Whitcliff any more but that I couldn't go for 4 days any more and Mum still got cross and said it was silly because I was doing so well and Sally said she had managed to get two days for me and Mum said does that mean that Claire can now always come for 2 days or will they mess her about again and Sally said that no they wouldn't mess Claire around any more and that she would have a per-ma-nent place-ment in the Centre for Outpatients. I said did I come to Whitcliff for 2 days on the bus with Mum and Mum and Sally looked at me as though they were a bit shocked. Then I said I would come on Tuesdays and Thursdays and Mum and Sally carried on looking shocked. Sally looked at Mum as if she was saying something that she wasn't saying to me then she said I thought that Tuesdays and Fridays would be better and I said I didn't like Fridays and that I liked Thursdays and Sally sort of coughed and said that didn't Mum agree with her that Thursdays were difficult. Mum didn't say anything and Sally had to carry on sort of talking as though she didn't want to talk and she said well she supposed that Thursdays were alright but that er Claire shouldn't that Claire. Then she looked at me and said that she thought that I didn't like Mike any more. I said that sometimes I liked Mike and that I hadn't liked him for a long time but that I liked his bus and that I liked him when we washed his bus and Mum said but I thought that Claire didn't see Mike any more and she looked at Sally as though something was Sally's fault and Sally said that she had thought so too but that Claire had obviously started it all up again. Mum and Sally looked at each other and I said so I will come on Tuesdays and Thursdays and Mum said yes, dear, you can come on Tuesdays and Thursdays and Sally didn't say anything. Then Mum said to Sally do you think she'll be alright on her own at home or will I have to cut my days at the Clinic and Sally said that no she should be alright and anyway it will be good for her to learn to look after herself a bit and that we had been learning life skills and I said I can make ham sandwiches but I can't use the cooker yet but Mike told me that he can cook baked beans in tomato sauce. Well that's alright then isn't it said Mum and she suddenly smiled because before she had looked all unhappy and worried. I moved my chair close to Mum and snuggled up to her but Sally just looked at us both as if she was afraid of something.

Kate

Five of us rattled away at the old Olympia manual typewriters. They'd been donated by a brewery in Dewsbury which had gone 'electric'. The sixth member of the Chosen Ones (as I thought of us), Tracy, took to computer programming like the proverbial duck. Tracy was a natural when it came to modern times but the rest of us were happy to remain forgotten in sixties technologies.

The cat sat on the mat. Which I was then meant to repeat several times. The mat sat on the cat. The cat on the mat sat (sic Latin syntax). My fingers were not strong enough and the little finger on my left hand invariably got stuck between the keys every time I went for the 'a'. The cat sat on the mat etc. While exercising my fingers into strong killing machines (I hoped that wouldn't come in handy) I decided with a vengeance that I was never going to do/study/think/believe anything as useful i.e. mundane as office work/computer studies/business studies/accounting if/when I got out of here. I was going to study. I paused in my typing at this point to think of the most useless thing I could think of to study. Philosophy; (which won by a slight margin over Latin and Greek, Latin and Greek being too good a basis for modern language study). And then I thought of Jeanette nastily, and psychology won hands down.

When is a cat a cat? Is a cat on a mat a cat? Is a mat with a cat a mat? Therefore can a cat not be a cat and can a mat not be a mat? Is the relationship between the cat and the mat more important than the cat or the mat on their own? Are we not important unless we exist in relation to something else? Do we only exist in relation to something else? Was this philosophy or psychology? Did it matter?

My little finger got stuck between the 's' and the 'z' and I had to stop to tug it out. I was also looking at the keys and the whole point was that one wasn't meant to look at the keys.

I exist because of the typewriter and the typewriter exists because of me. When we are separated we don't exist. Wrong. But we don't exist in relation to each other once we have separated? Right. Maybe. If I think about the typewriter I still have a relationship to it even though it isn't there, but the typewriter can't think about me, so it no longer has a relationship with me. But it still exists. At least I believe it still exists because I can imagine its existence but when I'm not with it I cannot prove that it still exists.

The others were now typing 'where is the gate'. (Was this existentialism – not that I really knew what existentialism was – or wish fulfilment or plain brutal cruelty? Indeed, where was the gate?) And of course Tracy wasn't typing anything, she was punching holes in green cards – at least she was doing that if that's what computer programmers did.

Bertha's departure had left not only a void but a longing for whatever it was that was out there now. And I was having a thing about bars and grids (and gates) and metal doors and metal beds and metal spoons and forks and knives. Not a very healthy thing. Bertha had reminded me that I was in and that I could get out again, one day. And I longed to get out. And this typing course was a most cruel carrot as it was leading me to a life outside of prison without any basis in fact. In fact, with complete disregard to the fact that I was a lifer, and that no amount of typing courses were going to procure my release.

I typed 'where is the gate' with a great deal of dramatic irony, if one can type with dramatic irony. Perhaps Virginia Woolf (I'd found a copy of 'A room of One's Own' in the library – now that really was random) typed with dramatic irony. If Virginia Woolf did type? Or did she write everything out in long hand. Like Tolkien who got his wife to type and re-type all (*all*) his novels six times (of course I can't remember if it was six times but it was certainly more than twice). But Virginia Woolf didn't have a wife (did she?).

'You've got a telephone message,' said Jeanette who had crept up behind me.

I jumped guiltily. I wondered how much of all this gibberish I was thinking I'd actually committed to the paper working its way around the roller bar on the typewriter and in my confusion I got my finger stuck between the 'a' and the 's' and the 'z' again.

But Jeanette was still being nice to me. She put a memo down on the desk by my typing exercise.

'Alan rang with the message that Jane had a baby boy at 8pm last night. Mother and baby are doing well,' I typed. (Just for the record it was 21st July 1974 which is a date I remember because it is

Sean's birthday and I also - usually - manage to remember how old he is and thus what year he was born in.)

For a moment I was just sitting by a window in an office typing and thinking about my best friend who'd just had her first baby. Just for a moment I was happy, like really normally happy. It was an odd feeling to remember what it was like to be normal and immensely reassuring to experience normality. It was generally all too easy to think that one would never be normal again.

And then I was worried. That wretched pink thing was nowhere near finished and without Bertha it had proved almost impossible. And then I was delighted because it was a boy and it didn't matter that I hadn't finished it. I can knit the pink thing for the next one, I though blithely.

And then I looked at the bar across the window and a little cold shiver ran up my body.

Kate

A little cold breath. Margaret came back. Yes, Margaret came back. This was not good news. At least it couldn't be good news could it? No one said anything; she just came back.

Eileen and I had had the cell all to ourselves since Bertha left. Things had been changing in the prison. The typing course for one but other things too. We had more privacy, or at least more space as less women were crowded into each cell. And because Eileen had two pills every day I was fairly confident that she would have had at least one of them each day. We didn't bother each other much. Sometimes we even did stuff together. Eileen was more sleepy than she used to be, but sometimes she could be her old chatty self, especially when she had picked up a friend she could mimic. Eileen herself didn't have anything to say so she had to have other people's things to say. I wondered if she said my things to other people. But she didn't say my things to me as she had done to Margaret.

Margaret was put back with us because 'we were all used to each other'. Margaret was just the same. Or almost just the same. There was a little thread of suspended tension, or was it excitement, I couldn't quite tell, which ran through her narrow shoulders. She wore glasses all the time now and stared, or seemed to stare, more than ever as the pale eyes were permanently magnified by the lenses in her glasses. I tried to tell myself that that was why she didn't seem to be normal and that being short-sighted wasn't a sin or even a sign of madness.

'Oh Margaret, how delightful,' cooed Eileen.

Was Eileen really that stupid?

'What a lovely time to come back. All the roses in the garden are in full bloom.'

We did have a prison garden. Some of the prisoners tended it. I didn't. I'd never been a great outdoors person myself. But flowers were meant to be therapeutic so perhaps Jeanette had encouraged the garden and the gardening. Of course, it was much nicer to go out into a garden than a brick courtyard. One almost felt guilty – prison wasn't meant to be nice, it was meant to be a punishment.

So what was Margaret being punished for this time? And was she in with us really just because 'we were all used to each other' or because she was joining the 'lifers' again? The first degree murder cases who might be a danger to society at large, but were not a danger to each other. And was I supposed to believe that? That Margaret was not a danger? I hoped desperately that she was in for stealing lipstick from the old people's handbags. Perhaps Margaret had developed a penchant for life, and lipstick was the first step towards joining the modern world and all its frivolity.

'We'll be going along for tea soon, Margaret. Will you join us?'

What was it about Margaret that so inspired Eileen?

The three of us trooped off to the canteen.

'You'll see there have been some changes here,' chirruped Eileen. 'And some for the better if you know what I mean.'

As if nothing had happened, as if no years had intervened between Margaret's release and her return. As if there had never been a release and therefore had never been a new crime committed. Because, and I had to face it, Margaret had now committed a new crime. A crime serious enough to bring her back to us.

'Now, I don't like to speak ill of the departed as it were, but I have to admit that it was a great relief when Bertha left. Really the likes of her are not a good influence.' Eileen turned to me patronisingly.

I was looking at Margaret who took the opportunity to eye up Eileen's throat. That was not good. That definitely did not bode well for Eileen, or me. I'd better keep up the typing exercises as perhaps those strong fingers just might come in handy. Oh dear, this was not the time for frivolity. But it was so hard to be serious with Eileen babbling on, pouring out the endless years and years worth of the errant nonsense she must have believed should have come out of Margaret's mouth. Although it wasn't errant nonsense to Eileen, it was sophisticated conversation.

It was bangers and mash for tea. With baked beans. Surely that would calm Eileen down. A warder came with her pill. I wondered if Margaret might also get a pill. She didn't. A pill would have been a good sign. It would have been a sign that they had finally worked out that Margaret was not just mad but dangerously mad. Couldn't anyone see through all that veneer of gentility? I would have to risk an approach to Jeanette. It was not allowed to discuss other prisoners with Jeanette but things had slipped before from her side so maybe I could do some 'slipping' from my side.

'Oh there's nothing like a good old cup of tea,' said Eileen. 'Do let me help you to some sugar,' she oozed over Margaret.

Margaret didn't care about the sugar but Eileen's prison dress had come loose at the neck in all the excitement and Margaret stared through her glasses to get a better view. Eileen's neck looked quite a challenge, thick and solid as it was, if one was contemplating strangulating her and of course all those well protected airways had implications when it came to smothering too. My neck was not challenging at all, me still being the thin scraggly thing I'd been when I came here.

Eight years ago – Sean's birth having given me – at least temporarily – a tighter grip on the actual date so that I made more attempt to type a correct date when we typed letters rather than just putting 1966 out of laziness or cussedness. Jeanette hadn't made up her mind about the latter yet but was still inclined to give me the benefit of the doubt. I'd better make the most of that benefit of the doubt if I was going to get her to take an interest in Margaret. The present Margaret I could not live with, or one way or another was not likely to live very long with, but it might just be possible to live with a Margaret who took (several) pills.

Claire

On Wednesday Mum went to the Clinic except she called it the hospital and she didn't come back all day and I spent the day on my own and the night. Mrs Cartwright came to see me. She came at 12 o'clock and made sausages and mashed potatoes for dinner. She brought the sausages and asked me to find some potatoes. At first I couldn't find the potatoes then I remembered that Mum keeps them in the cupboard next to the sink. Mrs Cartwright asked for 4 potatoes and she peeled them and cooked them on the cooker like Mum does. I can use the cooker now but I can't cook potatoes. Mrs Cartwright cooked 5 sausages and I ate 3 and she ate 2. We had Instant Whip for pudding and Mrs Cartwright said I could have the rest for tea if I wanted to. I said yes very politely but I don't really like Instant Whip very much. Mrs Cartwright did the washing up and I read my magazine. I read a story then Mrs Cartwright said she had to go and would I be alright and that Mrs Hunter would pop in and see me and did I have enough food for tea. I didn't say anything because I didn't want Mrs Hunter to do any popping in. I read the rest of my story and Mrs Cartwright went home. When Mrs Hunter popped in I watched Top Cat. I turned the volume up until Mrs Hunter went home then I made a ham sandwich and had a Bar Six which Mum said was for special occasions.

    I watched Coronation Street although I don't really like it because it is too noisy but Mum liked to watch it. Then I put my nightie on and went to bed. It was very strange going to bed and I thought it might be nicer in Mum's bed but it wasn't so I went back to my bed and then I fell asleep.

    The next morning I woke up and felt strange again. I walked around the house a bit but no one was there. The clock in the kitchen said eight o'clock and a bit after. I couldn't remember what was happening and felt a bit panicky so I went back to bed. Then I remembered that yesterday had been Wednesday and that Mum had gone to the Clinic called the hospital and that she was going to be away all night and that she had been away all night and that now it was the morning and that if it had been Wednesday yesterday then it was Thursday today which meant that I was going to Whitcliff. So I got dressed. I put on my blue skirt and my yellow blouse and my blue cardigan. Then I did a very clever thing and put my tights on without any help from Mum. Then I went downstairs and got the panicky feeling again because I forgot again what was going to happen then I heard a car and someone knocked on the kitchen door and that someone was Sally because she came into the kitchen.

Sally looked at me in my blue skirt and yellow blouse and blue cardigan and sort of clapped her hands and said clever girl well done Claire. Then I felt pleased and not panicky. Sally told me to get my coat and put my shoes on so I did. Then Sally helped me get in her car and I said are you taking me to Whitcliff and she said yes. I didn't tell her that I hadn't had any breakfast but I did make her drive me back home because I'd forgotten my sponge.

Claire

Jane came to see us with her baby called Sean. Mrs Cartwright came too. Sean was wearing the blue cardigan that I knitted for him. I thought he wasn't very nice because he was rude and blew bubbles and made smells but Mum seemed to like him a lot and cuddled him so I sat on the sofa next to Mum and cuddled her a bit fiercely. Everyone laughed except me and Sean. Sean gave a big shout and I put my hands over my ears and said that I wasn't sure if I liked babies. Everyone laughed again but I don't think that that was very nice of everyone.

I knitted a cardigan. It is for Janes baby. Janes baby is called Sean. Mum helped me.

by Claire

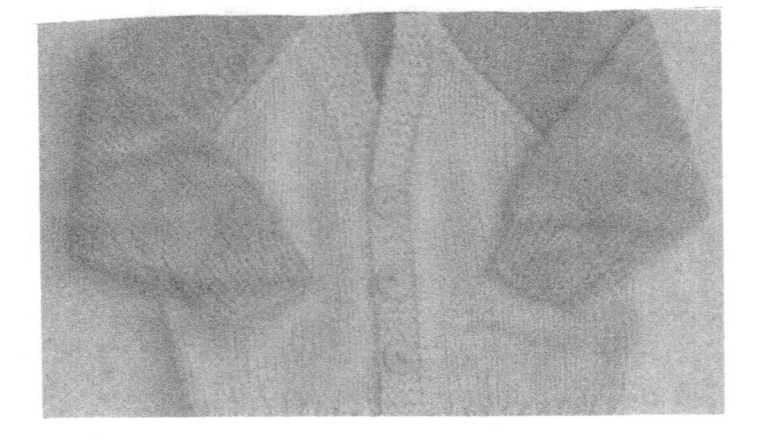

Kate

I was not a baby sort of person but little Sean was the most wonderful piece of engineering I'd ever seen. I leant over the table and put my finger inside his little fist. The little fist clutched onto my finger and the chubby cheeks gurgled and dribbled and snuffled and then the shining red lips opened in a broad smile revealing one sharp little tooth.

'He's gorgeous,' I said to a gratified Jane.

'Look, he's smiling for his Auntie Kate,' gooed Jane. 'Alan's waiting outside,' she added.

I wondered why Alan hadn't come in. I tickled Sean's tummy.

'He's amazing,' I said.

'Isn't he just,' said Jane. 'But he can be a little monster,' she said happily. 'When he starts creating I'll just pop out with him and Alan'll take him for a walk.'

So that's why Alan was waiting outside so that he could take charge of the baby when he became a monster.

'Is there anywhere to go for a walk?' I asked surprised.

Jane looked a bit non-plussed.

'Well yes, it's just normal outside you know,' she sounded critical like she had done on the few occasions when I'd been more stupid than her at school.

Gates and bars and grids suddenly shadowed my thoughts and I think I might have poked Sean a little bit too hard in the tummy instead of tickling him. The little red mouth began to wobble and Jane was up and out of the visiting room just before an enormously loud scream of outrage rent the air. Within moments she was back again smiling.

'I think he's got a dirty nappy,' she said.

Which was either true or kind. I pushed the shadows of bars from my thoughts.

'So how is it? How are you? What's it like?'

'It's hard work,' laughed Jane, 'and to be quite honest it's quite nice to get him off my hands for a few minutes.' She looked at me expectantly.

I felt a bit confused. Visiting me was a relief from looking after Sean? I didn't feel quite up to the task of helping Jane make the most of her few minutes. An uncomfortable silence drifted between us.

'How's the typing course going?' she asked at last.

'Okay.' I was more taken up with my project to get Jeanette to take an interest in Margaret than my typing just now. So far I wasn't doing too well on the Jeanette and Margaret front.

'You must be getting quite good by now.'

'Reasonable,' I said forcing my answers to relate to typing and not to Margaret.

'I wish I'd learnt to type. It must be so useful.'

'Yea, it's really useful.'

She looked at me sharply.

'Sometimes you haven't changed at all,' she said.

'Isn't that a good thing?' I asked.

'That depends on which bits of you we're talking about.'

'Perhaps you haven't changed either,' I said for something to say.

Jane looked interested.

'Is that what you think? That I haven't changed? You know, I don't think I have. I mean, I know I have but sometimes I still feel like the old me. Especially when I come here.'

'Is that good or bad?'

'I don't know.'

I smiled. I think that if she'd pretended to know at that point I'd have lost my best and only friend. Just the possibility made me feel shaky. Was I getting too dependent on Jane too? Would she inevitably leave me one day just as Bertha had had to? What if Alan got a job and moved to a different area?

'Does Alan still work at Rowntrees?' I asked suddenly.

'Yes, silly, I'd tell you about any major changes like that.'

At this point during visits – when the clock showed that we only had five minutes left – she usually said something about Mum and Claire. I braced myself.

'Claire loves the baby,' she said bang on cue.

'I expect she finished the cardigan for the baby, didn't she,' I said.

'Yes, she did,' laughed Jane.

'And is Mum okay?'

Jane hesitated.

'Yes. She went in for more tests a few weeks ago.'

'Oh.'

'She had to go in overnight.' Jane obviously wanted me to understand that it might be serious.

'What about Claire?' I couldn't help asking, the old responsibility sticking like a bur in my mind.

'Oh she was alright. Mum looked in and Mrs Hunter keeps an eye on her.'

'You mean she stayed at home on her own?'

'Oh yes,' Jane looked surprised at my alarm. 'She's quite capable now, you know. Mum says it's a blessing, especially if, well you know, if things aren't so good for your mum.'

Jane looked at me anxiously, wondering if she'd said too much.

Claire looking after herself? I couldn't do that, not any more, not now. I couldn't even have boiled an egg. So much for learning to type.

The bell went.

'Oh I brought you these,' Jane said hurriedly pushing a bag of toffees across the table.

I didn't eat toffees any more.

'Bye.' I watched her hurry from the room eager to get back to her 'monster' and her normality. I had to admire her loyalty to our old friendship as my normality must have been hard to stomach sometimes.

Kate

I was suffering from a complete character disintegration. I wasn't sure whether it started with Jane's visit with the baby or if it started before that with Margaret's return. Or Eileen's vociferousness. Or before that with the typing exercises. Or when Bertha left. Or my warped (or original depending on one's bias) view of history.

I could copy type a whole letter without looking at the key board and only occasionally having to stop to disentangle my little finger from its habitual battle with 'a', 's' and 'z':

The Manager,
Wigan Car Parts,
North Road,
WIGAN.

Dear Sir,
With reference to your letter dated 16th March 1975...

Or:

The Manager
Wigan Car Parts
North Road
WIGAN

Dear Sir

With reference to your letter dated 16 March 1975...

Being the modern and now quite acceptable form of layout. After which our teacher promised we would learn how to put in a subject heading and how to sign off our letter appropriately (on behalf of our mythical boss).

I had 'friends' as I limply followed Eileen and Margaret around from lunch to the dayroom to the garden to tea to our cell to the shower to the toilet to our cell to the canteen for cocoa to the dayroom for *Coronation Street* to our cell into our bunks to breakfast.

'Oh what a delight these daffodils are, aren't they Margaret,' chirruped Eileen.

'Oh what wouldn't one give for a nice cup of tea,' chatted Eileen (just stopping herself from saying 'cuppa').

'Really sometimes the meat they give us simply isn't fit to eat,' chimed Eileen watching Margaret push some gristle around her plate. Eileen had already eaten hers.

I watched the air coming out of Eileen's mouth and wondered how much breath she needed for each sentence. How much breath she needed for each word. How much breath she needed to breathe. Whether she needed breath at all. And did all that breath just slide happily down her throat and into her lungs and then seep out again as words until she took another breath. Without the breath she couldn't breathe but more importantly without the breath she couldn't talk. No more breath, no more words.

Dear Sir,

With reference to Eileen's breathing. Or should it be with reference to Eileen's talking?

The one good thing about Eileen's talking was that it meant that neither Margaret nor I need make any effort at all to keep the conversation going. We could appear to be making great advances in our socialising skills without doing anything. And even if we'd wanted to strike out on the lonely journey of developing our own friendships it wouldn't have been possible anyway. Eileen stuck to Margaret like a leech and I stuck to the pair of them.

Out in the garden Margaret suddenly bent over and plucked a daffodil. She bent over quite low so that her glasses fell a little down her nose. She reached down very carefully and plucked the stalk near its base. The little flower danced in her hand and the fresh sap from the broken stalk oozed out over her fingers. For a moment Eileen's monologue faltered and her mouth stuck in a soundless 'oh' and the breath that should have filled up her lungs never happened and the flow of words which should have flowed on the tide of her out-breath were lost. And in the silence the daffodil danced in Margaret's hand and Margaret smiled.

Eileen recovered herself, took in an enormous breath and carried on talking. I was helpless, lost in the endless trail of Eileen's words so that I couldn't think any more. Lost in reams of copy typing to mythical managers. Lost in Margaret's obsession with living things that could be plucked, with the sap that could be squeezed out of life, with breath that could be stopped.

Kate

'I keep having nightmares,' I said to Jeanette.

I didn't know whether I was having nightmares or not as everything seemed to have become one long nightmare. But I had to begin somewhere. I hadn't managed to explain about Margaret to her and she was too pleased to see me making 'suitable' friends and 'socialising' so that it was impossible to begin a conversation with: 'You know Margaret and Eileen? Well, they both need certifying and sending to a secure unit for the mentally deranged.' Besides which, who was I to make such accusations?

Jeanette looked interested and pleased that I'd initiated the conversation. I was rather pleased with myself as the ability to initiate anything had almost deserted me.

'Do you want to describe these nightmares for me, Kate?'

Initiating a conversation was one thing but sustaining it quite another.

'I quite understand if you find this difficult, Kate,' said Jeanette gently.

Suspicion about Jeanette understanding anything steadied me and I felt a little more confident in my own perverseness again with regards to Jeanette. I must believe that this had been a good idea, this idea of taking initiative.

'Now, how often do you have these nightmares?'

It struck me that Jeanette probably had a manual on how to question patients who needed to be encouraged to talk about their dreams. After all dreams were an easy way into someone's psyche. I would have to careful. I didn't want her to think that I was having evil thoughts. But whatever the incumbent dangers were, it was so good to think again that I almost felt grateful towards Jeanette for her 'understanding'.

'Most nights,' I said carefully. I couldn't honestly say that it was every night. I didn't manage to stay awake every night, but it was certainly most nights.

'And is it the same dream?'

'Yes.'

'Is it always a nightmare?'

'Yes.'

'Not sometimes a dream which turns into a nightmare?'

'No.'

'Or a nightmare that can turn into a,' she paused here perhaps wanting to find a more adequate word than nice, 'into a good dream, or into a normal dream?'

'No, it's definitely not normal,' I said quickly, then wondered if that was wise as Jeanette would be relating the not normalness to me not to anything else.

'Are there people in your dream, Kate?' she asked carefully.

'I'm not sure,' I equivocated.

'People you know perhaps?'

I looked at her reproachfully.

'I don't see anything,' I said. Which made sense to me but I immediately realised that it wouldn't make sense to Jeanette. 'I feel something,' I said before she had time to respond to my first answer. 'Like Jane Eyre.'

Jeanette struggled for a bit with this until she said.

'I don't think I quite understand you, Kate,' she said.

I had to applaud her honesty.

'I'm not sure I understand myself,' I said to be nice. I did understand, only too well.

I would have to get on with it. Our session would be over soon.

'I feel a cold breath on my face,' I said. 'So you see I don't see anything, I just feel something like Jane Eyre does when Rochester's mad wife is prowling round the house at night.' This was meant to make things clearer to Jeanette and to introduce the idea of an external mad person.

'Oh, have you been reading *Jane Eyre*?' asked Jeanette.

'No, not recently.'

'But you're having nightmares like Jane Eyre?'

'Yes,' that was the whole point, but I didn't quite like the way that Jeanette put it.

'Do you think that it could be something that you've read, Kate?' said Jeanette. 'You do read an awful lot, don't you?'

Damn it, I should have predicted that pitfall.

'It's nothing I've read,' I said starting to get frustrated and just a little panicky. 'It's just that I have an experience that feels like a nightmare but it could be something real. Like in *Jane Eyre*.' I.e.

it wasn't a nightmare that woke Jane Eyre, it was a mad and dangerous woman staring at her and breathing over her.

But I'd lost Jeanette.

'Would you like me to prescribe you some sleeping pills?' she said.

'No,' I tried not to shout. Sleeping pills were the last thing I needed.

'There's no need to shout, Kate,' said Jeanette sorrowfully. 'Well, I won't give you anything just yet but you must come and talk to me again if you keep having these problems with sleeping and we'll give you something for them.'

I got up to go. My time was up anyway. How had we gone from nightmares when sleeping to problems with sleeping? I must have completely mismanaged the whole session. I would just have to go on not sleeping which wasn't always possible. I burst into tears as I left Jeanette's office. But neither tears nor shouting nor in fact any kind of hysterical behaviour were a good idea as Jeanette would put it all in my records. 'Fantasising, overwrought, not sleeping, not admitting the reality of the situation to herself...'

Eileen and Margaret were in the day room.

'Oh, what a pity the rain won't stop, it would have been lovely to get a little fresh air,' babbled Eileen.

Margaret turned her attention, briefly, from Eileen's breathing to mine. I pulled up the collar of my prison dress and sat down next to Eileen. Eileen ignored me in full flow as she was but Margaret craned her own neck around Eileen and continued to stare at me through her glasses. At least I think she did because I could feel the cold breath. I could feel the fingers crushing the sap out of the daffodil. I was going into a blackout as the hysteria started to mount in me. The first blackout for many, many years. The first hysteria. Jeanette would be watching, especially after the shouting and the crying. I started to count under my breath, in a whisper. I got to twenty and the humming in my ears faded into snatches of Eileen's singing chatter. I carried on to forty this time. If I just kept still it would be alright. I was managing. I was managing to control the hysteria and managing to stop the blackout. I was so relieved that I burst into tears again, and muttering something loudly about a headache rushed off to the depths of the library – one would normally rush off to the toilets but people followed one to the toilets whereas no one went to the library. See, I'd even managed to think thus far rationally in the midst of my escape.

I'd taken an initiative. I'd controlled a blackout. I didn't have to fall prey to Margaret like a rabbit trapped in the headlights of her pale magnified eyes. I could begin at least by finding out more about Margaret. There was one sure way of doing this and that was to ask someone. Obviously not Jeanette, but someone important.

Claire

Mum didn't go to the Clinic anymore. She took me on the bus to Whitcliff and then she went home again. One day she stayed in bed and Sally came and took me to Whitcliff instead but usually Mum took me. I liked Mum being at home. When I wasn't at Whitcliff Mum made dinner and I made tea. I liked making tea. I made ham sandwiches and Mum said I was very clever but when I asked if we could go to Bettys Mum shook her head and looked sad and I was sad and a bit cross too because I liked going to Bettys. Then Sally said a very strange thing. She said that Mum was poorly. She said that Mum was very poorly and I said is she very very very poorly and Sally said yes but I didn't believe her because a very very very poorly person wouldn't have got up every day and made dinner.

Kate

I would have to risk Jeanette's black looks and talk to Dot. Dot was a 'crony' of Big Bertha's and now ran the knitting circle. I hadn't dared to join Dot's knitting circle as Dot had it in for anyone who could read, and she especially had it in for the 'Chosen Ones' who did the typing course.

At least my character had stopped disintegrating – in my opinion if not in Jeanette's. So I resurrected the pink thing for Jane's baby and trotted along to Dot's knitting circle in good time so that I could sit next to Dot.

Dot looked at me sardonically.

'Haven't you finished that yet, then?' she scorned.

'No,' I answered meekly.

'That baby'll be riding motorbikes before you've finished that sweater,' she said cackling smugly round at her cronies.

I took this to be a good sign and smiled carefully. I mustn't let her think that I was smiling at her and I mustn't let her think that I was too snooty to cope with being laughed at myself.

There followed some more jokes about the sweater being for a boy and being pink. I didn't point out that when I'd started the wretched thing I hadn't known whether the baby was going to be a boy or a girl.

Dot soon lost interest in me which usually would have been a good sign, but I wanted her to be interested in me so that I could ask her a question. Dot knew everything and in lieu of Big Bertha Dot liked to think that she controlled everything. Her present project was leading a character assassination of a warder who was currently very unpopular having disciplined one of the cronies by not allowing her to watch *Coronation Street*.

'Have you heard from Bertha?' I eventually said in a pause.

Dot looked at me sceptically. She wasn't likely to have heard from Bertha – no one heard from anyone once they'd got out again. But worse than that I'd made a big mistake by reminding her that this had been Bertha's group, that Bertha was my friend and that Dot was only leader of the cronies by default.

'Look, are you looking for trouble or something?' she said menacingly. 'Because we're quite happy the way we are, aren't we girls?' she appealed to the chorus who obligingly agreed with her in similar menacing tones. 'We certainly don't need toffee-nosed upstarts meddling in our business.'

'I don't want to meddle,' I said quickly.

'Just because you knew Bertha then has nothing to do with now, understood?'

'Yes.'

I went back to my knitting. It was so long since I'd done any of it that I didn't have a clue what I was doing.

Dot craftily moved the conversation on to the typing group.

'And that typing group is only going to give them prisoners ideas above themselves,' she said looking at me.

I bent over my knitting. But this topic of conversation didn't seem to inspire the cronies to the same level of vitriol as the disciplinarian warder. It struck me that some of them might even aspire to the typing course themselves. Especially those looking to be released within the next year or two. A typing job would be a good deterrent against thieving, which was what most of them were in for. But I didn't want to know what any of them were in for; I needed to know specifically what Margaret was in for.

I made a few more knots in my knitting, dropped a few stitches here and gained a few there – as one does. Perhaps I should wait until tomorrow. If there would be a tomorrow.

'Dot,' I said about five minutes before the bell went for dinner.

Dot ignored me, but not much else was going on at this point so I was fairly sure that she'd heard me. The others certainly had, as at least three of them stopped knitting to watch.

'Dot,' I continued, my urgency forcing me straight to the point, 'what did Margaret do to be put back inside?' Well, the boldest moves are the best or is it the safest? Something along those lines.

Dot stopped her knitting as well now and the whole group looked from Dot to me.

'And who needs to know?' asked Dot.

I'd expected 'what's it worth?' which would have been a real stumper.

'I do,' I said.

'Well, seeing as you're so pally with her why don't you ask her yourself?'

'Look,' that was a bad start but it held everyone's attention and as Dot didn't clobber me on the head I carried on, 'I didn't ask to share a cell with Margaret. Nor with Eileen for that matter. But I do, and I need to know what Margaret did.'

'Because?'

'Just because,' was as far as I wanted to speculate.

The bell went, but the cronies were still hanging on in suspense and expectation. Would Dot answer me or not? Did Dot actually know or not? The knowing bit was what did the trick. If Dot hadn't answered me she would have lost her reputation for knowing everything. Luckily she missed the trap I'd unwittingly made for her by testing her superior knowledge of all things prison related and beyond, added to which she experienced disproportionate gratification when able to demonstrate her all-knowing wisdom and power.

'She throttled a few of those old people,' Dot said.

'In the old people's home where she worked?'

'That's right. Smothered them in their sleep.'

'How many?'

'Two definites and three possibles,' said Dot, her reputation firmly renewed, established and even enhanced.

The cronies packed up their knitting and hustled off to dinner. The information about Margaret was perhaps old hat to them or perhaps dinner was just more important. They didn't share a cell with Margaret and they didn't in fact have anything to do with Margaret at all. I dropped any stitches that still remained on my needles and tried to hide my shock. After all it was old hat to me too, wasn't it? It was just that I did share a cell with Margaret. I flexed my fingers which were growing stronger by the day with all the typing. But would they be strong enough, I wondered, if it came to a tussle?

Kate

This time it really was a nightmare. Mr Rochester's mad wife was sucking the breath from me. Her teeth were sharp and dangerous like a vampire's and her eyes were wide and mad and darkened from lack of sleep. She started laughing and woke me up. Which meant I really had been asleep. The scream started in my sleep and carried on as I awoke so that I didn't realise at first that it was me who was screaming. My fingers were icy cold and stiff. In fact, my whole body felt as cold as a corpse. I decided to carry on screaming because I wasn't the only person awake in the cell. Margaret was awake. She was fighting with Eileen and Eileen would have been screaming too if she hadn't been covered with Margaret's pillow. Margaret didn't notice my screaming. All her concentration was bent on Eileen and the struggle Eileen was putting up. Margaret didn't want to be deprived of her quarry.

'You dirty bitch, you cow!' shouted Margaret. 'I'll finish you and your nasty little scheming words. Your ugly stinking breath.' These were words that the 'real' Eileen might have used herself. Had Margaret become Eileen and Eileen Margaret? But I decided that this wasn't the time for thinking.

I screamed. Then to give some momentum to my screams I screamed and shouted.

'Help! Help!' I shouted.

That Margaret might turn her attention from Eileen to me was a risk I would have to take. She might have turned her attention to me next anyway. I carried on screaming and Eileen carried on struggling. Margaret had become so obsessed with the ease of killing that she had forgotten that Eileen wasn't eighty nine. Eileen was forty one and strong. Eileen struggled and Margaret cursed. Now if Eileen had pretended to die Margaret might have crept back to bed as though nothing had happened, much as she no doubt had done after all her other murders. But Eileen was not a rational thinker at the best of times. She struggled and the more she struggled the more challenged and fascinated Margaret became. This was real killing, not just the easy snuffing as of a candle of the life already nearly drained from the elderly. This was Margaret's life's purpose to really kill something. All the other killings had been as an experiment until she should face her ultimate life's challenge. Eileen, whom she hated with a passion. Eileen who had sucked what was left of Margaret's old self out of her. Eileen who had tried to turn her into a nothingness. Now Margaret was taking all that life back and her vengeance and her strength were insurmountable.

I carried on screaming, wondering if my feeble cries could possibly be heard in the great empty vaults of the prison corridors. It didn't occur to me to try and do anything else. Everything was too supernatural and still more resonant of nightmare than reality. And having earlier solicited and failed to obtain help from the greater powers of the prison authorities in the form of Jeanette I did the only thing left to me to do: scream. Scream because my nightmare had returned. And perhaps it was just a nightmare. Perhaps Margaret wasn't really snuffing out the life of another human being because however much of a leech, even non-being Eileen had become, she was still human. At least I hadn't forgotten that. Even in the middle of my nightmare.

'At last I've got you, you vicious cow,' gasped Margaret.

'Help, please someone,' I gasped out hoarsely.

Keys were rattling. The grid in our door was opened.

I screamed to make sure and Margaret screwed her pillow into Eileen's face, just to make sure. The key struggled in the lock as though I wasn't the only person who was now in a panic and I could hear several agitated voices outside.

Three warders rushed in at once. One was a medical orderly who had probably come to administer Eileen with an extra pill. I screamed and pointed at the heap which was Margaret and Eileen. Eileen hadn't twitched for a while now and Margaret stood up and looked down on her. Her defamation had ceased and she was calm and collected and as refined as ever.

'Can I help you?' she asked the warders, much as Eileen might have done.

The medical orderly was leaning over Eileen.

'My God,' she was saying, 'oh my God.'

Deaths in prison were not good. A shocked silence had stunned everyone, except Margaret who was climbing into bed. A fourth warder appeared in the doorway. She made straight for me.

'Kate, are you alright?'

The voice was familiar. It couldn't be Bertha, could it? I thought, feeling even more confused.

'Come on let's get you out of here,' the voice continued, and I was manhandled rather roughly out of bed. At this point I might have struggled with the fear that I was being accused of something, like murder, again, but there was something about the voice.

The other warders seemed more stunned than me.

'What shall we do?' one of them asked.

'Get Kate out of here first,' was the reply, 'the child's frozen. Get her something warm to drink and wrap her in blankets.'

'Where?' asked one of the other warders.

'Bloody hell, I don't care, anywhere just as far away from here as possible.'

'But...'

'Take her to the staffroom then.'

However unconventional it was, this order must have been obeyed because I was hurried off through the murky night corridors of the prison and ensconced in a small but cosy room, wrapped up in a blanket, tucked into a large comfy chair and given some hot milk. I hoped that Jeanette wasn't right and that this was now my nightmare turning into a 'good' dream.

A warder – just a girl about my age or probably younger as I was no longer 18 – kept feeding me the milk and asking me if I was alright. I supposed Eileen was dead but I didn't want to ask anyone. I supposed that Margaret would now at last be put somewhere more appropriate, with many locks, no pillows and no free hands when she was anywhere in the vicinity of anyone else. And the magical pill at least three times a day.

I almost basked in the warmth and normality of a comfy chair and warm milk. In fact, I felt so normal that I was probably crying when Dickson walked in.

'Sorted, at least for now,' said Dickson as she sat down heavily in another of the chairs. 'Who on earth put that mad woman together with anyone?' she asked the room in general, accusingly.

'Dickson?' I said in wonderment.

'My God, I've been in charge of this section for less than 24 hours and I'm dealing with a murder.' She turned to me. 'And we'll start our investigations with you just as soon as you've finished that milk. And I want some straight answers from you, Catherine

Howard. Bloody hell, we'd better sort this out before we have all the authorities breathing down our necks in the morning,' she continued, turning her frustration away from me and towards the rest of the room.

'It wasn't me,' I said suddenly panicking. Perhaps they meant that the 'mad woman' was me.

'Bloody hell, I know it wasn't you,' said Dickson, 'bloody hell.'

Dickson's swearing sounded so blessedly familiar again that I felt faint with reassurance.

Kate

'You'd better start at the beginning,' said Dickson.

I looked at her uncertainly; that was an open-ended question. Dickson gave me a knowing look and groaned. She probably said 'bloody hell' again just for good measure.

'Okay smarty pants, start from the beginning yesterday.'

'From asking Dot what Margaret had done – just to make sure?'

Dickson looked a bit taken aback then said.

'No just start from last night, a couple of hours ago. How exact do I have to be for God's sake?'

'I was having a nightmare – a real nightmare.'

Dickson interrupted me.

'Someone had better take this down,' she said, surveying her night-duty warders.

The young girl found a pencil and a note pad and held the pencil between nervous fingers. Dickson took the pad and pencil from her and gave it to me.

'Here,' she said, 'you'd better write it down while you talk.'

One of the warders piped up anxiously.

'Isn't that a bit, not quite right?' she said nervously.

'Unconventional,' said Dickson. 'The whole bloody set-up's a bit unconventional. But Kate's the only person in this room, including me, capable of writing down anything more than a football coupon so the way I see it is that we don't have much choice.' Dickson scanned them all in big-time Dickson belligerent style. 'Any further comments?' she challenged her warders. Nervous silence ensued. She turned back to me. 'Well, get on with it then.'

'I was having a nightmare – a real nightmare,' I repeated so that I could write it down, 'which meant that I was asleep.'

Dickson pulled a predictable expression.

'I can't always tell,' I said, but I didn't write this down. I decided that Dickson wouldn't be very sympathetic to the details of the nightmare especially once I started to talk about *Jane Eyre*. 'I was having a nightmare and I think I started screaming in my sleep and when I woke up I just carried on.'

'Why?'

'Why?'

'For goodness sake Kate, why were you screaming?'

'Because I was frightened. I knew that something was wrong before I woke up and I think I was terrified because I thought that Margaret was going to kill me.'

There was a pause while I wrote all this down. Dickson used the time to assimilate the information. She decided not to comment but nodded her head when I'd finished writing to indicate that I should carry on.

'Then I saw that Margaret was trying to kill Eileen so I just carried on screaming.' I paused to complete the writing. 'Eileen was struggling which meant that she was still alive so I started shouting as well.' Another pause. 'I think I shouted 'help'.'

'Margaret was trying to kill Eileen,' said Dickson slowly. 'How did you know?'

'Because Margaret wanted to kill someone but I wasn't sure until tonight whether it was me or Eileen.'

'Don't write that down,' bellowed Dickson. She looked at me severely.

'Because she was suffocating Eileen with her pillow and Eileen was trying to push her off but she couldn't and Margaret wouldn't stop until she was sure that Eileen was dead so I had to carry on screaming. Shall I write that down?'

'Yes,' snapped Dickson.

There was a pause while I wrote it down. Dickson got up and looked over my shoulder presumably to check that I'd written down more or less the same things that I'd said. She grunted to imply that she was satisfied.

'You didn't try and intervene?'

I looked at Dickson anxiously. It had never occurred to me to intervene. I looked uncertainly at Dickson and shook my head.

'Write down my question and 'no',' she instructed me.

I still looked anxious and started to get a bit panicky.

'No one expects you to have done anything,' Dickson said wearily. 'This certainly wasn't your fault – no for God's sake, girl, don't write any more down. But,' she stopped and turned to the other warders, 'you'd all better go and do your rounds, better be extra vigilant the rest of the night and someone had better relieve whoever's still on duty with Margaret.'

'She's been sedated,' said one of the warders.

'Yes, I know, but she'll still have to be watched. Catherine can stay here for now.'

The other warders left and I gave the pad with my few notes on it to Dickson.

'Eileen is dead then,' I said quietly.

'Yes, she's dead right enough. But she must have put up a fight.'

I looked a bit queasy so Dickson stopped bringing to mind the graphic details of Eileen's suffocation.

'How did you know?' Dickson said, 'how did you know that Margaret was dangerous?'

'I wasn't sure at first whether she was dangerous, but I did think that she was mad, sort of unhinged. I didn't know she was dangerous, or at least I didn't know for sure until I checked with Dot today.'

'Bloody hell, I hope that Dot doesn't have anything to do with this,' exclaimed Dickson.

'No of course not. Margaret wasn't interested in Dot. Margaret was just interested in Eileen and me. So you see it could have been either one of us although I should have realised that it was always going to be Eileen. After all, she'd already tried to kill Eileen once before.'

'Now, steady on there Kate, are you telling me that Margaret has tried to murder someone in a shared cell before?'

'Yes.'

'Then why didn't anyone know?'

'Eileen said it was me and Big Bertha said it wasn't anyone and Margaret had already packed as she was being released the next day so I suppose everyone thought it was best not to enquire further,' I paused to take a breath.

'So how did you know that Margaret had tried to kill Eileen?'

'Bertha and I both knew. She was prowling about.'

'Who was prowling about?'

'Margaret.'

Dickson thought about this for a while.

'But there's no actual evidence that Margaret has attempted anything like this before in prison?'

'No.'

'Well, it might be best to leave it that way. Did you try to tell anyone else?'

'I tried to tell Jeanette. At least I tried to tell Jeanette that Margaret was mentally unstable and needed a pill.'

'Did you indeed,' Dickson almost looked impressed (for Dickson).

'But she didn't listen.'

'No we're not very good at listening in here, it goes with the job,' said Dickson sardonically, 'but as most of you are thieves and liars it isn't very surprising.'

'I'm not,' I began.

'Yes, I know you're not,' Dickson said crossly, 'that's why you're here and not just banged up in another cell for the night.

I looked at Dickson wonderingly, but decided not to say anything, not even to think anything, just to bask in the moment of being both believed and listened to all at the same time.

Kate

I had my own room (it was still a cell with a barred window and all the rest of it, but everything's relative). I had a bed and the compulsory table and chair, but I also had a bookcase and a small bedside cabinet with a drawer and a cupboard. Jeanette said that if I could get hold of one it would also be okay to have a portable typewriter in my room so that I could practice. Jane was on the job. Dickson had also returned for good and hadn't just been a figment of my imagination like a guardian angel on the night that Eileen died. I don't know what happened to Margaret. I didn't ask anyone but I did have to give evidence at a private inquest in the prison. I was only present for my bits though so I don't know what else went on. When Dot talked about Margaret I made sure that I was out of earshot. And Dot talked a lot about Margaret.

I'd made a point of telling Dot about Eileen and most of the whole business (being canny enough to leave out the bits that might look like fraternising with the enemy on my part). I'd decided that it was wise to make sure that it looked as though Dot was still in charge of all information that came into and went out of the prison and as a result of quietly empowering Dot with information I was allowed honorary membership of the cronies. This did not please Jeanette but then pleasing Jeanette had resulted in disaster. In any event, not pleasing her couldn't end up any worse.

Although having said that, a little bit of knowledge can be a dangerous thing and bolstered by such a large amount of insider information the empowerment went to Dot's head. Dot wanted to strike. Killings within prisons meant that conditions were bad and that the prison officials were incompetent and that the prisoners themselves didn't have to put up with this. So the prisoners would go on strike. Dot must come from a mining community, I thought inconsequentially.

'We stay in our cells all day and refuse to do anything,' announced Dot at breakfast about a week or so after Eileen's death. It was certainly after the inquest and after I'd been given my own cell.

The warders on duty looked nervously around at a room full of potential militants. I wanted to ask about food and what it was that we were all going to stop doing anyway.

Dot marched to the door of the canteen.

'Come on girls, if you're not with me you're against me.' (I'm not sure if she actually said that but she certainly meant that.)

We all stood up.

'Strike, strike,' Dot started dramatically and we all repeated after her: 'Strike, strike,' and marched through the corridors of the prison back to our cells.

I went back to my own little haven and was glad that I hadn't got the typewriter yet as I might have felt compelled to use it and practice my typing skills. But I did have Churchill's *History of the English Speaking Peoples* which Jane was borrowing from the library for me in instalments. They were rather long instalments as Jane didn't come that often now, what with the baby and things. She was going to end up paying a lot of library fines on the *History of the English Speaking Peoples*. I hoped Churchill was worth it.

I didn't get very far with Churchill because Dickson appeared.

'What's all this about then?' she asked aggressively, standing in the doorway to my cell.

'I don't know.'

'I'm not sure that I believe you,' said Dickson, which was disappointing after our last discussion.

'I don't know anything about strikes apart from the General Strike in 1926 because we studied that in history. However I don't think this is about wages, but it might be about conditions,' I said carefully.

'For God's sake, who do you all think you are?'

'I don't know, I haven't organised it,' which wasn't really an appropriate way to talk to a warder and Dickson seemed to be quite senior these days.

Dickson sat down on my chair.

'You'd better tell me all you know,' she said bitterly. 'This is about Margaret, isn't it?'

'It might be,' I said weakly. Dickson was putting me in a most uncomfortable position as Dot was bound to find out about this visit. I'd become one of those what do-you-call-ums that the police used. A snout? A grass? Surely Dickson must understand that I couldn't divulge anything that Dot might know about Margaret or even divulge anything that I might appear to know about Dot's motivations and plans for a strike.

'I think Dot's bored,' I said, figuring that unconscious motivations were exempt from grassing as long as I stayed clear of actual stated motivations. Anyway, Dickson could ask Dot herself the other stuff about conditions and such. I mean strike leaders aren't usually shy about publishing their demands, are they.

Dickson gave me her sharp look.

'I also think she's expecting, or at least hoping to be released in time for her daughter's twelfth birthday,' I continued.

'And what makes you think that?'

'She's knitting her a cardigan and she expects to be able to give it to her herself. It's quite a flashy modern looking thing…'

'Okay, Kate, spare me the details,' but Dickson was obviously coming up with a plan. 'If I was you I would go off to that typing course of yours.'

I looked at her helplessly.

'Well, suit yourself, but I'll have to punish the strikers.'

'But we're all striking,' I said dolefully.

'Not for long,' said Dickson and she stood up to go, looking decidedly pleased with herself. She'd obviously come up with something. Whatever it was I hoped fervently that Dot wouldn't trace it back to me.

Claire

Then one day Mum didn't get up and make dinner. I made tea at dinnertime but Mum didn't want any. She was a funny colour and looked very sad. I asked her if she was sad because of not having proper dinner but she just shook her head. Then I asked if she was sad because Sally hadn't come to take me to Whitcliff but she just shook her head again. Then I thought a very clever thing and I asked if she was sad because she was poorly and then Mum said yes she was sad because she was poorly and I said are you very very very poorly and Mum said yes again. And Mum looked so sad that I got into bed with her and cuddled up to her and put my head on her bosoms and I think that made her happy although she didn't seem to cuddle me very tightly. Then Mum said Claire and I said Yes Mum, Claire can you use the telephone and I said Jim's telephone a bit anxiously and Mum said yes the telephone downstairs and I said no not really because I didn't want to use Jim's telephone. Then I thought that Mum sort of sighed and she said then you'll have to go and ask Mrs Hunter for help but I said I didn't need help and that I could make ham sandwiches for tea as well. Mum carried on cuddling me and she said Claire you will have to go and see Mrs Hunter and ask her to come here to help me and she emphasised the help me bit so that I would understand that it was to help Mum and not to help Claire. Please Claire, it is very important that you do this for me Mum said. She has to come and help you I said and Mum said yes, not me I said and Mum said yes again. And then I did a very brave thing. I went out through the kitchen door and I walked down our drive bit then I walked down Mrs Hunter's drive bit and I knocked on Mrs Hunter's kitchen door. Mrs Hunter answered the door very quickly and she looked a bit shocked when she saw me and she said why Claire in her loud voice. I didn't want to look at her but I said very politely Mum says can you please come and help her but can you please come and not help Claire. Mrs Hunter got all agitated and fussed around finding her coat saying lots of things like I knew this would happen I told Margot that she couldn't go on like this.

    Mrs Hunter bustled me out down her drive bit and up our drive bit and into our kitchen then she bustled upstairs. I followed because I didn't really know what else to do. Mrs Hunter then said loud things to Mum and I wanted to say shut up but I didn't. Then I wanted to hit her but I didn't. Then she ran downstairs very noisily and picked up Jim's telephone. On the telephone she said she wanted an ambulance. It was like last time and I suddenly felt frightened and angry so I ran upstairs and shut myself in my bedroom.

I read my magazine and heard lots of noisy things. Then there were lots of noisy men as well as Mrs Hunter. Then I looked out of my window and saw the Ambulance but I couldn't see Mum. There was just the stretcher thing being put into the back of the ambulance and Mrs Hunter bustling around being noisy.

A long time later Mrs Cartwright came. She sat quietly on my bed and put her arms around me and said poor Claire but you're a good girl you'll be a good brave girl won't you and I said yes I would be a good brave girl because I thought that I had been very brave and good getting Mrs Hunter.

I had to be on my own again but it was alright. Sally came the next day. I asked if she was taking me to Whitcliff in a puzzled sort of voice because it was a Wednesday. She said no she wasn't taking me to Whitcliff and I said is that because it was Wednesday and she said no it was because she was taking me to the hospital to see Mum and I said you mean the Clinic that is a hospital and Sally looked a bit puzzled but she still said yes. When I saw Mum in the Clinic that is called a hospital there was a woman in a uniform like on the telly and she was called a nurse. She was very nice to me and she was very nice to Mum and gave Mum lots of pillows so that Mum could sit up. Mum smiled at me a lot and the nice nurse gave me some orange squash and 2 biscuits. Sally didn't stay and talk to Mum but she said that she would be back soon to take Claire home and Mum said is Claire managing in a worried sort of voice and Sally said yes she's managing very well and then Mum smiled again. I held Mum's hand and smiled back at Mum.

Kate

'We went on strike a couple of weeks ago,' I said to Jane.

'Gosh, there's nearly a pound to pay on this book,' said Jane. She was examining the third volume of the *History of the English Speaking Peoples* and trying to work out the library charges.

'It was because of Margaret, I think. At least that was how it started but it was just an excuse.'

Jane was still doing her library fine calculations. I chatted on.

'I hope Alan and Sean are alright, it's a bit cold out there.'

And as I still hadn't got Jane's attention I continued, 'Do you want me to send the books back to you in the post when I've finished them? It's silly to pay charges – especially for Churchill.'

'You went on strike?'

'Yes,' I tried to make it sound exciting.

'Like the miners? And everyone else for that matter. Alan's never going to vote Labour again.'

'Oh?' I thought that middle management never voted Labour anyway. 'I've never voted for anyone,' I said.

'Haven't you? Why not?'

I looked at Jane with a resignation worthy of Dickson.

'What does that mean? You can't vote in here?'

'Nope.'

'Well, how was I to know that?'

'What's the matter Jane?'

She relaxed a bit.

'I want to send Sean into pre-school and start working again.'

'So?'

'And Alan wants to have another baby.'

'Oh, I see,' although I probably didn't see at all, jobs and babies and pre-schools were all incredible luxuries from where I was sitting. 'Don't you want another baby?'

'Yes, I suppose so, but not yet. I don't want life to only be about babies, it's like being in a ...' she just stopped herself.

Jane rebelling? I felt quite pleased and almost included in this new phase of Jane's life.

'So you're on strike too,' I stated happily.

Jane looked startled, then grinned.

'I hadn't thought of it like that. I'd better be careful or Alan won't vote for me either,' she laughed. 'Er, I don't mean to be rude or insensitive, but what can you strike about in here?'

'Oh you know, the usual things, conditions, free-time, rules, wages.'

'You're having me on.'

'No, we did go on strike, but it only lasted half a day.'

'What did you do?'

'Stayed in my room and read the *History of the English Speaking Peoples*.'

It didn't sound much like a strike.

'I usually go to my typing course,' I said, trying to explain the huge break with normal routine. But Jane wasn't listening. She obviously had something else to talk about.

'Your Mum's in hospital again,' she said suddenly.

'But it's not four o'clock yet,' I said unthinkingly, which even sounded ridiculous to me, but the tradition of Jane talking about Mum and Claire just before the visitors' bell went was ingrained in my heart. 'Oh,' I added quickly, hoping she hadn't heard me.

'It's not good, Kate,' she said.

'Oh,' I said again.

Jane took a brave breath.

'She's dying of cancer, Kate,' she said.

There were lots of questions I should have asked at this point. For example, my obligatory one about Claire. I wished that Jane had waited until her usual five minutes before the bell. Now there was too much time to have to do something and to have to say something. The minutes crawled by.

'I thought you should know,' Jane said, trying to fill in the gap. 'She's in the new hospital.'

'New hospital?'

'Yes, it just opened earlier this year.'

'Oh, so what happened to the old city hospital and the county one?'

'I don't know. There's just the new one now, of course.'

Of course.

'It's really nice.'

A hospital, like a prison, could never be really nice.

'Where is it?' I asked, not wanting to think about Mum.

'On the Wiggington Road,' said Jane.

'Oh, just by Rowntrees?'

'Yes, but not so far down.'

I'd equivocated long enough and Mum wasn't really that far from my thoughts. I tried to rally some rational response.

'How long?' I managed to say.

For a moment Jane paused.

'Not long,' she said quietly. 'She stayed at home as long as possible because of Claire.'

'So she's known for some time?'

'Yes, I suppose so, but she never said anything. The first we knew was that she was going into hospital.'

'So Claire's on her own?'

'Yes.'

I didn't ask if she was okay.

'Does she understand about Mum?'

'Oh, I don't know, she must do.'

'Has Mum…' but I didn't finish the sentence because the bell went and I hurried off to my room as quickly as I could. Has Mum asked about me, was what I'd wanted to ask Jane, but then again I hadn't really wanted to hear her answer.

Kate

'You've got parole to visit your mother,' said Dickson.

'It doesn't matter, because I'm not going to visit her anyway,' I said.

'Were you this difficult when you were a child?' Dickson said.

'Yes,' I said. I was glad I wasn't having this conversation with Jeanette (now tell me Kate, why do you feel like that? Have you thought about how your mother might feel?). Dickson was much tougher than Jeanette. Like an old boot in fact.

'I'm not going because,' I said.

'I'll give you the rest of the day to think about it and when I come to collect you tomorrow you'll say, 'yes of course Mrs Dickson' and you'll be all ready and waiting with teeth brushed and hair washed.'

'Give me one good reason.'

'You mean apart from the fact that you have to do what I tell you to do anyway?'

'No, perhaps not.'

'And all the obvious ones about your mother dying?'

'Certainly not those.'

'Then how about your first day outside prison in ten years or thereabouts?' At which point Dickson left the room.

'Are you coming with me?' I asked, but Dickson was out of earshot and anyway making too much noise to hear anything as she stomped down the prison corridor away from my room.

My room wasn't canary yellow but there were elements of full circle or déjà vu about being on my own again. Sometimes I thought that the tape would be re-wound and we would all start from some point at the beginning again. Preferably at the point where I bought an iced bun and didn't catch the bus home but went back into school to meet Jane after her exam instead. At a point before Jim died whenever that point had been. Or even after that, mightn't there have been a point during the trial when I could have been found innocent and not guilty?

The illusion that time had stood still wasn't entirely unpleasant. If ten years hadn't passed then none of this would ever really matter would it? I would still be eighteen and still have the same future ahead of me however long the present kept rolling along. *I'm sitting on top of the world, just rolling along just rolling along* – where on earth had that popped up from? Sometimes I had very bad control over my thoughts. Wasn't it from a song or something? I hoped to goodness that it wasn't anything that Jim used to like. Imagine having any part of one's thoughts – especially the unconscious parts of one's thoughts – influenced by Jim. No, I wasn't going to see Mum. It would look like I'd forgiven her.

The other illusion was that suddenly things were changing, moving. People had gone or moved on – Bertha, Eileen, Margaret and now even Dot had been released. This certainly was an illusion as lack of change was the one constant in my life, hour after day after month after year. I was the old timer. A dingy mousy old woman who no one really bothered with anymore. I was part of the fabric of the place, unchanging and unchanged.

I'd completed the typing course and could type at fifty words a minute, punctuate and layout a business letter and do simple accounting. Perhaps the prison authorities would employ me as a secretary and I could become their most faithful employee instead of their oldest prisoner. (I'm sure I wasn't really the oldest prisoner or more accurately the longest serving prisoner but whether I was or not didn't really matter.)

I'm going to die in here, I thought. Which wasn't a very reassuring thought, the kind of thought in fact that got one into trouble with Jeanette. We're all going to die anyway, I countered belligerently, which was neither helpful nor original.

'I can't go because if Claire's there it might upset her,' I said out loud to Dickson who of course wasn't there to hear me. And why should it upset Claire? Claire probably wouldn't know who I was anyway. Would my mother know who I was? And who'd applied for this parole? I certainly hadn't. My mother? How could she apply for parole for me, dying as she was in hospital? Indeed, had she even asked to see me at all? That was the question I should have asked Dickson. Has my mother asked to see me and does she know that I might be visiting her? And why would she suddenly want to see me now after all these years? Is that what happened when you knew you were dying, you suddenly wanted to see people again? I didn't remember wanting to see my mother when I thought that I was dying – or at least thought that Margaret was killing me or had been about to kill me when she'd finished with Eileen. My experience of dying was that there wasn't time to think about niceties like seeing people. When you thought you might be dying you screamed as long and loud as possible just in case someone could stop you from dying. Which in my case they had. Damn it, did I want a day out? Did I want a day out possibly in the company of Dickson? I certainly didn't want a day out to see my mother, dying or not.

Kate

The duty warder collected me after breakfast the next morning. We went through a lot of locked doors. It was a bit like coming up from a submarine as one began, tentatively, to feel one could breathe real oxygen again. The warder locked the sixth door behind us and ushered me into a room with a table and chair. On the table was my school skirt, the blouse with rosebuds on it, the purple cardigan that Big Bertha had helped me to knit (someone must have gone into my room to find that) and a new pair of stockings. I knew they were new because they were still in the pack. But they weren't stockings, they were rather ugly flesh coloured tights. I grappled with the tights and decided I was happy that stockings were a thing of the past. I felt very modern until I put my school skirt on. It was too short but still showed a tendency to twist around my waist.

'I must have grown,' I exclaimed to no one in particular although the duty warder was still in attendance.

Dickson came in just as I was pulling my arms into the endless sleeves of the purple cardigan.

'Bloody hell, I thought you'd look better in civvies,' she said.

I'd been feeling almost chipper until then.

'I said I wasn't going,' I said miserably.

'Well, it's already decided that you are,' said Dickson.

'Do I have to?'

'Yes, all arranged, you're coming with me.'

So Dickson was going with me. That was a good thing, wasn't it?.

The Duty warder looked on askance at this conversation. Perhaps she didn't know that Dickson and I went back a long way. My shoes were too big with just the tights so I put my prison socks on over the tights and fiddled with my shoes while Dickson disappeared. She came back with two coats over her arm. One of them apparently was for me.

'Come on then,' she said, 'or we'll miss the train.'

I followed Dickson out. It was that easy. We just walked out of a few doors and someone even waved at us as we strode by the front entrance and headed to the side of the building. There was a big wall behind us and a car park in front of us and an ordinary street with cars rushing by. I stared at the cars. They were all square and squat and there seemed to be so many of them.

'Is this where Alan has to walk with Sean when Jane visits me?' I said. 'It's not very nice is it?'

Dickson wasn't listening; she was opening one of the cars. She got in the driver's seat and suddenly there I was standing all on my own with the whole free world around me. Dickson opened the passenger door from inside the car.

'Come on, Kate, in you get,' she said as she twisted her neck around to see where I was.

I climbed into the car and pulled the door closed with an enormous crash.

'Bloody hell, don't pull the bloody door off will you.'

'It's a funny car,' I said as if I was an expert. I'd been in more prison vans than I'd been in cars.

'What do you mean, it's a funny car?' said Dickson as she started the engine and drove off out of the car park at great speed.

'Well, it's different.'

'Different,' scoffed Dickson, 'it's about the most ordinary car you can buy – and the cheapest. It's the successor to the mini,' she continued as she drove into a long line of cars waiting at some traffic lights.

'The mini,' I said disbelievingly, 'but the mini…'

Dickson applied the accelerator and we roared through the lights just as they were changing back to red.

I held on to my seat.

'Are we driving to York?' I asked.

'No, we're taking the train. The authorities thought I'd have more control over you on a train,' Dickson said wryly.

'Why?'

'Bloody hell child, you don't give up do you? Because on a train I have two free hands to contain you if you get difficult and I can even apply handcuffs if necessary whereas in a car I have to use both hands to drive. Have you got the picture now?' she finished sarcastically.

I sat meekly in the passenger seat next to her and nodded my head.

'Have you got handcuffs with you?' I asked.

'No,' said Dickson with a glint in her eye.

'There's not much point me trying to escape anyway, is there,' I said.

'No, not really.'

A big sign said National Rail and we swung into another car park. There were so many cars everywhere. We drove up lines and lines of cars until Dickson started fiddling and manoeuvring into a narrow space between two cars. She then applied the handbrake, pulled the keys out of the lock and got out of the car. While she rummaged in the back of the car for her bag and the coats I climbed out of the passenger seat.

'*What brave new world is this?*' I said under my breath, muddling my Shakespeare as I breathed in the damp fumy air of Wakefield station.

Dickson pushed one of the coats into my arms and I followed her at a fast trot towards the main station entrance and the ticket office.

'Two day returns to York,' she said.

I was still getting over the shock of how much the tickets cost when Dickson marched me to the platform just in time to board the next train going to York.

Dickson barged her way to a window seat and I sat down opposite her. I was on my own again, no restraining arms, handcuffs, bars, grills, locks. Dickson rummaged in her bag and brought out a flask and two cups.

'Want some coffee?' she said.

At this point in the journey I think I experienced happiness, although it was such a strange emotion that I could have just felt confused. But what I was quite sure of was that whatever happened next it would be worth it just to be sitting here for this moment in time watching that *brave new world* whiz by outside. A *brave new world* that I was a fleeting part of.

'Okay,' I said to Dickson.

Kate

When we arrived at York Dickson insisted that I put the coat on. Amazingly, it fitted. Dickson grunted in satisfaction.

'Shelly lent us it,' she said.

I didn't have a clue who Shelly was but the coat was a huge improvement on the rest of my get-up – and it could have been a lot worse and still been an improvement.

Dickson marched us out to the station forecourt then paused uncertainly. She looked a bit cross.

'The new hospital's on the Wigginton Road,' I said. 'I don't know exactly where, of course, so it could take half an hour to walk there.'

Dickson still looked a bit cross.

'We could probably catch a number 10 or 11 bus and get off at...'

'Okay, okay, miss know it all. Where do we get these buses from then?'

'Just here,' I said pointing up at a bus stop sign which said (amongst other things) numbers 10 and 11.

'And how do we know that these buses still go where you think they go – it's a long time since you were last here.' said Dickson.

I thought that was a bit below the belt.

'Because here's a number 10 and it says Wigginton on it,' I said politely.

We launched on to the bus. Dickson bought two tickets and suddenly grinned.

'Bloody hell,' she said.

I smiled nervously and found I was chewing my lip. I hadn't chewed my lip for nearly ten years. I was sitting by the window with Dickson next to me. It would have been less nerve-racking to look at Dickson or examine the inside of the bus which eerily or reassuringly – I wasn't sure which – hadn't changed in ten years. But my eyes strayed to view my old stamping grounds. York city centre. It must have been spring because the banks below the city walls were covered in daffodils. There were a lot of people about. Tourists? There were a couple of groups that could only have been tourists and other people loitering around with cameras.

I pressed my cheek against the bus window as we went over Lendal Bridge, drinking in the familiarity of the Minster. Again I noticed how many more cars there were. We turned into Saint Leonard's Place and there was the new Theatre Royal looking rather drab. Tourists were gathering by Bootham Bar and the bus swung into Gillygate, which looked as disreputable as ever. The bus was rattling along and my original euphoria at being free was slipping away. A train journey and a bus journey, that was all.

When we got to the junction with Wigginton Road and Clarence Street I noticed a signpost saying 'Hospital' and I indicated to Dickson that we should get off at the next bus stop. And there we were crossing the road and heading in the direction of the new hospital.

Everything was happening far too quickly. But I wasn't a donkey; I couldn't just dig my heels in and refuse to move, I just had to keep trotting on after Dickson. I must have been dragging my feet and slowing down though because Dickson stopped and turned around, irritated.

'Get a move on, for goodness sake. And don't walk three yards behind me. It makes me nervous,' she snapped.

My mouth felt dry.

'I didn't want to come,' I said pathetically.

'I thought you enjoyed the train ride,' said Dickson.

'Yes, but that was then,' I said childishly.

Dickson stopped so that I had to catch up with her. She looked at me sternly but she didn't say anything. I wondered if I'd have felt better if she had had the handcuffs with her. As things were now there was too strong an element of free will in the whole enterprise. I mean, it looked as though I was choosing to go and see my mother. And of course that's what I should have done, I should have chosen to make this visit and not just be here because Dickson said I had to be and had bullied me into it.

We had arrived at the reception desk of the gleamingly new hospital and Dickson was making enquiries about where we should go.

'I really don't think...' I was trying to say as Dickson set off down a long corridor. A long, pale, quiet corridor without locks at every junction.

'At least tell me one thing, Dickson,' I said desperately.

Dickson paused.

'Well, what then?'

'Has my mother actually asked to see me?'

Dickson remained still for a split second, then carried on marching down the lock free corridor and I just had to wash along in her wake.

'How should I know?' she said. 'We just got notification from the hospital and I applied for a visit on your behalf on compassionate grounds. Most prisoners would kill for a day out like this, even if it was with me.'

'So this was more about me having a day out than about visiting my dying mother?'

'Bloody hell child, what a way to put it,' said Dickson.

I continued to follow Dickson sullenly or nervously, I wasn't sure which, until we turned into a quiet ward. A window was slightly open and the curtain drifted gently on a light breeze. A nurse who was arranging some tulips in a vase turned to face us with a friendly smile.

'Can I help you?' she said.

'We've come to see Mrs Margot Brown,' said Dickson.

'Ah, yes, of course, this'll be Margot's younger daughter,' she said looking at me. Her smile looked uncertain. Her breezy nursing confidence was deteriorating into an anxious insecurity.

'Older daughter,' I said.

'Yes, please come this way,' she carried on. She was decidedly flustered as well as uncertain and nervous.

My reputation goes before me, I thought bitterly. Dickson suddenly looked every inch the prison warder and my clothes something fished out of the ragbag, which in fact they were. It wasn't right, it wasn't me who should suddenly feel ashamed, I thought, and I wanted to cry.

Mum was in a side ward on her own. She was sleeping. She was grey. Her hair, face and skin were all grey and she had lines of pain engrained into her skin.

'Don't wake her,' I said and sat with a dump onto the nearest chair. The tears were running through the fingers I'd put up to my face to try and hide them and I sobbed quietly while Dickson pulled up another chair and sat next to me.

Kate

'Kate.' It was Mum's voice. She must have woken up.

She was holding out her hand to me. If this was meant to be some bedside reconciliation scene then I wasn't quite up to it. I stood up and went over to her but I didn't put out my hand.

Mum was smiling.

'You haven't changed a bit,' she said.

I didn't say anything.

'You're not still angry are you?' she said. 'You were always so angry about everything.'

'I'm not angry,' I said stiffly.

'I know I should have, well I shouldn't have let things happen the way they did, but I didn't have any choice.' She held out her hand to me again. 'Come, Kate, you'll be alright, you've always been the strong one.'

I did take her hand. It was thin, like paper.

'How's Claire?' I asked unable to help myself.

Mum smiled again.

'She's alright. I think she'll be alright,' said Mum. 'She'll have the house and there's a bit of money saved up. In fact I think there's a young man interested as well.'

'A young man,' I exclaimed, sounding more alarmed than surprised.

'And why shouldn't there be?' said Mum proudly. 'Claire's really come on a lot you know, since you last saw her.'

'Since I last saw her,' I exclaimed loudly and indignantly. I took a deep breath. 'Does she, does Claire ask about me?' I said more quietly.

Mum carefully didn't look at me.

'She thinks you've gone,' she said with a hint of embarrassment.

'Bloody hell. Gone. You mean like Jim? Claire thinks I'm dead? Mum, how could you,' I think I was shouting.

A spasm of pain flitted over Mum's face.

'We mustn't quarrel,' she said. 'Claire's alright. I just wanted to see that you were alright too.'

There should have been no answer to that but too many old wounds were being rubbed.

'Yes, Mum, I'm fine. I've just been in prison for ten years because your wretched husband decided to get himself killed,' I said loudly again, 'but perhaps everything's been so hunky-dory with me out of the way that you've forgotten what actually happened. You certainly seem to have forgotten me.'

Dickson coughed loudly and deliberately. And the nurse who was still hovering around looked disapproving as well as nervous. But I didn't care.

'Mum, what do you really believe actually happened on June 15th 1966?'

Mum remained silent and full of pain.

'I don't know,' she said, looking past my right ear.

'I'm sorry,' I mumbled. It wasn't fair to have to deal with all these untended wounds while Mum bravely tried to smile through her pain.

'I just need to know that you're okay, Kate, that it's been alright,' she repeated.

This was ridiculous. I started to back away from the bed.

'What is it you want, Mum? What are you trying to say?'

'I just want,' Mum said weakly.

'What do you want,' I was shouting. Dickson stepped forward before the nurse could. I took a breath. 'What do you want?' I repeated more quietly. 'To forgive me for killing Jim? Is that it? You think I killed Jim and now you want to forgive me because everything's worked out alright in the end anyway?'

'No, I know you didn't kill Jim,' Mum said calmly.

I stared at her.

'Then what then? Who did?' It was hard not to shout and at this point hysteria would have been a comfort.

'I don't know.' Mum looked confused, as though this conversation wasn't going where she had intended it to either. 'I just hoped that you would forgive me,' she said her voice drained and her eyes looking past me again. 'And,' she was making a huge effort now and the nurse had stepped forward, 'and that you would understand, Kate.'

'I really must insist,' the nurse was saying.

Mum had laid back on her pillows and shut her eyes.

'Is that it,' I said a little wildly.

'Margot just needs to rest,' said the nurse primly.

'Yes, that's it,' said Dickson. 'Come on let's go home.' I'm sure she said home although it's more likely that she said back, 'let's go back.'

I looked at Dickson, confused and bewildered as I was, and followed her blindly out of the ward. I think one of us must have knocked into the table where the tulips were on our way past because our exit from the ward was accompanied by a loud crash as of glass exploding into many splinters.

Claire

I went to see Mum for 7 days and she always asked Sally if I was managing and Sally always said yes. The last day when I went to see her the nice woman called a nurse looked cross and said we would have to wait a bit because someone had broken a glass vase with flowers in it all over the ward and it had made a big mess and could hurt someone because of all the glass. When she let us in to see Mum Mum was sort of asleep and only opened her eyes 3 times to look at me. But she did hold my hand and she did smile and I think she said you're a good girl Claire but it was a bit difficult to hear what she said.

We didn't go to see Mum at the Clinic called a hospital again. Sally just sat with me in my house and looked very serious. She said that a very sad thing had happened. She said that Mum had died in her sleep in the early hours of the morning. I think I said is that the same as Jim? Does that mean that Mum has gone? And I think that Sally cried. That is very very very sad I said. I went to my bedroom and it was very very very sad.

Lots of people came to see me and I got anxious and didn't like it. They kept saying that it was very sad and I kept saying very very very sad and then on Sunday Mike came. I made ham sandwiches and we watched telly. Mike didn't say it was very sad although he did look a bit sad because usually Mike only smiles. We sat on the sofa eating the ham sandwiches and Mike held my hand and it was nice. Then I put my head on his bosoms and that was nice too. Mike said I was nice and although I still felt very very very sad about Mum I also felt a little bit happy about Mike.

Kate

I didn't get to Mum's funeral. Armley prison had had a break out and all the prisoners were striking on the prison roof and as a result all prisons in the area were on high security alerts to prevent copycat action at other prisons. No one was allowed parole for anything.

So I hadn't killed Jim. At least that was Mum's assertion. But how could she be so sure? Unless she had killed him herself. But that was impossible, wasn't it? Perhaps I'd heard it wrong; I'd been so bloody confused. Perhaps she said I know you killed Jim, but it doesn't matter. And it was all over so quickly. There I was shouting at Mum as if I was still 18 and then suddenly I was on my way back to the prison again with Dickson.

Bloody hell.

It was easy to have that thing about bars and metal doors and keys and locks again. And all this extra security didn't help. I was locked in my cell for hours on end – as, I had to presume, were all the other in-mates. Even Margaret would have been better than this. But that wasn't quite true. I resigned myself to Churchill instead. At least Churchill wasn't a pathological smotherer. Churchill wrote rather well. I tried to bask in the words without really worrying about what they said but the bars on the window wouldn't go away. Neither would the conundrum of the bedside scene with Mum.

She must have asked for me to go and see her otherwise she'd have been surprised when we showed up. And she wasn't surprised. She almost seemed to have been expecting us. So that was one question answered. But she must have had a reason for that, requesting to see me. Unless that's what one did when one was dying. One thought about things and revisited the past and put everyone into their right places. One forgave people or if it was more appropriate one asked people for forgiveness – forgive us our trespasses as we forgive those and all that stuff was very relevant for a bedside death scene, but I felt that it was less relevant for ten years and counting of incarceration. At least that's how I saw it but I was never that switched on when it came to questions of theology. Perhaps a childhood deprived of The Church had left me unable to deal graciously with bedside dying scenes.

Added to which the calm dying and bedside thing wasn't entirely clear to me yet. In my world, people didn't die with time to ask for anything. They died when they weren't meant to die. I think. I presumed that Jim wasn't meant to die and therefore that I wasn't meant to go to prison. So what went wrong? Eileen wasn't meant to die. I was sure about that. That was an accident, or an incompetence or a failure in prison procedure, however one wanted to look at it. But it wasn't meant to happen and could so easily have been avoided. But could Jim's death have been easily avoided? In Eileen's case I knew who the murderer was and what the motivation was (if an unhinged mind and an obsession with the ability to kill can be called a motivation). But as it seemed no one knew who killed Jim then how could we work out the motivation and assess whether it was meant to happen. Of course if Mum was right and she had known who killed Jim, and just say for the sake of argument that it had been Mum herself then perhaps it had been meant to happen. Perhaps Mum had planned it all and got the insurance money and I was just an accident that got in the way. Was she apologising because I got in the way? And if I'd killed Jim was that meant to happen? Presumably not as I would certainly know if I'd premeditated it. I could at a pinch believe in a blackout that somehow included killing Jim but one that blanked out several days of planning as well was not possible. And by premeditated I don't mean wishing that Jim would fall off the face of the earth in general, I mean cold blooded pre-mediated murder, not just wishful thinking.

Churchill words slipped in and out of my mind without so much as a whisker of a thought giving them any attention. Having so much time to think was not good.

Mum seemed convinced that Claire was okay. Unless that was wishful thinking too. There might be a lot of wishful thinking about the living if one was dying and unable to do anything about the living any more. Of course Mum wanted to believe that everything was fine with Claire. She'd even convinced herself that things were positively rosy in the home that Claire had now presumably inherited in its entirety from Mum. I didn't need a home, did I? Her Majesty was providing me with a home, food, clean sheets, clothes and even an education. That Claire had a boyfriend I doubted. Claire didn't cope with other people. It had been okay with a few people that she knew, people who were predictable (and I supposed Jim had to come into that category, however reluctant I was to admit it). But Claire didn't like having strangers around. Unless that had changed too. Claire seemed to have changed in so many other ways that there was no reason why she shouldn't have changed in this way as well. I would have to ask Jane. Does Claire have a boyfriend? Although a young man who is showing an interest is a long way away from having a boyfriend. And what kind of freak would go for Claire? Whoops, there I was again making assumptions about Claire based on the handicapped teenager I'd left behind – and at this point I made myself remind myself – ten years ago.

With a huge effort of will I surveyed the barred window calmly for several minutes, then went back to Churchill.

Claire

Linda was in the drive talking loudly to Mrs Hunter and Mrs Hunter was talking very loudly to Linda. They kept pointing at my house and I thought that they kept pointing at me. I got very cross and I got so cross that I went outside through the kitchen door but I didn't like the shouting. They kept saying Jim and I didn't like them saying Jim. Mum had said that no one should say Jim's name. I put my hands over my ears and I said very loudly I don't like it then I went inside and into the back room. I shut the door and put the radio on very loudly.

Kate

Jane was wearing a navy suit with neat black court shoes and a navy striped shirt with turned up collar. Her hair was cut short and styled away from her face. She must have gone back to work.

'You're looking pleased with yourself,' I said. 'You've gone back to work, haven't you?'

'Yep.'

'What about Sean?'

'Oh, he does pre-school every morning and Mum looks after him in the afternoons.'

'Oh.' It all sounded very convenient.

'So I've got my old job back with Yorkshire Life.'

I thought of asking if it was worth it but decided not to.

'You didn't go to the funeral,' said Jane.

Was that a criticism?

'There was a high security alert here which meant that no one was allowed anywhere because of all that business at Armley.'

'Oh, I see.' Jane looked relieved.

'Didn't Alan and Sean want to come in?' I said wanting to change the subject. I didn't want to hear all the gory details of Mum's funeral.

'No, I came on my own.'

'Where's Sean?'

'With my Mum.'

'He's spending a lot of time with your Mum, isn't he?' Now I sounded critical.

'Alan's gone to the football match,' said Jane as if that explained it. 'Anyway,' she leant over the table, 'I thought it best to come on my own.'

'You don't usually,' I said.

'Yes, but there's been things happening since the funeral.'

'Bloody hell, what sort of things?' I couldn't imagine Mum coming back to haunt anyone unless it was me and I hadn't seen any sign of her.

'Kate, are you taking me seriously?'

'Not really.'

Jane sat back in her chair exasperated.

'But I haven't even told you anything yet.'

'Bloody hell, just tell me then.'

'And why do you keep saying bloody hell?'

'Do I?'

'Yes, but never mind. Everyone's suddenly started talking. After your Mum died all sorts of rumours started flying around.'

I looked blank.

'About Jim,' exclaimed Jane.

'About Jim?' I felt suddenly annoyed. 'Why drag all that up now? It's bad enough Mum dying without having to re-live the whole killing of Jim thing all over again.'

'No, it's not about you, Kate, I think everyone's forgotten about you.'

'Well, that's very comforting, I'm sure.'

'Kate, don't keep interrupting.'

I looked at Jane silently, waiting and sulking.

'There are rumours about Jim and goings-on.'

I kept silent.

'Affairs and things.'

'Affairs?'

'Yes. All the time apparently. Three women in York and two in Doncaster – isn't that where he used to travel to with his job?'

'Bloo…but how does anyone know? And why does anyone care now?'

'Well, don't you see, Kate, it makes him look bad and,' she leant back towards me, 'it gives lots of other people a motive for murdering him.'

'How come?'

'Don't be obtuse, Kate.'

'I'm not. Why would Jim having a few affairs here and there – and the number is probably exaggerated – give us any clue as to who murdered him?' I decided not to confuse the discussion by mentioning Mum's statement that she knew. At least she knew that I didn't kill him, which of course didn't necessarily mean that she knew who did kill him. 'It does give Mum more of a motive though, doesn't it,' I said quietly.

'Exactly.'

'But Mum had an alibi.'

'But perhaps one of these other women don't have alibis.'

'How is anyone going to remember what they were doing on 15th June 1966?'

'I'd remember what I'd been doing if I'd been murdering someone.' Jane's logic was getting as good as mine. Perhaps going back to work had been good for her. At least, good for her brain.

'Okay, smarty, what's your theory then?'

'I don't have one,' said Jane disappointingly.

'So all these rumours don't amount to anything more than malicious gossip which is having a field day because Mum is not there to give the lie to it or to make people feel embarrassed enough to tone it down. After all no one was going to malign her beloved Jim while she was still alive, were they?'

'There's no smoke without fire,' said Jane weakly, and not wanting to be so easily put off she continued, 'but it does make people feel better.'

'Bloody hell.'

Jane looked at me reproachfully.

'Sorry.'

'I mean it makes people feel better towards you, and not think such bad things because if Jim was bad then it makes you less bad.'

'So now that everyone else thinks that he was a bastard and not just me it's okay to kill him?'

'Kate, why are you being so difficult?'

'I'm not being difficult. I just don't see what difference this makes.'

'It means that if you come out people won't think such bad things about you,' said Jane in exasperation.

'But I'm not coming out, am I?'

'No, but I've never ever given up the hope that you will do one day, and one day sooner rather than later.'

And I'd never ever had that hope from the moment I was incarcerated in that cell with Big Bertha and Margaret and at some dim distant point in time Eileen as well. I looked at Jane astounded.

'Have you really believed that all this time?'

'Of course, what else can you believe when your best friend is put in prison? It just can't be forever, can it?'

'Unless I did murder Jim in cold blood.'

'Bloody hell,' said Jane with a broad grin, 'don't start that again, Kate.'

Claire

Linda came on Mondays and Wednesdays and Fridays and Sally came on Tuesdays and Thursdays and took me to Whitcliff and Mike came on Sundays. I liked Linda. I wrote a list of shopping things and then Linda bought them.

Claires List

bread in the blue bag.
ham.
orang squash.
crisp.
biscuits.
blue pengins.
mangerin.
By Claire

Kate

Jane's prescience was unnerving. About a month later Dickson came wandering into my cell pretending to want a friendly chat.

'How are you getting on, Kate?' she began.

'Okay.'

'I'm sorry you missed your mother's funeral. I think that in other circumstances you would have got a further parole to go.'

'It doesn't matter,' I said. 'I'm not sure that I'd have wanted to go. Having an excuse made it easier.'

Dickson didn't say anything.

'Your behaviour throughout your time in prison has been what a Parole Board would call exemplary.' This didn't quite sound like Dickson.

'Has it?' I said, not quite liking posh Dickson talk.

'Bloody hell, Kate, don't play smart with me.'

'I've just kept out of trouble.'

'Successfully, is the point, despite teaming up with Dot for a while.'

'Perhaps Dot was a plant by the Parole Board to test prisoners' resolve.'

Dickson looked at me painfully.

'You have even been out for a trial day.'

'Was that visit to hospital a trial?' I asked appalled.

'I recorded it down as such, just in case.'

I looked at Dickson suspiciously.

'You managed well outside of prison. You found your way about and you behaved normally. Most prisoners don't, you know. It can be very difficult to readjust to life back in the world after such a long stay in prison.'

Normally! Bloody hell, what I remembered best were the hysterics, the paranoia, the shouting, the angst, the broken vase shattering all over the clinically quiet ward.

'You sound like Jeanette,' I said accusingly, although one thing was for sure Jeanette would never have complimented me (or insulted me) with the accolade of normal.

'Bloody hell, Kate, do you want us to help you or not?'

I wasn't sure.

'What do you mean?' I said.

'I'm recommending you to the Parole Board for early release.' Dickson wasn't quite looking me straight in the eye which meant there was a catch and she had no intention of telling me what the catch was. She was going to spring it on me at a point of no return.

I stared at her suspiciously.

'You have a good prison record. You will easily adjust to life as a law-abiding civilian. You have modern working skills so that you will find it easy to get work.' Was she reading this from a book?

'So I can be useful,' I said, 'even with a record?'

'Yes, of course it is easier without a record, but we'll send you off with a reference both for your skills and for your good conduct.' This definitely wasn't Dickson talk; it was more like Jeanette jargon.

'It can't be that easy.'

'Crying out loud, child, do you want it on a spoon?'

I was still suspicious but at least I'd provoked Dickson into sounding like Dickson again.

'And I will strongly recommend an application for early release.'

'This isn't just a ruse, is it?'

'Do you need more time to think?' demanded Dickson.

'No,' I said quickly. 'When, when is all this going to happen?'

'You're due to go before the Parole Board Thursday week.'

Dickson hovered around the cell for a bit then left abruptly. I had the worrying feeling that I'd disappointed her. Or more worrying still that she was debating with herself whether or not to tell me the thing she was keeping from me.

But how else was I supposed to react other than with paranoia and angst? There was I a 'lifer' suddenly being told that perhaps I wasn't a lifer after all. Was there to be no reference to Jim and my heinous crime? Or would that all come up at the Parole Board again? Would I have to admit it all to secure my release? Damn it, why hadn't I thought of all these questions while Dickson was still with me?

Bloody hell, though – that was it, wasn't it? That was the snag that Dickson hadn't managed to come straight with me about.

After all Dickson had also heard my mother say that she knew I hadn't killed Jim, and knowing that could she still expect me to perjure myself? On the other hand, Dickson was a pragmatist and getting out was getting out. Dickson wouldn't care two hoots about perjuring.

Could I, however, admit to murdering Jim? Could I admit to murdering Jim to secure my release? For money? For eternal youth? I liked to think not, but on the other hand the world was a *large price for a small vice* (and much good did an insistence on innocence do that other Catherine Howard). Especially as now, apparently, no one cared much for Jim anyway and the general consensus was no doubt that he had got his just deserts. I hated to find myself veering over to Jim's side in all of this, as it were sticking to the rights of it, sticking to the truth when no one else cared a bean. The truth! Well, that was an open ended philosophical thing wasn't it? And if I started going on like this at the Parole Board there was no way they'd accept Dickson's verdict that I was normal. Perhaps I'd be sent off to a secure psychiatric unit and meet up with Margaret again.

At which point in the flow of self-debate I decided that perjury along with purgatory was a sure winner. There was no way I intended to end up in hell with Margaret (sic. a secure psychiatric unit) or in heaven or the land of the righteous with Jim (sic. stay in prison on a point of principle). No, all things considered I might even be prepared to behave with Jeanette, and going along with Jeanette certainly would be a perjury of the soul.

Claire

Linda stayed and watched telly with me today. We watched Blue Peter and I made a ham sandwich. Linda didn't want a ham sandwich but she did have a cup of tea. There wasn't any milk so I had to put milk on my shopping list and Linda said I should put cornflakes on it as well but I don't like cornflakes. I thought that I would ask Mike if he likes cornflakes. Then Linda said that I should put baked beans on the list. I like baked beans.

Linda said I had to have a new telly because there was a bad bit in it and the picture went all wibbly. Linda said I would have to ask Sally about the telly but I said I didn't want to ask Sally so Linda said that she would ask Sally.

Kate

Jeanette had the task of preparing me for the Parole Board and the world beyond. Given a choice I'd much preferred to have gone through the hoops with Dickson. (Bloody hell, child, pull your socks up and get on with it, end of interview – but life wasn't meant to be that simple, was it?)

'Well, Kate, the P.P.O. is really sticking her neck out for you isn't she?'

The P.P.O.?

'Personally I think that you should have had more time.'

Jeanette really knew how to encourage someone. And anyway, more time might just be more time to get into trouble.

'But I have to admit that you really tried hard with the typing course.'

I was by far the best student – even though that wasn't saying much.

'And you have responded exceptionally well to having a room on your own. Prisoners can often find that very hard, especially after sharing with the same women for many years.'

'It wasn't hard,' I piped up.

How ridiculous to find it hard not to have to share with Eileen and Margaret; really, sometimes – if not usually – Jeanette just didn't get it.

'It is a very important step when we first consider a prisoner for release.'

I dwelt on the word release. It was starting to sound good.

'Especially in cases like yours where the prisoner will have to live in the wider community on her own. Have you thought about this, Kate?'

'Yes, no, I'm not sure what you mean.'

'I mean you don't have family, so if you are granted early release you will have to live on your own.'

I had Claire.

'Oh, I see,' I said.

'Have you thought about where you want to live?'

'No, not really.'

'You do have to make plans you know, Kate.'

'What if I don't get early release,' I said.

'Now, you mustn't think like that, Kate.'

'Well, I'd go back and live in York, wouldn't I? I don't know any other towns.'

'Okay, that's a good start. Have you thought about the implications of this?'

'No.'

Jeanette looked at me carefully.

'You are aware that people may remember what happened and you may have to deal with unpleasantness if anyone does.'

'No one remembers,' which wasn't quite true, but I was fairly confident that no one would remember me. I decided not to explain to Jeanette that no one cared about Jim any more, that in fact Jim had become the two-timing villain of the piece. 'I could live on the other side of town just to be on the safe side,' I said.

'Good,' said Jeanette, 'it is so much more constructive when you think positively, Kate. I'll look for some suitable housing for you away from your original home address,' Jeanette continued.

'Okay,' I said, deciding to go along with the co-operation theme. Sometimes it was worth staying on the right side of Jeanette.

'And then there's the question of a job,' continued Jeanette.

'Well, I can type and stuff, can't I,' I said.

'Good, Kate,' repeated Jeanette.

This was almost as easy as being awkward, and almost as enjoyable. When praise has always been thin on the ground it's surprising how long a way just a little can go.

'Is it that easy?' I said.

Jeanette looked surprised.

'Of course it's not going to be easy,' she said.

I couldn't help but look disappointed.

'Your release is just a beginning and from there you must take little steps, Kate.'

Meaning?

'Do you still have that nice friend?'

Big Bertha? Dot?

'You mean Jane?' I said. 'Yes.'

'And do you think she'll be supportive?'

'Oh yes.'

'You sound very sure.'

'I am.'

'You must remember that Jane will have her own life now, Kate, and it may be difficult for you to be a part of it. You must be sensitive to that, Kate. It won't help if you get too dependent on Jane, you know, Kate.'

Bloody hell. I managed, with difficulty, to bear all this in silence.

'I will recommend that you are assigned a Parole Officer in York and she can also be a 'friend' for you.'

Jeanette had very deliberately put inverted commas around the word friend. But she needn't have bothered; the last thing I wanted was a 'friend' like Jeanette.

'What about money?' I asked.

'Very good, Kate,' said Jeanette, 'it really is most encouraging how well you are applying yourself to the whole idea of having to go out into the world again. Really, you seem to be getting the idea much more quickly than I had expected.'

Was she going to answer the question?

'Of course we hope that you'll get a job quite soon, and of course we'll assist you with that process in every way we can, but in the meantime you will get social security and a housing allowance to tide you over.'

No cash, no real money. 'Is that it, then?' I asked.

'What do you mean, is that it, then?'

'I mean, is there anything else we should discuss?'

Jeanette looked almost alarmed.

'Well, no I suppose not…'

'So I can go now then?'

'Well yes, but aren't there any questions you want to ask?'

Yes, but I wasn't sure I wanted to hear the answer. Will I have to admit to killing Jim? For starters. And how about… How likely was it that I was going to get early release? Because if after all this I didn't it was going to be unbearably disappointing.

June 1976
PAROLE

Claire

Mrs Cartwright came with some wool. It was red wool. She said that she thought I would like to knit a jumper for Sean. Sean is Jane's baby that smells bad. I was very polite and said thank you to Mrs Cartwright but I don't want to knit a red jumper for Sean I want to knit a blue jumper for Mike.

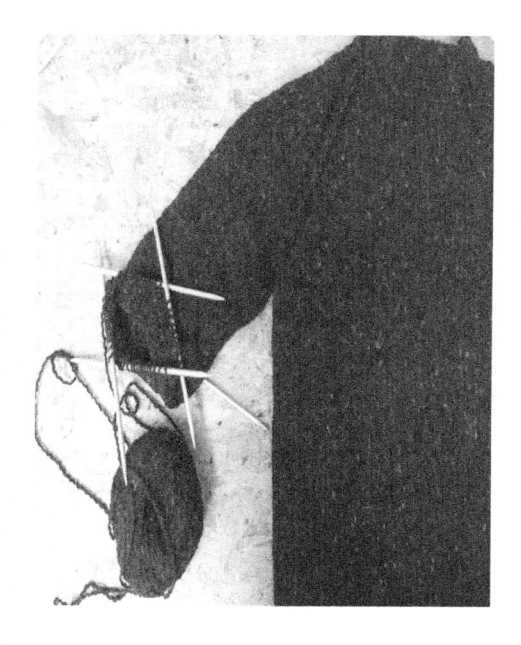

Claire

I didn't want to write in my diary at Whitcliff. I stayed at home and watched telly.

Kate

I sat in an interview room by the table. I had a large floppy bag which Jane had brought for me stuffed with my belongings, which were mostly books. It was a good job that Jane had never managed to remember to bring me the long ago promised typewriter as that would never have fitted into the floppy bag. I had several of Jane's library books, all the books she'd bought me and a copy of *Wuthering Heights* which I'd found in the prison library and grown so fond of that I couldn't bring myself to put it back. So I'd gone into prison an honest person and was coming out a thief without a twinge of conscience. (In fact I'd come out a lying thief if I was still in the belief that I hadn't killed Jim but if it's all the same I'd rather not go into that.)

The books hung heavily in the bag as the only thing I had to pad them out a bit was my purple cardigan. I was wearing my school skirt, the rosebud blouse and a pair of sandals that Jane had lent me. I'd had to give back my prison shoes. I'd also been given back my mother's watch and the key to our shed. The key to the shed made me feel a bit hysterical so I'd pushed it to the bottom of my bag. Mum's watch, which she'd obviously never come to collect, I decided was now mine, after all it seemed that Claire had everything else. I'd put it on and it hung loosely round my wrist. I was going to have to concentrate very hard on the fact that I was twenty eight and not eighteen.

Everyone was being very nice to me and someone had brought me a cup of tea. Jeanette however had been hopping around trying to spread doom and gloom because my Parole Officer 'friend' was apparently on sick leave so she was not coming all the way from York to collect me. I would have pointed out to Jeanette that I didn't need a Parole Officer 'friend' to tell me how to get to York but rather disturbingly I felt incredibly insecure. And this was not an emotion I wanted Jeanette to pick up on. Especially not at this precarious juncture of the proceedings. What if they changed their minds – the sort of opposite of a reprieve – and put me back in my cell?

I turned round from the table to see that Dickson was standing in the doorway.

'Still here, then' she said.

'Yep.'

'Can't get rid of you, can we.'

'No, I'm waiting for Jeanette,' I said.

'Bloody hell, that bloody woman couldn't organise a...' Dickson looked at me crossly. 'You didn't hear that, Howard,' she said. I returned her belligerent gaze meekly and she went over and stood by the window ostensibly looking at the view of concrete and tarmac. After a while she turned back to me and looked at me closely.

'Are you going to be okay, then?'

'I don't know. I guess so.' I didn't have to pretend with Dickson and the relief calmed me down a little.

'Bloody hell, it's been a long time. This place won't seem quite right without you.'

'Is that meant to be a compliment?' I said.

'Bloody hell,' repeated Dickson grinning. 'You can't just start where you left off, can you?'

No, I was now a copy typist secretary, a library book thief expert and swore like a trooper. I looked at Dickson wondering whether to voice these thoughts.

A warder came up behind Dickson.

'Psychologist's organised the paper work, Gov.,' she said.

I looked at Dickson covertly. I still couldn't square this idea of her being someone important.

'Okay, tell her we're on our way down.'

'You don't want to check it yourself? Jeanette thought...' Jeanette's thought died on the Warder's tongue as Dickson gave her a withering look.

'No, we'll come down. I think this prisoner's waited long enough for her release without waiting for everyone to double check triplicate copies of a release already ratified by the Parole Board.'

'Whatever you say, Gov.,' the warder said and left us rather sharpish.

I stood up but Dickson was still leaning against the window looking at me. I tried to pull the school skirt into a better position.

'It worries me that I've been released because I'm contrite and not because I'm innocent,' I said bravely and because Dickson was probably the only person I'd ever be able to say that to and I wasn't ever going to see Dickson or her prison again.

'Does it matter? You're getting out, aren't you?'

'I don't know.'

Dickson walked across the room and picked up my bag and I followed her out of the door.

'Did you tell them what Mum said?' I asked Dickson's back.

Dickson turned around to face me.

'Just drop it, can't you, Kate?'

'But no one said anything at the hearing. I mean about other, well other possibilities.'

'There wasn't much to say, it was hardly new evidence. Your Mum's bedside testimony was meant for your ears only. And anyway it couldn't be proved as your Mum's dead.'

'I suppose it was just Mum's opinion,' I said sadly, 'something she said to make me feel better. A sort of reconciliation kind of thing. I wasn't very good at the reconciliation bit, was I?' There was an uncomfortable tone of regret in my words. Dickson said nothing.

'Dickson,' I continued suddenly as she turned her back on me and walked on, 'do you think I did it or did you think I'd done it? I mean I know how Mum's words sounded but she didn't do it.'

Dickson paused yet again and turned to face me.

'That's as may be, but I'm as one with your Mum.'

'What do you mean?'

'Bloody hell, child, enough's enough, but if you want to carry on believing that you did it, far be it for me to persuade you otherwise.'

'But I don't think I did it.'

'Really?'

'No,' I said lamely

I supposed that the Parole Board thing had all just been one big farce (which sounds better than one big lie) orchestrated by Dickson as the only way in her opinion of releasing an innocent prisoner. It was all a bit much to take in so I decided to let it go. The sun was shining. If there were any birds in Wakefield that morning they were singing. And Jeanette was waiting by the main exit door with a big wad of papers. Dickson dropped my bag and took the papers and silenced the anxious looking Jeanette.

'I'll sort them later,' she said. 'For god's sake just get this child out of here.'

Dickson balanced the papers on one arm. I imagined her dropping them in the bin and wondered if this should make me feel better – wiped out of my old world and now wiped out of Dickson's world. But not entirely, as Dickson was holding her free hand out to me. I felt confused, but it wasn't to shake hands it was to give me a scrappy bit of paper with her telephone number written on it. I took it. No, not entirely wiped out.

'Well, you never know,' said Dickson and with a hefty pat on the back she pushed me towards the prison gate which meant that Jeanette reluctantly had to retrieve my bag and follow me.

Claire

Sally said I had to go on holiday. Sally said I was de-pressed but I don't know what de-pressed means. I asked Sally if de-pressed means going on holiday and Sally said no it means being sad. I said I'm not sad and asked Sally if a holiday was like going to Bettys because I liked going to Bettys with Mum and I am sad about not going to Bettys anymore. Sally looked surprised and said yes a holiday was like going to Bettys but for a whole week and I said that was silly because you couldn't go to Bettys for a whole week because you wouldn't have anywhere to sleep. Sally looked a bit cross so I put my hands over my ears and Sally said very loudly that a holiday wasn't actually going to Bettys it was just like going to Bettys and I said that there was no need to shout I wasn't deaf and Sally started to laugh which I thought wasn't very nice. Sally got a big magazine thing and showed me a picture of a beach then she showed me a picture of a bed in a room then she showed me a picture of a café which was a bit like Bettys and Sally said that this was a holiday. Sally said that you sit on the beach and sleep in the bedroom and eat in the café. I said I didn't want to go and Sally showed me a picture of a big blue bus and then I said that I would go.

 I asked Mike if he had a big blue bus and Mike said no he only had his yellow bus. I asked Mike about the holiday and he said that holidays are nice things and that I would like going on the big blue bus on the holiday.

Kate

Jeanette led me purposefully towards the prison gate. You'd think she couldn't wait to get rid of me. But as it was now generally accepted that I was, after all, the perpetrator of a heinous crime it wasn't that surprising. We didn't say much. At least I don't remember anything being said. Jeanette might have been wittering on about something, giving me lots of instructions about my new flat and stuff. I suppose she also gave me a key but if she did I lost both it and the address somewhere deep within the realms of Jane's floppy bag. More usefully she gave me £10 for my train fare to York. At the gate a warder let me through then locked it again. Jeanette on the inside and me on the outside.

Oh brave new world indeed. Last time it had been all cosy with Dickson mouthing off. Bloody hell was this what happened when you got released from prison? Bertha must have done this, stood by these very same gates. It was a happy thought; Bertha marching off to a new life via the station. Margaret? Was a less happy thought; Margaret marching off to discover her true *modus vivendi*. Or perhaps their Parole Officers hadn't been on sick leave or perhaps they'd had friends to meet them; Margaret's old people eagerly colluding in their own deaths as they welcomed Margaret into their home.

I found my way to the station, bought a ticket and missed the next train to York. I'd had this sludgy underground feeling before, trying to drag my thoughts and person through something unreal which finally took over and became reality.

Surely Dickson could have given me more than a bloody telephone number, I thought sullenly. But if I wanted to return to the utopia of Dickson's regime I would have to kill someone else. Or at least be accused of killing someone else and then spend a further ten years professing my innocence, as admitting guilt resulted in being released from utopia.

I nearly missed the next train as well but a guard got cross with me and when he blew his whistle and pointedly stood by an open door which led into a dark and unwelcoming interior I obediently dragged myself and my bag onto the train and he banged the door shut behind me. After about ten minutes I realised that no one else was going to tell me what to do so I dragged my bag further along the train and sat down on the first empty seat I came to.

Of course, all this happened again when the train arrived at York. Luckily the train terminated at York and the guard came along and shooed me off before the doors were locked. I dragged my bag along in York for a bit until I found myself at the number 2 bus stop in Exhibition Square. As I pulled my bag up to the top deck of the bus I wondered vaguely who would be at home. Mum? Jim? Claire?

Kate

With a bit of a struggle I managed to remember that it was a Tuesday and that it was about two o'clock in the afternoon. I wasn't sure about the two o'clock bit though as Mum's watch only worked when I shook it about a lot.

The bus was quiet. It was the time of day when there weren't many witnesses to prove that you were or weren't on a particular bus. The time of day when only renegade pupils, or those who'd just done their last exam got on the bus at the stop by the girl's grammar. No school age children got on the bus. Only me in my school uniform skirt.

We rattled on at great speed down the Old North Road and I winced every time we scraped under the low hanging trees by Whitcliff Park. The bus overran the Whitcliff stop and had to backup. The unease of an unpleasant altercation drifted up to the top deck and I watched a bent old lady struggle off the bus clutching a walking stick and a shopping bag on wheels. I'd seen her before, hadn't I? Getting off the bus on a June afternoon laden with newspapers and oranges to give to a demented husband or a heroic son wounded beyond all recognition in a war which for the rest of us had ended more than three decades ago. But she hadn't seen me. She hadn't seen me clamber up the stairs and hide up on the deserted top deck.

In a sudden panic I pressed the stop button and stood up while the bus was still rushing onwards. It screeched to a halt, overrunning my stop as well. My bag left me behind and hurtled down the stairs while I chased after it. The bus driver didn't back up for me and I looked guiltily at the one remaining passenger on the bus as my bag and I fell out of the bus and on to the road side about twenty yards from the bus stop and about fifty yards from the phone box by Potter's Farm further up the Old North Road. The phone box which smelt of sick and urine and blood and guilt.

A big lorry roared past, hooting loudly. I was standing in the middle of the road. A car steered round me crossly and a third one stopped. A man wound the window down.

'Are you lost, love?' he said.

I panicked and dragged my bag onto the other side of the road. Other cars were coming up behind the man and he carried on, forgetting me. My alibi, I thought numbly.

I tried pulling the strap of my bag over my shoulder. The books had all got wedged into one corner and jabbed into my hip with every step. I tried to put on a prodigal daughter returning air but in my case the proverbial bad penny was more apt.

What time was it now? Three o'clock? Half past two? Mum's watch said half past two. I gave it another shake and moved the hands on to three o'clock as I turned into the side entrance at number 12 Potter's View.

The curtains twitched in number 14 and I dropped my bag on the back doorstep of my old home. I had to scatter a few contents about on the cracked concrete drive – Mum and Jim's new-built semi wasn't looking so new any more – until I found the key to our shed.

The shed looked innocent. Like big dogs do before they bare their teeth. I could feel the curtains twitching in the back at number 14. 'That's right, make sure you get a bloody good eyeful, Mrs Hunter,' I muttered under my breath. Or shouted out defiantly. It was one of those crucial details that are so hard to remember.

The key fitted into the lock like it was yesterday and the door swung open like an absurd horror movie. For a split second I saw Jim's shoes, the white bit of bone sticking out of his arm and I bent down to pull the plug of the circular saw out of its socket. The socket was still there. But the circular saw had gone as had Jim's whole wretched workbench with zero safety features and an armoury of lethal weapons. Leant against the back wall were the remains of the wonky shelf that Jim had never finished.

'Bloody hell,' I said out loud, steadying myself.

Claire

On Monday Linda didn't come then Sally said that Linda wasn't coming anymore. Sally said that Carol was coming to help instead and I said that I didn't like Carol and Sally said that was silly and that Carol would be just like Linda and I said I wasn't going to Whitcliff and Sally made a big sighing noise and said that Carol would come the next day which was Wednesday but Sally was wrong because Kate came and it was Tuesday.

Kate shouted at Mrs Hunter then she made lots of noise in the shed. I don't like the shed so I went into the back room and put the radio on loudly. Kate came in and sang all the wrong words like she always does. I switched the radio off and asked her if she was Carol just to check. Kate said that she was Kate and I told her that Carol was coming on Wednesday and Kate said that it was Tuesday and I said that I knew that it was Tuesday and I felt cross because Kate always knows everything. I said that Emmerdale Farm was on the Telly and Kate looked surprised and I felt happy because Kate didn't know about the telly and she didn't know about Emmerdale.Farm.

Kate

The back door was open so I went in. Claire was sitting by the radio crooning. I joined in. *'Are you lonesome tonight,'* I sang. I could hear Jim in the front room rustling his newspaper crossly and sniffing through his big hairy nose. *Is your heart filled with pain, shall I come back again? Tell me dear, are you lonesome tonight?*

Claire switched the radio off. 'I don't like Elvis Presley any more,' she said crossly. She'd got fat. All that pink prettiness had gone blousy. 'Are you Carol,' she said.

'Umm, I'm Kate.'

'Carol's coming on Wednesday.'

'Ah, well it's Tuesday today.'

'I know it's Tuesday today. Emmerdale Farm's on the telly.'

'Have you got a television?' I exclaimed before I could stop myself.

'Of course I've got a telly. Linda got me one.'

'Oh. Who's Linda?'

Was I stupid or something? 'Linda who used to come.'

'And, er, who's Carol?'

'Carol's coming on Wednesday.'

Ask a silly question.

'Does anyone else come?' I nonetheless tried to continue.

'Mike comes on Sundays and you've come today and today is Tuesday.'

Slight pause.

'Claire, do you know who I am?'

'You're Kate,' she said and switched the radio back on. It was some song I'd never heard before.

Claire

Then Kate asked lots of questions and I put the radio on so she went away. I could hear her making lots of noise so I turned the volume up and sang 'Water Loo my Water Loo doody doody doo'.

Kate

I went back into the hall. Jim's telephone was still on the hall table by the front door. The one we weren't allowed to use. 'I don't want Kate using that phone. All her friends ringing up day and night. I might miss an important call.' It was Jim's business phone, but perhaps it had been for all his floozies. I turned my back on the telephone and peeked into the front room. A large television occupied the corner where Jim's record player used to be. There were three dirty plates on the coffee table, a glass of squash half drunk with a dead fly in it and an empty crisp packet on the sofa. I picked it all up and took it into the kitchen.

I was just trying to scrape congealed beans off the last pan when Claire joined me in the kitchen. She produced a large loaf of sliced bread from a kitchen cupboard and ham and margarine from a small fridge. The fridge was new too. She was humming the song I didn't know while she made her large white sandwich.

'Are you going to make me one too?' I asked.

She looked a bit taken aback. 'Do you want one?'

'Yes, I've just done all your washing up and I'm hungry.'

'Linda didn't used to have a sandwich,' she said uncertainly.

'Yes, well, I'm not Linda, am I.'

'No, you're Kate.' She made me a sandwich. I winced at the amount of margarine she spread on the bread. 'Linda used to stay sometimes and watch Emmerdale Farm with me. But not anymore.' Claire suddenly looked a bit lost.

'Would you like me to stay, Claire?'

'But you're Kate.'

'I can still stay though, if you like.'

She picked up the two plates of sandwiches and went through to the front room. She was smiling.

Claire

When I went in the kitchen it was all nice like it was when Linda came so I made a ham sandwich but Kate said that I had to make her a ham sandwich and I said that Linda didn't have a ham sandwich but then I did a very kind thing and I made Kate a ham sandwich and I said to Kate that Linda stayed to watch telly and then Kate said that she would stay and that made me feel happy.

Then Mrs Hunter came and that made me unhappy. Kate ran away like she always does and Mrs Hunter made lots of noise. I turned the telly up until Mrs Hunter went away.

Kate

Feeling punch drunk with the connivings of Jack Sugden I left Claire to watch the second half of Emmerdale on her own and went upstairs. Someone was knocking on the kitchen door and I remembered that my things were still scattered all over the doorstep.

'Hello. Hello there. Claire?' I recognised Mrs Hunter's voice and loitered on the upstairs landing listening. 'Is everything alright, dear?' Mrs Hunter was now standing in the hallway right underneath the upstairs landing by the doorway to the front room.

'Emmerdale's on.' I could hear the indignation in Claire's voice.

'I thought perhaps you had a visitor?'

I imagined Mrs Hunter trying to peer round the door to spot the intruder. I held my breath.

'It's only Kate,' Claire said loudly and crossly. I heard the volume on the TV increase and I thought I heard Mrs Hunter retreating and closing the kitchen door behind her. I moved carefully to the landing window to check. I sat on the top step of the stairs and listened to Jim telling Mum how useless I was. 'The only thing she seems to do without shouting is reading.'

'I wish there was more we could do for Claire.' Did Mum say that or did Jim? It made me feel a bit queasy. I didn't know why so I stood up again and went into my bedroom.

It was suspiciously tidy. Someone had been in here. All my stuff in its organised heaps all over the floor had gone. Was it still my room? The bed was made up. Perhaps someone else slept here? Linda? Carol? Or, God help us, Mike, whoever he was.

Jim's wallpaper was still on the wall though. I opened the top drawer in my little dresser. My underwear was all washed and ironed and folded in neat piles next to the little hankies I'd had when I was five which were embroidered with my initials, C. H. I started to cry. I stumbled over to the window and flung it open. Kill Jim, I thought. I said the words out loud, tentatively, into the early evening of the dull June day.

Kate

Carol was a bit put out.

'They didn't tell me there was two of you,' she said putting two plastic bags on the kitchen table next to the new mini fridge.

I eyed up the plastic bags, trying to think of something sensible to say.

'This is Kate,' Claire said as she started ransacking the plastic bags. They were full of cheap food. Not proper food like we got in prison but cheap bread and ham and beans and crisps and biscuits.

'I don't suppose there's any eggs in there?' I asked tentatively.

Claire and Carol turned on me in mid rummage.

'Or peas or apples...?'

'Now look here,' Carol paused trying to remember my name.

'Kate,' I said helpfully.

'Kate. There's nothing in my book about no Kate, Just a Claire.'

'That's Claire,' I said pointing to Claire as she disappeared out of the kitchen clutching a glass of orange squash and a packet of biscuits.

'I'm here to do for a Claire.' Carol looked at me appraisingly hands on hips studying me with a disconcerting intensity. 'You're not one of them are you?' Carol jerked her head in the direction of the vanished Claire and looked at me almost conspiratorially.

I tried not to look too shocked at her turn of phrase and attempted to see it as a compliment, anyway I reckoned that conspiratorially could go in my favour.

'No, you don't need to do for me, just for Claire.'

'So you do for yourself?'

'Yes.'

'So if I do downstairs,' I could see Carol assessing the possibilities here, 'you can do upstairs?'

I nodded.

'And if I was to finish a bit earlier it wouldn't be bothering you, would it?'

'No.'

Carol smiled smugly.

'But.'

Carol was immediately on the defensive.

'About the food.'

'I can't be getting more food, and', she paused threateningly, 'I'll have to tell that Sally about you.'

Did I want 'that Sally' to know about me? I pushed my point about the food instead. 'We don't need more food. I mean who decides what food to buy?' Carol looked a bit non-plussed. 'I mean do you just get what you think or does Sally or…?'

'Oh,' the light dawned, 'she writes me a list.' Carol jerked her head in the general direction of Claire again.

Ah ha, this was something I could probably manage, although how on earth could they let someone of Claire's increasing proportions decide what food she ate? I thought crossly.

'I'll be getting on, then,' Carol interrupted my thoughts.

About an hour later she called upstairs where I was hiding out of the way to say she was off now and that she'd see us on Friday. I galloped down the stairs and caught her just as she was about to go out of the back door.

'List,' I said. She took it without comment, which was more than Claire was going to do when she ransacked the next lot of shopping bags. 'And…'

'Get on, dearie, the bus goes in two minutes.'

'Who comes tomorrow?'

'Tomorrow?' Carol sounded indignant. 'I shouldn't think anyone comes tomorrow. She goes to Whitcliff on Thursdays and Tuesdays.'

'She wasn't at Whitcliff yesterday,' I said, feeling suddenly anxious.

'Well, I don't know,' Carol was getting irritated again. 'You'll have to ask Sally about that.' And she scuttled off up the road in a brave attempt to catch her bus.

Claire

On Wednesday the new person called Carol came. I thought that Carol didn't look very nice but she had brought me some food like Linda and when I checked in the bags it was the same food that Linda brought. I was trying to eat cornflakes for breakfast because Mike said that he liked cornflakes but Kate was making lots of noise and being cross with Carol and Carol was being cross with Kate so I found the jammy biscuits and the orange squash and went into the back room and put the radio on. I sang 'Water Loo my Water Loo doody doody doo' and then when Kate started being noisy again with Carol I turned up the volume. When it was quiet again I wrote my list but when I tried to find the new person called Carol she had gone and I just put my list on the table in the kitchen.

Claire

The next day was Thursday. I always go to Whitcliff on Thursdays because that is when Mike and I clean his yellow bus. Kate was being quiet so I tried to eat some cornflakes then I went into the front room. I always go into the front room on Thursday mornings because then I can see when Sally comes. Sally comes in her car to collect me and take me to Whitcliff. She comes on Tuesdays as well but I don't always like to go on Tuesdays. The clock said half past nine when Sally came in her car. Kate was in the kitchen and she was saying things to Sally so I got my bag and went into the kitchen. Sally hadn't come to get Kate she had come to get me and I didn't like it that Kate was talking to her as if she had come to get Kate and that I wasn't important any more. I got into the front of Sally's car because no one told me not to. I was cross and I was going to press the horn and make a big loud noise so that Sally would stop talking to Kate but Sally's car wasn't the same as Mike's bus and I couldn't find the horn to make a big noise.

Kate

The next morning – I hadn't seen so much action in three days since, since when? Since all those episodes in my life best forgotten? A car pulled into the drive and a thin woman with permed hair let herself in through the back door.

'I'm here,' she shouted helpfully as she closed the door behind her.

'Hello,' I said. 'I'm Kate,' I added anticipating the question. Claire was in the front room looking optimistically at a blank television screen. The woman looked at me carefully and I could see her mind's eye doing a quick scan of Claire's files. Was I someone she should know about? Was I even still in Claire's files? Or had I been erased out of those too? Jim and I both erased from the era of life after Jim. Her mind's eye was struggling so her gaze focussed more steadily on the actual me.

'Er, Kate?' she asked slowly.

I wasn't a very inspiring sight, dressed as I was in clothes that Mum had thought were suitable for an eighteen year old in 1966.

Claire now joined the party carrying a large handbag.

'Ah, Claire, are you coming to Whitcliff today?'

Bloody hell, did she get to choose? We didn't used to let her choose as she'd never have chosen to do anything. Claire pushed through the door and turned back to look at the woman. She was clutching her handbag aggressively. The gesture meant, of course I'm coming are you stupid or something.

'I see you have a friend staying, Claire,' the woman said matter-of-factly.

Suddenly inspired I said. 'Are you Sally?'

'Yes that's Sally and you're Kate,' Claire butted in crossly.

'Are you…?' Sally began, her mind's eye in fast recall.

'Yes,' I said.

'And have you…?'

'Yes,' I answered. Could they stop me? Could Sally stop me living at home? 'So I could bring her to Whitcliff on Tuesdays and Thursdays? Those are her days aren't they?' I charged on, desperately trying to turn my appearance into a convenience not a nuisance.

Claire had climbed into the passenger seat of the car and slammed the door shut pointedly. Patience had never been one of her strongest points.

'Is Claire...er, how does Claire feel about this?'

'About me?'

Sally nodded.

'She likes company,' I said. And as far as I can see she needs someone to keep a closer eye on her, but I didn't add that. 'Shall I collect her this afternoon?' I said instead.

This was all going a bit quickly for Sally, 'Er yes,' she said uncertainly.

But I was feeling quite confident suddenly, after all if Claire had choices and if Claire chose to live with me then surely there was nothing that Sally could do about it. Apart from persuade Claire to make a different choice.

'Is it the same place as before? The Centre for Outpatients?'

Sally nodded. 'You're Kate?' she said and the remembrance of who I was can hardly have been reassuring. 'You can collect her at 4,' she added and marched briskly out of the door just in time to stop Claire discovering the whereabouts of the horn.

It was a pyric victory because that afternoon I would have to walk out of the house and down the street like normal people did.

Claire

When the clock said four o'clock I went to find Sally's car but I didn't find Sally's car because Kate found me instead. I liked seeing Kate but I felt funny inside because it was like it used to be and it was different from what it used to be. I walked to the bus stop with Kate but Kate said that unless I had 20 new pennies – I don't know why she called them 20 new pennies – we couldn't get the bus. I said that I did have 20 pence so then Kate said that we could get the bus but when the bus came she said I had to give the 20 pence to the bus driver. I didn't want to give the bus driver my 20 pence so we had to get off again and Kate said that if I didn't give the bus driver 20 pence then we would have to walk home then she said that it would do me good to walk home and I thought that that didn't sound very nice and I put my hands over my ears and said that I wanted to go in Sally's car and Kate said that I couldn't go in Sally's car. Kate sounded cross. Then Kate did a nice thing like Mum used to do. She put her hands over mine which were over my ears and said that we would walk home together and that it would be nice and that it was sunny and that we could count blue cars on the way home. I didn't want to count cars but I decided to walk home with Kate.

    At the weekend Kate made me very happy because she said that if I paid the bus fare we could go to Bettys. I said that it would be very nice to go to Bettys and Kate was all smiley. She held my arm like she used to do. I'd forgotten about Kate holding my arm but I liked it and we had a nice time on the bus because Kate chatted a lot like other people do and we pointed and giggled because an old man got his walking stick caught in an old lady's bag. It wasn't very nice to point and giggle but it was nice to giggle with Kate like people do on the telly.

    At Bettys we both had Welsh rarebit and a pot of tea and I ordered chocolate cake for two. Kate was very pleased and told me I was very clever but then the woman called a waitress came and Kate said I had to give her some money and I said I didn't want to give her any money and then Kate did a bad thing. She pinched my purse and took 2 pound notes out of it to pay for the Welsh rarebit and the tea and the chocolate cake. I told Kate that that was very naughty and that Mum never ever stole my money and made me pay and Kate said but that was then not now and now Mum wasn't here and that meant that I had to pay if we went to Bettys. I asked Kate why she couldn't pay and Kate just said that she didn't have any money and I thought that that was a fib because everybody has money.

    I didn't like Kate talking about Mum and saying that things were different and I felt sad on the way home. I told Kate that the next day was Sunday and that she would have to go away. Kate looked surprised like Sally sometimes does and said that she had thought that I wanted her to stay and I said that I didn't want her to stay on Sundays then Kate looked as if it was alright again and said oh you mean you want me to go away just for the day tomorrow and I said yes because tomorrow was Sunday. Then Kate had her clever look and she said is that because Mike is coming but I didn't say anything because Mike was my special friend and he wasn't Kate's special friend. I said to Kate that she could go and see Jane because Jane was her special friend and Kate looked surprised again and said yes she could go and see Jane and then she said that I was very clever again and when we got home I let her sit next to me on the sofa so that we could watch telly together.

Kate

I did a lot of walking. There wasn't really any option because if I started using the bus then the £2.65 I had left after my journey from Wakefield would soon be all used up.

I walked Claire to Whitcliff on Tuesdays and Thursdays. She didn't like it but neither did she like the idea of using her own money to get the bus. Claire seemed to have quite a lot of money but I hadn't quite yet succumbed to stealing from her. I had some vague plan that the healthy eating and exercise I was subjecting her to would help her lose weight – except at Whitcliff someone always seemed to be having a birthday and Claire always seemed to be stuffing herself with cake and when I collected her I would be given a piece to take home, which Claire would then appropriate and eat herself. But at least on the cake front I had apparently been accepted at Whitcliff as Claire's what? Carer, I supposed.

Then I walked to the library and walked home again where I locked myself in my cell and read for the rest of the day. When Carol came I hid upstairs and on Sundays I walked somewhere so that I wouldn't meet Mike. Until Jane finally caught up with me and then I walked to Jane's on Sundays which was a long walk and took most of the day. Walking was the ultimate passer of time and should have been introduced into prison routines in preference to almost anything else.

When I walked past a phone box I rang Dickson's number and listened to her swearing until the pips went.

And when I wasn't walking or reading in my cell I sat at the top of the stairs and listened in to the murmur of Mum and Jim's conversations drifting up from the front room.

Kate

'Don't you think you should get a job?' Jane was looking at me trying to be sympathetic and not impatient. 'Don't you think you should move into that flat they organised for you? Are you allowed to just live with Claire like that without asking anyone? What do her helpers say? You've got that typing diploma. I'd have thought that you could get a job easily with good typing skills.' And more relentless questioning.

I looked at her sullenly and shrugged. Sean toddled back from menacing a duck and fell into her lap. We were sitting in the Museum Gardens having a picnic. Alan was at a football match, or a cricket match or cleaning the car or whatever it was that husbands did on Sundays.

'You have to do something, Kate.'

I'd spent the last ten years being trained to do nothing. Failing to learn how to knit.

'I think Claire likes me being there,' I said.

'Oh well, that's good, isn't it. I thought she thought…I thought, well, that your Mum…' A big splodge of rain exploded on the sandwich paper. 'Oh lord, at least I've parked the car close by.'

Alan wasn't washing the car then. I packed the picnic things into Jane's hamper and she packed Sean into his pushchair and for want of anything better to do I ran back to her car with them.

We sat in the car watching the rain streaming down the windscreen. It was one of those cloudbursts you get out of clear blue skies in July. Sean leant back in the backseat sucking his thumb, tired after all the duck chasing.

'Come back to our house. I'll dig out those old clothes I said I'd give you.' She looked at me for encouragement.

I shrugged again. I didn't want to go home. It was Mike's day and I didn't want to meet Mike.

Claire

I was packing my bag to go on holiday. Mike had told me lots of times that I would like going on holiday and Sally had told me that I had to pack my things in a suit-case and I said do you mean in Mum's suit-case and Sally said yes. Then Sally gave Kate a list of things that Sally said I had to pack in the suit-case and I was cross because it was my list not Kate's list and I was going on holiday and not Kate and Sally should have given the list to me. Kate read the list that Sally should have given to me and sighed a lot and I watched telly with the door closed so that Kate couldn't watch it with me. Then Kate came into the front room and switched the telly off like Mum did when she had something very important to say and Kate said in her sighing voice shall we write a list together Claire so that you have a proper list of what to take and I said so that it will be my list and not yours and Kate said yes it would be Claire's very own list and not anyone else's. I felt happy then and we wrote the list together.

Claire's holiday list.

Sponge bag: tooth brush
tooth past
flanel
soap
shampoo
towel
towel

~~Swimsuit~~ no swimsuit
Light cardigan Claires blue Cardigan
Claire's blue dress
Claire's white blouse with blue flowers on it
Claire's blue skirt
Claires skirt with blue flowers
Claires white blouse
Claire's dress that Jane gave her
2 sandels
~~crisps~~
~~ham~~ ~~no food~~ food for the bus journey
~~bread~~ blue pengins
purse
Magazine
6 socks, ~~tights~~ 7 pants 4 bras

by Claire and Kate

Claire

Then I told Kate that we had to go shopping. We had to go shopping because Mike said that I had to have a t-shirt because when I am on holiday I have to wear a t-shirt. Mike showed me his t-shirt. It had big writing on it but I didn't want big writing so Mike said I could get a t-shirt with a picture on it so I said I would get a picture with Mike on it and Mike said that he didn't think he was on a t-shirt so I said I would get a picture with a yellow bus on it and that made us both very happy.

Kate said that if we went shopping I would have to take my purse and use my money and I said would I have to use my money on the bus and Kate said yes and I said would I have to use my money in the shop to buy the t-shirt with the yellow bus on it and Kate said yes and I said would I have to use my money in Bettys and Kate said yes so we counted my money very carefully and Kate told me that I had lots of money so we went on the bus into York to go shopping.

We went into 3 shops but they didn't have t-shirts with yellow busses on them. Kate found a t-shirt with a red bus on it but I told her that red buses were very silly and Kate dropped the t-shirt on the floor and the woman in the shop got cross and Kate said something noisy and I didn't like it so I said that we had to go to Browns and Kate said that Browns didn't sell t-shirts and that they cer-tain-ly didn't sell t-shirts with yellow buses on them and I put my hands over my ears and Kate said it was alright and she said we could go to the shop called Woolworths. In the shop called Woolworths I found a blue t-shirt with a big yellow flower on it and I said that I liked the blue and yellow t-shirt and Kate said in her way when she is not being nice that a yellow flower was not the same as a yellow bus and I said that it was big like a bus then Kate laughed and I went to the woman where you pay and I bought the blue t-shirt with the yellow flower. Kate carried on laughing and said well at least its big and I said yes it is big and then we were both happy so we went to Bettys.

Claire

On Sunday Kate made me get up very early and eat cornflakes. She told me lots of times about going on holiday and getting up early so I was very good and I put my new blue t-shirt with the yellow flower that was big like a bus on. Then Kate said we had to go to the bus stop very quickly. I didn't like to go very quickly but Kate had my suit-case and she went very quickly so I had to follow her. When we got to Whitcliff there were lots of people. I told Sally that I had packed my suit-case and that me and Kate had made a special list but Sally had that look on her face that meant she wasn't really listening so I just stood with Kate because I didn't know what to do and it was all strange and I wondered if it was going to be frightening and then Kate asked me if Mike was going and I said that Mike wasn't going but that a big blue bus was going. Then I saw the big blue bus and I was happy so I went to where the big blue bus was.

Kate

Claire was going on holiday. We had to be at Whitcliff by seven. We were going to be a bit late because the number 2 bus didn't leave our stop until two minutes past seven. I wasn't very worried; Claire's list of things to take said that the bus was leaving at 7.30.

Claire had a roller bag which she'd packed herself, reading her list out loud. She'd been packing it for two weeks and unpacking it and making me take her shopping because she wanted a t-shirt with a pink kitten on it to take with her. I tried to tell her that it wasn't on the list but she just gave me the look that meant she didn't like Elvis Presley any more. She found a t-shirt in Woolworths with a big sunflower on it and bought that in extra large. I didn't point out that a sunflower wasn't a pink kitten and took her to Bettys for a cup of tea (or more accurately, she took me). She went a bit quiet in Bettys and looked at me for a long time without saying anything. Mum had always gone to Bettys when she was out shopping.

I was now manhandling the roller bag onto the bus and buying tickets (after an incident about payment for the tea at Bettys I had finally taken to stealing the odd ten pence here and there from Claire – enough to cover another trip to Bettys and a few bus fares) and Claire was sitting in regal splendour on one of the front seats with her hefty handbag on her knee. If one can sit in regal splendour wearing a t-shirt with a large sunflower stretched over one's bosoms.

The Whitcliff car park was full of parents and carers and eager happy Claires. Claire had found Sally and was proudly telling her that she'd packed everything herself. I trailed up behind, dragging the evidence.

'Hello Kate,' Sally started to say until another proud Claire came up and interrupted her.

There was a bus on the far side of the car park and people were starting to queue by it. I suggested to Claire that we join the queue and we made our way over to the bus. There were about twenty young people all apparently handicapped in one way or another. I glanced at Claire. She just stood next to me and made no obvious contact with anyone else.

'Is Mike going?' I asked casually.

Claire's lips twitched and she looked past me carefully. 'No,' she said.

I didn't say anything else because the bus driver opened the big luggage space under the bus and Claire dived to the front of the queue to put her bag on the bus first, expecting me to follow her. She then charged onto the bus and sat at the front, handbag on knees and t-shirt stretched regally.

'Bye,' I said amidst the mêlée of other parents.

Sally was standing with her list by another older woman. 'That's Claire's sister,' I overheard her saying.

'Oh.' The older woman didn't say anything. I imagined her looking disapproving but daren't turn to look at them in case I drew their attention.

'It's so nice that Claire still has family. I thought that she might have had to move here after her mother died.' Sally was smiling benignly on all us anxious carer-parents. 'But now her sister's come home again she'll be able to stay at home. I'm so happy for her.'

I looked up at Claire occupying the entire front seat. She'd already forgotten me.

Claire

I got on the big blue bus and sat at the front like I did in Mike's yellow bus. I liked sitting on the big blue bus and I decided that I liked going on holiday. I had 3 blue penguins in my handbag.

Kate

I indulged in a bit of Jim taunting and didn't wash up for a week. Carol was on holiday too. My books were all over the coffee table in the front room vying for place with six empty coffee cups. I was getting even worse than Claire.

There was the Kafka novel I'd bought second hand in 1965 but never read. I still didn't want to read it but its presence added a certain symbolism to the mess. Jim didn't like D H Lawrence either so I piled these books on his chair. Jim, of course, didn't like anything. Not to mention my stolen copy of Wuthering Heights. But it was Mum who hadn't liked that. 'You're not reading that old thing,' she'd said when I'd borrowed it from the school library and she'd made me take it back the next day.

I put Claire's radio on loudly and watched Emmerdale Farm on the TV. I was under strict instructions to recount all the goings on to Claire when she came back at the weekend.

I rang Dickson occasionally just to hear her voice. I went to the phone box at the end of our street. The one that I'd rung the ambulance from. I just managed to hear her swearing, 'Is this a funny phone call or something,' before the pips went. I never put any money in.

Jane bought tickets for the theatre on the Saturday night. I didn't hear what she said we were going to see and Claire was due back the next day at 6pm.

Claire

Claires Holiday By Claire

Claire staying in a hotel

Claire walking

Claire eats Chips

Claire on the beach

Kate

I walked to Whitcliff to meet Claire off the bus and arrived half an hour early. Claire gave me her roller bag and someone called Janice gave her a lift home. I faithfully wheeled the roller bag all the way home because the buses only went every hour on Sunday evenings. I hadn't seen anything of Mike all day – I had been a bit interested to see if he'd turn up. (I still hadn't met Mike – I usually went to see Jane on Sundays but what with the theatre and Claire coming home ...)

Claire

I made a new friend on my holiday. She is called Janice. When we got back to Whticliff in the big blue bus Janice said that I could go home in her car so I said yes thank you because I'm a very good girl and I went home in Janice's car. But when I got home Kate wasn't there and I had to wait ages for her to come home and I was cross because I was very hungry but when Kate came home she asked me if I would like bacon and eggs and that made me happy because it was like Mum.

Kate

Claire told me that her dirty washing was in the plastic bag and that she was hungry. Jim said something about me being useless and Mum made Claire bacon and eggs.

Kate

Jane plonked a big form on the table in the kitchen, next to the little fridge. It said UCCA all over the top. University Central Council for Admissions, or something like that. I wondered whether to pretend that I didn't know what it was. Claire was watching Coronation Street in the front room, which meant that it was either Monday or Wednesday.

Jane was bristling with news that had nothing to do with UCCA forms and I reckoned it would be easy to distract her.

'Well, aren't you going to make me a cup of tea then?'

'Sure you wouldn't rather have coffee?'

'Don't be difficult, Kate,' Jane said with a smile in her voice.

I sighed inaudibly and put the kettle on the gas. It was too difficult to explain about my current cup of tea phobias – Mum, Bettys, my tea cosy in Jim's workshop, Jim's enormous breakfast mug which I longed to smash into smithereens, police stations, prison. I got the teapot off the shelf and two of Mum's best cups and saucers. I asked Claire if she wanted any but she just turned the volume up on the TV.

I carefully moved the UCCA form out of the way, sliding it under the fridge so that you could only see the bottom bit where it said *for official use only*.

'You're expecting another baby aren't you.'

Jane opened her mouth to protest and then smiled so smugly that I almost wanted to hit her. I made the tea instead and Jane sat down.

'I can't keep anything secret from you, can I,' she exclaimed happily.

'Does Alan know?'

'Of course he knows.'

'Does he mind?'

'Of course he doesn't mind. Kate, you are funny sometimes.'

Sometimes?

'Isn't it a bit soon after…'

'Kate!'

I poured tea into the posh cups. 'I suppose you'll be wanting sugar as well,' I said resignedly.

'Anyway,' Jane continued sipping her tea gingerly. A few globules of milk fat floated on the top, just to make me feel at home. 'I didn't come here to tell you about the baby,' she said and she retrieved the UCCA form from under the fridge. I'd scarcely been able to take my eyes off it the whole time and she knew it.

'Please, Jane,' I said hoarsely.

She looked at me for a long time. I mean really looked at me without normality and ten years getting in between. 'Mum reckons it's going to be a girl this time,' she said.

'I suppose your Mum knows about things like that,' I said and Jane started to laugh.

Claire

Kate and Jane were in the kitchen talking. I didn't want to talk because Emmerdale was on the telly. On the telly a man called Joe was doing some thing that wasn't very nice and I didn't know whether I wanted to watch it or not. I would have liked to watch it with Kate but Kate was talking to Jane. I went into the kitchen to check. Kate and Jane were drinking tea out of Mum's cups that are very special. I was going to say something about them being Mum's special cups that we weren't allowed to use unless we were very good but Jane said hello in her way which is very friendly and Kate didn't say anything. Sometimes I get confused because Kate does the things that Mum would have done but she is not like Mum so I just felt confused and went back to watch Emmerdale which I didn't like very much either.

Kate

I now had three UCCA forms on my bedside table. Two for entry in 1977 and one for entry in 1966. The one for entry in 1966 was carefully filled out in my best handwriting. First choice Manchester to read English Language and Literature, second choice Leeds, ditto, third choice Bristol, ditto, fourth choice Oxford to read English Literature and fifth choice Cambridge, ditto. At some point I'd obviously decided that that form was never going to be sent off. At the point where I'd put Oxford fourth.

I went to the window and said rather feebly, 'Kill Jim.' Then I wandered out onto the landing and sat down on the top step. Claire was watching the TV as usual. She listened to the radio less and less and watched the TV more and more.

I'd asked Mum if she would sign the UCCA application for me and she'd said that she would have to ask Jim, which is probably when I'd put Oxford down fourth. That night I'd sat at the top of the stairs and waited for Mum to have the conversation with Jim. I didn't hear much to start with because Jim had a record playing. Luckily it came to an end and Jim didn't put another one on. It was all quiet for at least a minute and I could hear Claire murmuring in her sleep from her little bedroom at the front of the house.

I think they'd been talking about Claire, though, not me and when they carried on I didn't listen very closely until Mum suddenly opened the door to the front room and went into the kitchen to make their bedtime cup of tea. (No wonder I hated tea, it was so bloody ritualistic.) Mum had left the door open and I could hear Jim rustling the late edition of *The Press*. When she came back with the tea her hands were full and the door remained open.

'Kate asked me if I'd sign some form for her. I think it was her university application thing,' Mum said. I wished I could see their faces. I heard *The Press* rustling as Jim put it down either to take his tea or listen to Mum more carefully.

'Did you?'

'No, of course not. I said I would have to talk to you first.'

'We've been through all this, Margot,' Jim said. I put an unpleasant expression on his smarmy features, the lips just a bit too wet and his nose more than a bit too big. 'Look, Margot.' Look your bloody self, Jim. 'Maybe, maybe it would be for the best.

Maybe Kate should go away. She's never settled with us. If she goes to university – and I think she'll even get money to go or something – then it'll just be the three of us. It'll, well it will make life much easier.'

'I don't want her going away.' Mum's voice was high and strained as if she was trying to make it sound normal and unstrained.

'It's not as though she ever does anything to help,' Jim continued.

'She has to stay.' Did Mum even sound hysterical?

I went to bed. Perhaps that's when I'd filled in the Cambridge bit. When I'd planned what I'd say to Jane about how Jim wouldn't let me go to university. I was so confused that I had a *Jane Eyre* nightmare. Except this time I was the mad woman and I didn't know properly what was then and what was now.

Claire

I think Kate was talking to someone. I didn't like someone being in the house so I did a very brave thing and went to tell Kate that I didn't like someone being in the house but when I found Kate in her bedroom there wasn't anyone else there. I told Kate anyway that I didn't like someone being there. Kate had her shocked look on then she laughed which I didn't like because it was how she used to laugh. Then Kate said a very strange thing she said that she was talking to herself. I'm just talking to myself she said and laughed in that way that is horrid like she used to laugh. I didn't think that it was possible to talk to no one so I asked Sally but Sally just looked surprised and I couldn't understand what she said. I asked Mike and he agreed with me that you couldn't talk to anyone if there was no one there. Mike kissed me on my cheek three times and I liked it.

Kate

Eleven years later I filled in the new UCCA form. The one I'd sent off for not the one that Jane had got for me. Durham to read History, Newcastle to study Psychology (although I didn't fulfil any of the requirements), Kent at Canterbury to do English and Drama, SOAS to study African Languages and LSE to study Philosophy. I don't think they even had a Philosophy course. I tried to explain this to Jane as she ransacked through my junk on the bedside table. Sean was on the floor in the kitchen ransacking Claire's handbag. Claire was watching TV and Alan was at a football match – he really was at a football match this time. It was a Saturday. I think Jane had come especially to rootle out my UCCA form. She was noticeably pregnant now, and had given up work again.

Jane exclaimed in triumph and clutching my UCCA form went back down the stairs to the kitchen. I followed her obediently.

'I'm going to post this, to be sure,' she said.
Sean had found some chewing gum in Claire's bag. I wondered what would happen when he got around to putting it in his mouth. Jane looked at me severely to get my attention. 'I'm going to post this form,' she said, waving it at me.

'I haven't signed it,' I said.
'I'll forge all the bits you haven't filled in.'
'Sean's just put three pieces of chewing gum in his mouth.'
'For God's Sake, Kate, you're so irresponsible.'
It was hardly my fault.

'Anyway, I've got to go. I promised Mum I'd help her choose a suit for my cousin's wedding.'

'Do you want me to look after Sean?'

'No.' Jane was almost yelling. She scooped him up and my UCCA form got all scrumpled. She juggled Sean, bag, UCCA form and car keys and let herself out of the kitchen door.

She didn't need to shout. After all, I looked after Claire. All the time. Apart from Sundays and when she was at Whitcliff and when she went on holiday and when she did secret things and told me to go out. Hadn't I promised someone that I'd look after Claire? That I'd stay at home and not go to University, or prison, so that I could look after Claire? But I'd killed Jim so that I could go to

University. I hadn't killed Claire so that I could go to university, had I?

    I wandered off to the phone box and rang Dickson. 'Bloody hell,' she said and hung up.

Kate

Durham didn't want me, but Newcastle did (Jane must have done more than forge my signature on the form) as did also SOAS and Canterbury. I never heard back from LSE. I just had to tick one of the boxes and say that I was going. It was already March.

There was a daffodil out in the garden. Claire was sulking because I'd put her on a diet and I hadn't slept since I'd got the first acceptance letter. At least I don't think I'd slept because I was either not sleeping or having nightmares all the time. It had been bad enough listening in on Mum and Jim's conversations but now I was going through that whole cold breath phase all over again.

Except that this time I was the mad woman. I was locked in a cage, but if I killed Jane Eyre I would be able to escape.

Claire

Mike and I had a plan. Mike said he was going to come on Saturday as well as Sunday. Mike's plan was that we were going to watch football. My plan was that we were going to eat crisps and that Mike was going to kiss me more than three times. I didn't like being kissed before but someone called Kathy was kissed on the telly so I thought that it must be alright to be kissed. I was going to ask Kate but I think that Kate thinks that it is very bad to be kissed. When I saw Sally at Whitcliff I asked her if it was alright to kiss someone like on the telly but Sally looked surprised in a bad way and asked in a voice that was frightening if anyone had kissed me and the way she said it didn't make me think of Mike it made me think of something else that I'm never ever ever going to talk about so I said no to Sally and decided that I would just ask Mike. Mike said that it was very nice to kiss someone and he said that it was e-spe-ciall-y nice to kiss me.

    I told Kate that she had to go away on Saturday. I don't think that Kate liked me telling her that she had to go away because she looked very serious and she said that she was going away and that it might be difficult for me and that if I wanted her to stay she would stay and not go away and I said it wasn't difficult and that she had to go away on Saturday. Then Kate suddenly looked surprised and said you mean you just want me to go away for the day on Saturday and I said yes because that was what I had said in the first place and then Kate said why? Why did I want her to go away on Saturday and I said I'm not telling you and Kate said is that Mike coming and I said that Mike is not that Mike he is Mike and Kate started shouting and saying that she couldn't leave me on my own with Mike so I put my hands over my ears and said that I wasn't listening.

Kate

Claire had sent me off to the cinema. It was a Saturday and I was usually allowed to stay at home on Saturdays. The cinema was crowded because it was raining and the only film showing was *The French Lieutenant's Woman* which I didn't want to see because it didn't have a proper ending. Once you started speculating about what *could* happen you ended up sitting on Claire's bed in the middle of the night thinking of possibilities. After all, it was only a matter of re-writing a bit here and there.

I wandered through York disconsolately, getting wet. I was wearing Bertha's purple cardigan, which didn't keep out the rain but was a sort of talisman against evil doing. Everyone thought that I was at the cinema. I'd even bought a ticket with Claire's money. I'd asked Jane but they'd just had a baby.

I'd been to see it, the baby I mean, and we'd quarrelled about the name. 'You can't call it Dawn,' I'd said. (Who wouldn't quarrel with a friend who tried to call a baby Dawn?)

'She's not an it,' Jane had said. She was all pink and gleaming, in fact she and the baby looked just like each other, pink and gleaming. Except the baby smelled.

'Sean and Dawn, it sounds like some silly TV thing.'

'Alan and I think Dawn is a pretty name. You see she was born at dawn so that's what we're going to call her.'

'You could call her June.'

'Why June?'

'Because she's been born in June. You could call her June Dawn.'

'Kate, are you taking the mickey?'

'No, not really. Just pointing out the ridiculousness of the name Dawn. You could call her something sensible like Maud.'

'Kate.'

Dawn had snuffled and screwed up her little face and wrists.

'You look really well,' I'd said, changing the subject.

'I feel really well. In fact I could have lots more babies the way I'm feeling.'

'Well, don't,' I'd said.

Alan had appeared around the hospital bed curtain.

'Hello sweetheart,' he'd said to Jane, bending to kiss his wife and new baby girl. 'Hi, Kate.'

'Hi, Alan,' I'd said moving away from the bed. 'I'll be going then.'

I'd backed away from them, waving. Domestic bliss; perhaps it really was possible. The husbands I came across usually got murdered.

After which happy notion I decided that no one would remember a wet person in a purple cardigan so I caught the bus home.

The old woman got off at Whitcliff. It was about two o'clock. I gave Mum's watch a shake and moved it onto three. A few people got off at my stop. I pulled the cardigan over my head as if to protect myself from the rain and hurried home.

A car was in the drive. A Ford Escort. I know what make it was because I stood and looked at it for about five minutes. I listened to see if I could hear the circular saw going in our shed, but Jim didn't have a car.

I knocked on the door. How ridiculous was that? No one answered me so I went in. It was quite noisy inside, upstairs, in Mum and Jim's room. I ran upstairs, a huge hurt clenching at my heart, and pushed their bedroom door open. Claire and a man were in a heap on the bed, fighting, making love.

Claire

Mike and me were on the sofa watching football on telly. I had put some crisps in a bowl because it looked nice like Mum did when we had my birthday party. Mike kissed me three times and I kissed Mike once and Mike said that he liked to be kissed. Then a bad thing happened. There was a big noise and someone was upstairs shouting. They were shouting bad things and it sounded like Kate used to sound before she started to be more like Mum, but it couldn't have been Kate because Kate had gone away for the day. I think the person who sounded like Kate used to sound was shouting bad things about Jim and that was very very very bad because Mum had said that we were never ever ever to say anything about Jim.

Then Mike said he would go upstairs and tell the person not to shout because it was upsetting me and I said that Mike wasn't to go upstairs because something bad might happen. Then the shouting person ran downstairs and I heard the kitchen door bang and after that there was lots of noise outside. Mike looked worried and I said that Mike was not to look worried because I only liked it when Mike smiled so I turned the telly up and I told Mike that it was only Kate and that it was like last time but then I remembered that I hadn't liked it last time so I did a very brave thing and told Mike that he had to go but that he could come back tomorrow because a bad thing was happening but that it wouldn't be happening tomorrow. Then I thought that I would go and help Kate but I didn't like all the blood so I watched the telly instead.

Kate

I ran out to the phone box and dialled Dickson's number. And when she answered, by some miracle of science, I managed to push ten pence into the slot.

Claire

Mike came the next day which was Sunday. Mike asked me why the shed was in a big mess and I said that I didn't know it was in a big mess so Mike showed me the shed in a big mess and I said that it didn't matter because it was Jim's shed anyway.

Kate

Dickson was due in on the 11.28 from Wakefield. I'd demanded that she come and see me – and believe you me it had been demanding, hysterical, the full works.

'This is my day off, Kate,' Dickson said loudly and crossly behind me.

'Isn't York quite a nice place to come for a day off?' I said. I felt absurdly pleased to see her.

'York might be,' she said belligerently. It was hard not to smile. 'Why couldn't you just tell me whatever it is you've dreamt up this time on the phone?'

'We can go to Bettys,' I said.

It was the most ridiculous place to discuss a murder. We both ordered a chicken salad and a pot of tea. I expected Dickson to say, 'Who's paying', but she didn't so I could deal with that particular problem later. She looked around at the splendours of Bettys, not sure whether to be uncomfortable or chuffed.

'Well, have you murdered someone else then?' Dickson asked loudly.

I winced. Not yet.

'I er, I moved in with Claire,' I said cautiously.

'You did what! You stupid…bloody hell and I thought I'd driven some sense into you.'

Dickson's loud exclamation nonplussed me so I didn't know what to say. Had anyone told me I couldn't go home? It was confusing, irrelevant. The tea arrived.

'I, I had nowhere else to go,' I said pathetically.
Dickson looked at me less than sympathetically.

I tried again. 'If I hadn't moved in with her Claire would have had to live in at Whitcliff.' I wasn't even convincing myself.

'And exactly why was that anything to do with you?' Dickson poured the tea noisily – only Dickson could pour tea noisily – and looked at me sternly. 'You were not, I repeat, not meant to return to the scene of the crime.'

Dickson sounding like a rulebook frightened me. I tried to say something, failed, and drank some tea instead.

'We learnt our lesson with Margaret.'

I dropped my teacup back onto its saucer with a loud clatter. Did Dickson think? Did Dickson think that I'd do it again? I looked carefully past Dickson's left ear and counted the times I'd sat on the side of Claire's bed in the past month.

'I'm moving out,' I said sounding just a little hysterical. 'I'm going to University.'

'Where?'

'Newcastle,' I said, quickly swallowing the list of ors and buts and possibilities.

'Then go back home and pack up your bags and move to Newcastle.'

An uneasy silence was broken by the arrival of two chicken salads. I think I said, 'I can't.' I must have looked desperate but I should have known not to run to Dickson for comfort.

'Kate, cut the crap. This is all very nice, bloody expensive chicken salad and all, but what is this all about? You didn't get me to come all the way from Wakefield, on my day off, to tell me you were going to University.'

'Claire either has a boyfriend or someone from Social Services who's abusing her.' I blurted out. I didn't say *again* and I still didn't look Dickson in the eye.

'So what's new,' she said.

I looked at her carefully. 'Someone called Mike visits her on Sundays.'

'Boyfriend, then. Social Services don't work on Sundays.'

'I'm sure Sally at Whitcliff does,' I said unhelpfully.

'Well, bully for Sally, but I bet Mike doesn't.' Dickson munched on her chicken salad. 'Kate, what does any of this have to do with me, or even you for that matter?' She repeated.

'I just told you.'

'You just told me what?' Dickson reposted stubbornly. She was chewing a large piece of chicken. I tried to eat some of mine.

'I told you about Claire, about Claire and Jim.' I was shouting now.

Dickson raised an eyebrow and stuffed some more chicken in.

'You told me about Mike, in your words, *abusing* Claire, not Jim.'

'But it was Jim. It was Jim.'

'Eat your chicken up Kate, everyone's looking at us,' Dickson said calmly. 'So you've finally worked out what happened?' She sighed heavily. 'Like I said, you should never have gone back home.'

'But it means we all had a motive to kill Jim, didn't we?' I was whispering now.

'Yes.'

'But.'

'And as long as you stay in that house you'll be chief suspect again next time.'

I think I sat looking at Dickson with my mouth open for five minutes.

'Dickson, do you think I *did* murder that bloody man?' I was speaking too loudly again but Dickson didn't care. She took another huge mouthful of chicken and carried on talking and chomping at the same time.

'No, I don't think you killed Jim.' I'm sure she sighed heavily.

I looked at her startled, she sounded so sure.

'But how...'

'It just seemed apparent to me right from the start that an undersized scrap of a thing like you couldn't have committed that particular murder. Bloody hell, how were you supposed to wield a shovel powerfully enough to knock a fully grown man off his feet and sufficiently hard enough also to knock him senseless onto a circular saw blade whether it was operational or not.'

I looked stubbornly at Dickson.

'If I'd really wanted to kill him badly enough mightn't I have found some super human strength?'

Dickson slurped her tea and gave an exaggerated shrug of her broad shoulders. 'Big girl, is she, your sister?'

A potent pause hung like a silent cloud over the happy lunch eaters surrounding us.

'But what if.... What if it happens again?' I whispered.

'You get yourself off to that bloody university and it won't be our problem, Kate.' I wished she could look smug and more confident. But another thought seemed to strike her and she cheered up, stuffing in her chicken salad. 'That'll be D.I. Slater's problem,' she said and burped loudly.

Claire

I didn't like it when Kate came back. Kate shouted a lot and Kate said a very bad thing about Mike and I cried.

    I told Kate that I wanted Kate to go away again for a very very very long time because I didn't want her to do bad things to Mike and I told her that I didn't need her because I'd got Mike and I liked Mike and I didn't always like Kate. And anyway nothing bad could happen now because there wasn't a shed any more. I think Kate cried which was sad but Mike didn't cry. He was very very very happy and that made me very very very happy.

Kate

Jane was late. I heard the car draw up and the car door slam almost immediately afterwards. I was waiting in my bedroom. My bag packed. Well, Jane's bag was packed and most of Claire's savings were in my purse. I'd been waiting all morning, or a few months or years depending on your point of view.

Claire obviously thought it might be Mike because I heard her charging officiously into the kitchen. Twelve stones of woman rushing along a small hall was fairly easy to hear. I'd failed on the diet front and Carol's bags were once again filled with white bread, biscuits and pop.

Claire had been very interested in my announcement that I was going, or might be going or perhaps might be away today and had asked careful questions about my movements. Which was why I knew that Mike was coming.

'Hello Claire,' I heard Jane say.

I imagined Claire's grunt and her retreat into the front room.

Jane was going to ask where I was next so I pulled myself together and went down the stairs. I met Jane awkwardly in the hall. The door to the front room was open and Claire was standing by the window looking out for Mike.

'Sorry I'm late,' Jane said.

I shrugged. I had bigger problems than Jane being half an hour late. Somehow or other I had to get on and out and through the door into another Brave New World. I pushed past Jane and walked quickly out through the kitchen. As a last thought I called out goodbye to Claire, but not wanting to hear her response, or lack of response, I didn't pause. I just dived into the passenger seat of Jane's car and hugged my - Jane's - bag to my knees.

Jane was babbling on as she manoeuvred the car out of our drive. Claire's drive. Perhaps about to become Mike's drive.

'Sorry, Kate, there was a bit of a crisis.'

I didn't listen. We sped on up the Old North Road and I watched the familiar landmarks vanishing. A derelict phone box by Potter's Farm. The Whitcliff bus stop. The turning at the traffic lights and the twisty back way to the station.

'Gosh there's never anywhere to park. Do you mind if I just drop you here?' Jane was still talking as we drove into the station forecourt.

I shook my head then forced myself to look at her.

'You will be alright won't you?' she was saying, or thinking, I'm not sure which. I headed off in the direction of the ticket office and buried into Claire's money and bought a one-way ticket to Newcastle.

That was the easy bit.

Two hours later I was still sitting on platform nine. About every half an hour a train pulled in heading for Newcastle. I hugged Jane's bag and imagined Claire at home watching the football on telly with Mike and eating junk.

Mum sat on the bench beside me. She was crying. 'You can't leave her on her own.' I could feel her tears on my cheeks and the guilt of Claire's disability blacking out the future. I put my fingers in my ears and said, shouted, whispered, thought. 'But she doesn't need me.' Mum was clawing at my arm and then someone poked me hard in the back. I leapt to my feet and turned round to see Jim. His big smarmy face was leering down at me.

'You're not needed, Kate,' Jim was saying, 'leave the three of us in peace. It will be for the best.'

But I couldn't trust him, could I?

I think I decided to go back home and rescue Claire but another train was waiting at the platform and I found myself by an open door to the last carriage. The guard was walking down the train blowing his whistle. He stopped by me and said crossly,

'Get a move on, lovey, we can't wait all day.'

So I did and the door slammed shut behind me.

Claires diry

Kate went in Janes car with Jane. Janes car is blue. Kate had a big bag. Kate has gone away for a very very very long time. Kate has gone on a train. Mike stayed in my house all nite. I like Mike.

Mike and Claire
By Claire